DYED AND GONE TO HEAVEN

AIMEE NICOLE WALKER

Dyed and Gone to Heaven
(Curl Up and DYE Mysteries, #3)
Copyright © 2017 Aimee Nicole Walker

ISBN: 978-0-9974225-6-6

aimeenicolewalker@blogspot.com

Cover photograph and interior photos © Wander Aguiar – www.wanderaguiar.com
Cover art © Jay Aheer of Simply Defined Art – www.jayscoversbydesign.com
Editing provided by Pam Ebeler of Undivided Editing – www.undividedediting.com
Proofreading provided by Judy Zweifel of Judy's Proofreading – www.judysproofreading.com
Interior Design and Formatting provided by Stacey Blake of Champagne Formats – www.champagneformats.com

Copyright and Trademark Acknowledgments
The author acknowledges the copyrights and trademarked status and trademark owners of the following trademarks and copyrights mentioned in this work of fiction.
Copyrights and Trademarks:
Word of Warcraft – Blizzard Entertainment
Miami Vice – Universal Television, NBC
Elle and Warner – Legally Blonde (Metro-Goldwyn-MGM)
Teenage Mutant Ninja Turtles – Mirage Studios
Mini Cooper – BMW
AG Jeans – Adriano Goldschmied, Inc.
Hermes – Hermes International
Gucci – Gucci Group
Vick's VapoRub – Richardson-Merrell Inc.
Home Alone – Hughes Entertainment
Scooby Doo – Hanna-Barbera
Andrew Christian
Walt Disney – Disney theme parks
Dr. Phil Show – Harpo Productions, CBS
Friends – Warner Bros Television, NBC
Netflix
Absolute Black and F-150 – Ford Motor Company
McDonald's
The Closer – Warner Bros Television, TNT
Twitter and tweeting – Twitter, Inc
Facebook and Facebooking – Facebook, Inc.

Other Books by Aimee Nicole Walker

Only You

The Fated Hearts Series
Chasing Mr. Wright, Book 1
Rhythm of Us, Book 2
Surrender Your Heart, Book 3
Perfect Fit, Book 4
Return to Me, Book 5
Always You, Book 6
Any Means Necessary, Book 7

Curl Up and Dye Mysteries
Fatal Reaction (Series Prequel found on author's blog)
Dyeing to be Loved
Something to Dye For

Undisputed – coauthored with Nicholas Bella

DEDICATION

To Kim Hay,
You were a beacon when I needed it the most. To the moon and
back, lady!

ONE

Josh

I couldn't stop myself from glancing at Gabe across the table in the fancy restaurant where we went on a double date with Adrian and Sally Ann to celebrate the upcoming birth of their baby girl. They'd just discovered they were having a daughter the day before and invited us to dinner with them. As happy as I was for them, and I was over the moon and back at least three times, I was even happier that I got to go home with Detective Delicious sitting across the dinner table from me—the one engaged in a hushed conversation with his partner.

I knew what the leaned-in heads and lowered voices meant. They were discussing their cases, most likely Billy Sampson, and Gabe didn't want me to overhear and become upset. He was protective and cute like that, but I was certain he would learn that I was made of much sterner stuff than he ever imagined. I had survived Billy's heinous treatment of me in high school and his childish attempts at harassing me as an adult wasn't even a blip on my radar. Billy Sampson was a man who hated himself and turned to drugs in his attempt to escape the truth. He would have to live with his actions for the rest of his life, but I didn't.

"What do you think about this crib mobile I found on Pinterest?" Sally Ann asked from beside me. She held up her phone and showed me a picture of a mobile with miniature stuffed animals that looked like zoo babies. "I think I want to keep the theme neutral," she told me. "At first I thought it would be pink or blue everywhere depending on the gender, but I've changed my mind. Maybe my daughter will hate pink stuff. Maybe she'll want to wear baseball jerseys instead of dresses. Yeah, I think I need to let her decide what her personality is rather than cramming it down her throat from day one."

"If I weren't gay as fuck, I'd steal you away from Adrian," I told her.

"Shucks," she replied, blushing. "You say the most charming things." Sally Ann batted her eyelashes playfully at me.

I looked over at Gabe for the hundredth time in twenty minutes and thought about the lovely burgundy color of his tie. It was one that I found scrunched in the back of his dresser drawer when we moved him out of his house and into mine. *Wow! It was still so shocking to me that we had made such a bold step and that I was the one who suggested it.* I remembered how cool the silk felt against my fingers when I handed it to him to wear that evening—after I got the shameful wrinkles out, of course. I silently observed how lovely the color looked against my fair skin and was shocked that I'd even consider letting Gabe tie my hands up during sex.

I had never given that kind of trust to anyone because they had never deserved it, but Gabe did. I had found a man—or maybe, like with trouble, he found me—who was steeped in goodness. I admired his dedication to his family, friends, and justice. I loved that he was patient with me when I struggled at times to fight my demons and that he accepted me for how I was, not who he thought I should be. Of all the gifts that Gabe brought to my life, those were my two favorites. And somehow, someway, that beautiful soul was in love with me.

"He's crazy about you too," Sally Ann said, nudging me with her shoulder. "I've never seen Gabriel so happy as he is with you." Her words meant a lot to me because Sally Ann had gotten to know Gabe when he first moved to town with his ex-boyfriend, Kyle. She would've seen them together as a couple and saw their connection. Even though Kyle himself told me that Gabe and I had something they never did, it was great to hear it from someone outside of the relationship. Sally Ann had no reason to blow smoke up my ass; if she didn't believe it, then she wouldn't have said it.

"I know," I said softly, but not arrogantly. I never took Gabe's affection for me for granted, but I wouldn't pretend I didn't know it existed either. I was never one to fish for compliments. My days of begging for crumbs of attention were over.

"How's cohabitating going?" she asked.

"It's been surprisingly easy so far," I replied honestly. "I expected it to be more challenging in the beginning as we got used to one another's personalities and habits, but it's great. There's a big difference between sleeping over a few nights a week and living with someone."

"There sure is," Sally Ann agreed. "I'm glad it's going so smoothly for you both. It wasn't the case for Adrian and me."

"Really?" I asked in surprise. They seemed so in tune with each other, and it was obvious how much they loved and respected one another. I leaned closer, lowered my voice, and asked, "How so?"

"We were both thirty years old and had lived on our own pretty much since college, which meant we were fairly set in our ways. Like with you and Gabe, our personalities are so different, but Adrian and I are both stubborn and don't compromise as well as you guys do."

I laughed then because I was quite stubborn and Gabe did most of the compromising when we first met. I guess you could say that he was equally as stubborn because he refused to give up on us when all I did was pull him close then push him away. Luckily for me, Gabe knew it wasn't done in a manipulative way and was astute enough to realize I was afraid and fighting my growing feelings for him.

"Give me an example," I told Sally Ann.

"Toilet paper."

"As in you liked different brands?" I asked curiously.

"No! He," Sally Ann pointed across the table at her husband, "puts the roll on wrong."

"I do not," Adrian fired back instantly, letting us know that we weren't as quiet as we had thought. "There's no such thing."

Sally Ann shook her head vehemently. "There's scientific evidence that you use less toilet paper if you pull the paper over the roller versus under." *Wow! Sally Ann was serious about her toilet paper.*

"You're so fucking cute with your science talk," Adrian said to his middle school science teacher for a wife. "According to the Debunkers," he said referring to a new show that debunked common myths, "that's not true at all."

Sally Ann threw her head back and laughed. "Those guys aren't *real* scientists," she shot back.

Adrian looked at me and asked, "Do you know how Gabe and I yell at the referees for getting the calls wrong in football?"

"And basketball," I reminded Adrian.

"Wait until baseball season starts," Sally Ann said to me beneath her breath.

"I heard that," Adrian said, good-naturedly.

"You were supposed to," Sally Ann replied in a sing-song voice.

"Well, anyway," Adrian said, trying to get back to his question to me, "she is so much worse when I watch Debunkers." Adrian laughed hard when his wife flipped him the bird across the table. "She yells, 'that's not scientific' or 'that isn't how you measure it,' every five minutes."

"Or less," Sally Ann added. "I'd rather watch sports any day of the week."

Gabe and I sat smiling at each other over the table while Sally Ann and Adrian playfully bickered about his favorite show. It wasn't that Gabe and I liked the same shows because that was the furthest thing from the truth, but we compromised or watched television in different rooms. To be honest, we didn't watch a lot of TV when he first moved in because we were too busy entertaining ourselves in a more mutually pleasing way.

After the cute little tiff was over, Sally Ann returned her attention to me while our guys resumed their case-talking positions.

"Josh, I've meant to ask you something, but I wasn't sure I should," Sally Ann said. Her worried tone and the way she wrung her hands had me curious.

"Sally Ann, you can ask me anything."

"Will you teach me to pole dance after I recover from having my baby?" She grimaced once the words left her mouth.

"Why do you look so nervous about asking me that?" I asked her.

"Well, you've never told me about your pole dancing studio, which means I either heard it from Gabe or Adrian. Logic points to Adrian, and I don't want you to think that Gabe is telling him intimate details of your life together."

She had a point, and I could understand her hesitation. I had to admit I was curious about how the conversation came up, but I was certain that Gabe wasn't telling Adrian details of how I worked the pole. Six months earlier, I wouldn't have felt the same way; I would've jumped to all kinds of conclusions. "I don't think you said anything bad or inappropriate about me and I would love to teach you how to pole dance. It's amazing exercise for strengthening your core muscle groups."

Sally Ann leaned over and hugged me. "You're amazing, Josh. I'm so lucky to call you my friend." She pulled back and looked at me appraisingly. "Do you want to see more nursery ideas or is that boring you to death?"

"It's not boring at all," I assured her. "I'd love to paint a picture for her nursery once you decided on a theme."

"You paint too?" she asked.

"It's just a hobby," I replied. "I'm not sure I'm all that great at it, but I will make it with love for baby Adrianna."

Sally Ann tilted her head, and she got a faraway look in her eyes. "Why had I never thought of that name?" she pondered out loud. "It's a combination of both our names. It's perfect!"

"Sunshine," Gabe said. The shock in his voice pulled me away from my conversation with Sally Ann. I looked over at him, and he asked, "Are we," he gestured back and forth between him and Adrian, "tripping or did Nate Turner just walk into the restaurant?"

"What? Nate's dead." I turned my head in the direction that Gabe and Adrian were looking and said, "I'd say there was something psychedelic in those stuffed mushroom appetizers, but you didn't eat them."

"You see him too?" Gabe asked like he truly saw a ghost.

"Hell yes, I do," I replied in awe.

We watched as the ghost of Nate Turner stopped, smiled, and spoke to a waiter in the dining room. That was odd because I'd never seen Nate Turner smile, although I didn't know him well and

I refused to think about how well Gabe did. He also came off as someone who thought that speaking to a waiter was beneath him. The new Nate Turner, though, clapped the waiter on the shoulder before he joined a group of people at a table.

"I don't fucking believe it," Adrian said. "I saw his photos from the morgue. You ID'd his body at the scene."

"I gave a visual ID that the dead man in the car was the man I knew as Nate Turner. I know for a fact they made a fingerprint and dental record comparison to validate my identification," Gabe said. "Who the fuck is that guy?"

"We're about to find out," Adrian said. He raised his hand and waved the waiter over who'd been talking to the doppelganger.

"Yes, sir?" the waiter asked.

"What's the name of the gentleman you were just talking to?" Adrian asked, nodding his head in the direction of the table our mysterious man just joined.

The waiter hesitated as if he wasn't sure he should say. "His name is Jonathon Silver, sir."

"Thank you," Adrian said pleasantly. "He looks so familiar, but that's not a name I recognize."

"He's relatively new in town," the waiter replied. "Is there anything else? Would you like more bread for your table?"

"No, we're fine, but thank you," Gabe told him. I could tell that he was eager for the guy to move on so he and Adrian could discuss the new development. I counted to four after the waiter moved on before Gabe said, "Has to be a twin brother."

"No other explanation," Adrian agreed, "but why in the hell had no one told the cops about his existence? Not Nate's attorney, not his silent business partner, and not his staff. No one mentioned this guy at any time."

"The only thing the Cincinnati police told me was that he had adoptive parents. There was no mention of a brother—identical twin or otherwise," Gabe told Adrian. "They must've been raised by different families."

"Which means that the CPD probably didn't know either. What are you going to do about this discovery?" Adrian asked Gabe. Adrian didn't include himself in the equation because Gabe was the one leading the joint task force investigating Nate's homicide while Adrian wrapped up any investigation that involved Billy Sampson since Gabe was obviously biased against him.

Gabe shook his head and shrugged his shoulders slightly before he replied with, "Not much I can do about it until Monday. I can do a basic internet search on the guy and try to get some background info, but I guess there's not much out there if the CPD didn't know about him. He's either kept his nose clean or has evaded capture." Gabe looked at me across the table then said, "There's no need ruining our evening over something we can't resolve tonight."

I knew that the investigator in him wanted to fight that logic, but I also knew from previous conversations that he felt his hectic, long hours on the Miami Police Department played a big part in his failed relationship with Kyle and he wasn't willing to let the same thing happen between us. I loved that about him, I truly did, but I'd rather him do what he could right then so that his attention would fully be on me when he was home.

"I can ride home with Sally Ann and Adrian if you…"

"Nope," Gabe said emphatically. "Yes, my mind will be spinning in a million directions tomorrow, but it's not fair to call in the task force on the weekend with nothing to go on except his name. Like I said, I'll do some research tomorrow and formulate a game plan for Monday."

"If you're sure," I told him.

"I am," he replied. "Let's go back to enjoying our dinners and later you can tell me why I'm just now learning that you can paint." So he had overheard what I said to Sally Ann. "I expect you to show me your stuff when we get home. Your *artwork*," he corrected when he could tell I was about to snark about how often I show him my stuff.

"The bloom is already falling off the rose," I woefully told a laughing Sally Ann. "Gabe, you've seen my artwork already."

"I have? When?" he asked.

"The studio in my attic," I told him.

"Are you telling me those paintings of the ballet dancers are your creation? That's just…wow, Sunshine. What other talents are you keeping from me?" he asked in awe.

The attention he was giving me in front of Adrian and Sally Ann made me feel anxious, so I did what I did best in that type of situation. "Baby, you've barely scratched the surface of my talents." Sally Ann and Adrian laughed, but Gabe just studied me quietly for several moments.

"There's no time like the present to find out," he told me. The look he gave me promised that he wouldn't let up that night until I shared a new talent with him.

Once we got home, I showed him how I could tie a cherry stem with my tongue and how useful a strong tongue could be once I had his dick in my mouth. I could honestly say that his case was the furthest thing from his mind right then. I also forgot to ask him how in the world Adrian found out about my pole dancing, but then I decided it didn't matter because I trusted and believed in Gabe.

TWO

Gabe

I HAD MEANT WHAT I SAID ABOUT THERE BEING NO POINT IN calling in the task force on the weekend on just the discovery of Jonathon Silver's existence. Time away from the job was important for a well-balanced, happy life. I was also right that my mind would constantly spin as I tried to figure out what role, if any, Silver may have played in his brother's death.

Instead of being angry that my mind was preoccupied, Josh went upstairs to his attic and began working on the painting for

Adrian and Sally Ann's nursery. It still blew my mind that Josh had created those gorgeous paintings. Why the hell would he hide that kind of talent in a room that only he saw? It was baffling to me. I also thought that it was slightly unfair that he had been blessed with so many talents when so many of us could barely walk and chew gum at the same time. I could lift weights and play a few sports, big deal. Josh lit up a room with his personality, made people feel good about themselves, and made it a prettier world with his hidden art. I just shook my head and went back to doing a basic internet search on Jonathon Silver.

As I suspected, I hadn't learned much from public databases. There were no mentions of Jonathon Silver's name in any online or print articles. He didn't appear to own any residential property in the northern counties of Kentucky or southern counties of Ohio. It was trickier searching for commercial properties unless you knew the address or the proprietor's name. There were many sites that offered to give me the contact information for Jonathon Silver, but I wasn't about to pay for it when I could get that information myself at the police station. I blew out a frustrated breath that what I predicted had come true—I knew absolutely nothing new. I had hoped to get a head start for our Monday morning task force meeting.

"Why don't you call John and ask if he wants to leave earlier tomorrow, so you have extra time to gather information before your meeting?" Josh asked. I wasn't aware I verbalized my irritation for him to hear or maybe he read my mind. Was that another skill he had been hiding? *I want sex. I want sex. I want sex.* "Why are you making that cheesy porn face?" he asked me.

I threw my head back and laughed at the confused expression on his face. "I was trying to see if you could read my mind because you commented on what I was thinking before I made the cheesy porn face."

"You want to watch cheesy porn?" he asked.

"No," I replied. "I want to know if you can read minds or if I talk out loud sometimes when I'm not even aware of it."

"You didn't verbalize your thoughts out loud, babe," Josh replied, shaking his head. "I'm not a mind reader either, but I could tell how anxious you are by the tenseness in your body and the way you keep tapping your pen on the notebook. So, why not give John a heads-up about who we saw last night and find out if it's possible for you to pick him up earlier. If not, you can always go to the station early in the morning and get started on the background searches."

He was right, and I told him so. "I'll go into the station early tomorrow and work for a bit before I pick him up. I can fill Dorchester in during the drive to Cincinnati." I liked my temporary partner and didn't want to screw up his weekend for no good reason.

"Great. Now hopefully you'll be able to relax and enjoy Sunday dinner with our friends," Josh told me. He never failed to call Meredith and Chaz "our" friends, and that meant a lot to me. It made me feel like our relationship was more like a partnership, that we were truly one.

"If not, I know what always makes me feel better." I made the most lecherous facial expression I could. I narrowed my eyes into a sultry look that was supposed to be sexy and bit my lip. Instead of Josh jumping me as I'd hoped, he howled with laughter.

"You look constipated," he managed to wheeze out in between peals of laughter. "I love you so damn much, Gabe. Never change." I was so glad I could entertain him, but damn my ego took a dive when Josh couldn't tell my constipated face from my sexy face. His next words soothed my wounded pride. "You don't need a sexy face for me to want to throw myself in your arms, Gabe. You just need to keep breathing."

"You say the sweetest things." I set my notebook and pen on the coffee table and pulled him until he was in my lap. "I love you so much, Sunshine, so I want to be better about leaving my work outside these walls."

"That's not how guys operate, Gabe. Regardless of our

profession, work drives us. You don't complain to me when my last client's appointment runs thirty minutes over so why would I hold it against you when you're trying to solve a case?" What Josh said made sense logically, but in theory, it didn't stand up. I saw too many relationships die for other officers when disappointment over canceled dates and late nights turn into resentment.

"You have to let me know when something isn't working right for us. I need you to tell me when I've done something to upset you, instead of suppressing things." I ran my fingers through his platinum blond hair and smiled at the way his hazel eyes turned a shade darker with affection whenever I touched him in the simplest of ways. He was a man who was truly starving for love and affection when I met him, and I was a man with an abundance of love and affection to give to the right man. We were made for each other.

"It's like you don't even know me." Josh shook his head sadly. "Have you ever known me *not* to tell you how I feel in one form or another?" He hid behind snark when he felt most vulnerable, he got very quiet when he got angry, and expressed his love for me with his body—either during a dance, sex, or both. Technically, I would know by his reaction how he felt, but I would prefer that we just said what was on our minds. "I can tell how important this is to you. I will try harder to be upfront with you about my feelings without all the extra stuff tossed in."

"Thank you."

"You're welcome." Josh leaned forward and gave me a quick peck on the lips before he stood up. "I need to get started on dinner now, but we'll talk about ways to relax you later."

"What are you fixing tonight?" I asked.

"Roasted chicken, stuffing, green beans, and rolls." He looked back over his shoulder on the way to the kitchen and said, "Apple tarts for dessert." Josh laughed wickedly because he knew what cinnamon, apples, and pastry did to me. "I got you that fancy vanilla bean ice cream you like."

"I swear I've gained ten pounds since I started dating you," I told him.

"I guess we'll just have to double down on your cardio work-outs, babe." He had a suggestion for every scenario, and for the most part, I found no fault with them.

Meredith arrived at her normal twenty minutes before dinner, but Chaz wasn't with her, and he didn't show up during the final minutes of Josh putting his masterpiece together. I could see Josh and Meredith's posture becoming more and more rigid from worry as time ticked by so I took the plates from Meredith's hands.

"Why don't I set the table while you call Chaz to make sure he's okay?" I suggested. It wasn't like Chaz to be late, but both Josh and Meredith had remarked on separate occasions that he'd been run-ning late in the mornings to open the shop. He seemed tired and quieter than his usual demeanor which earned him the nickname of Spaz.

"Thank you, honey," Meredith replied. "He never misses dinner and… hey, sweetie. Where are you? Dinner is almost ready, and we were getting worried. You fell asleep?" she asked in disbelief.

"Tell him I'll hold dinner for him," Josh yelled over his shoulder.

"Just come on over, Chaz. Josh is holding dinner for you." Meredith pocketed her phone and worried her bottom lip between her teeth. "Do you think he's sick?" she finally asked. "The exhaus-tion and the dark circles under his eyes makes me think he's sick."

Josh came out of the kitchen and pulled Meredith into a hug. "Let's try not to jump to conclusions, okay? It's obvious we need to have a come-to-Jesus talk with him because letting him come to us on his terms just isn't working. Let's wait until he has a full belly to strike."

"Deal," Meredith said, nodding.

The close bond of friendship they shared always made me smile. It made me even happier that they opened that circle to in-clude me too. Still, I knew we could be heading into territory where my objectivity might come into play if Josh and Meredith didn't get their way.

It didn't take long for Chaz to show up and I was shocked by his appearance when he arrived. His hair was sticking up everywhere, his eyes were red and puffy, and his skin had an unhealthy pallor. His clothes were rumpled, and he wore a look of complete bewilderment on his face. Meredith took one look at him and burst into tears.

"Sugar, get in the car, and I'll take you to the ER right now," she told him. *So much for waiting until after dinner.*

"I'm not sick," Chaz told her. "I was just up late last night—well, early this morning—playing video games."

"Video games?" Meredith's tone and demeanor had changed from distraught to disbelief in a second.

"Yeah, it helps me relieve stress," Chaz said with a shrug of his shoulders.

"Stress?" she asked, placing her hands on her hips. I could tell she was about to give Chaz a piece of her mind. I opened my mouth to do my peacekeeping routine, but Josh shook his head. As much as I loved Chaz and Meredith, he knew them a lot better than I did so I heeded his warning.

"Yes, stress," Chaz said defensively. "I don't have a built-in stress reliever," Chaz said, pointing in my direction, "like Jazz does, and I'm not as kickass as you are. Nothing seems to faze you, Mere."

"That's a bunch of bullshit if I ever heard it. Don't make excuses for bad behavior and then play the poor pitiful me card," Meredith told him. No lie, I took a step back because I hadn't seen her so angry in the short time that I'd known her. I would've agreed with Chaz's assessment that nothing got her down until I saw her in action. "Josh and I have been worried sick to death about you for months. You've turned us down to go out, you've been late to work, you've been absent-minded at times, and you nearly missed Sunday dinner with your family. You look physically ill right now, baby,"

Meredith added, but with a softer tone of voice. "What can we do to help you?"

I saw all the starch fade right out of Chaz. He pulled a chair back from the table and flopped down in it. Josh and Meredith moved to stand on either side of him. Meredith ran her fingers through his hair, and Josh rubbed his back.

"I feel so immature and ridiculous, but that's what I've gotten caught up in," Chaz said. He looked up at Josh and then Meredith. "I'm sorry for worrying you. I promise you that I'm not sick and I'll do better about getting to work on time."

A sudden thought occurred to me while the trio made up. "What game are you into these days?" I asked. What was the likelihood that Chaz was the same guy that Kyle had been playing with online?

"*World of Warcraft*," Chaz replied. *Same as Kyle.* "I know, you probably think I'm acting like a ten-year-old."

"No, I don't think that. You're not the only guy I know in this town who's hooked on that game." Josh narrowed his eyes at me as he considered my words.

"You don't say?" he asked.

"I just did," I replied smartly, earning myself a glare from my guy.

Chaz looked back and forth between us in confusion. "Um, I hate to break up whatever is going on here, but do you think we could eat now?" he asked. "I haven't eaten all day." As if to emphasize his misery, his stomach growled angrily inside his thin frame.

"I do believe Gabe and I can table this discussion until later," Josh said somewhat huffily as he returned to the kitchen.

We gathered around the table, Meredith said grace, and then we began passing around the platters and bowls of food. Conversation lulled while we piled our plates high with food but kicked into higher gear once we'd had a few bites. I wasn't exaggerating when I told Josh on numerous occasions that he made the best food I had ever eaten. I would've been happy to worship his skills in silence, but I didn't consider myself to be a rude person. I answered whatever questions I could about my time working on the task force, which basically left me with discussing the people I worked with rather than the details I had discovered, which weren't many. So, I stuck with discussing the individual personalities and skill set of the members.

Josh snorted when it came time to talk about Paul. His reaction drew odd looks from Chaz and Meredith. Paul and I had hooked up once after my breakup with Kyle. Somehow Josh knew it immediately the night he and I ran into Paul at Vibe. I momentarily thought Josh would get mad that I had kept the secret from him, but I assured him that I made Paul aware that I was off the market. That seemed to be enough for Josh, who then asked me to take him to a hotel and fuck him like a stranger. What could've been a big fight turned out to be one of the most memorable nights I had with him.

I tilted my head to the side and considered his facial expressions. It was one of those times that I needed him to tell me how he felt because the expression on his face gave nothing away. I learned firsthand at my parents' house just how brilliantly Josh could play poker. I filed away a mental note to ask Josh about the situation with Paul later and finished telling Mere and Chaz about the rest of the team.

"It sounds so…" Meredith broke off as she thought about the words to use.

"*Miami Vice*," Josh supplied for her.

Meredith laughed. "I was going to say exciting, but I guess that works too."

"Task forces are only fun when the actual busts are made," I told them. "Until then, it's a lot of boring legwork and planning. It often feels like you take one step forward and ten steps back."

"Blissville must seem dull in comparison to Miami," Chaz tossed out there.

Had I not been looking into Josh's eyes just then, I might not have noticed the subtle tensing of his body when he heard Chaz's comment.

"Quite the opposite actually," I told Chaz, "and there's no place I'd rather be." Well, maybe someplace naked with the man I loved, but for the moment I'd settle for being in the same room with him.

Josh smiled sweetly at me then said, "Who wants to play Monopoly after dinner?"

We all groaned because Josh killed us every single time he played, demonstrating how good his business skills truly were. I blew out a resigned breath because it looked like I wouldn't be getting my guy naked for quite some time.

THREE

Josh

IT WAS MORE THAN JUST MY EARS THAT PERKED UP WHEN GABE
announced he knew another guy in town who was hooked on
playing *World of Warcraft* online. It wasn't jealousy, but intrigue
that prompted my response to his statement. I recalled that Gabe
once mentioned that there was an online gamer that caught Kyle's
attention. What if the world truly was smaller than we thought?
I was sure the odds of Chaz being the same guy that Kyle met
online were slim, but that didn't mean impossible. Besides, I saw

the attraction between Chaz and Kyle whenever they were in the same room together. Hell, Kyle had noticed Chaz when he was in a relationship with Gabe, not that he ever acted on it or behaved inappropriately. Quite honestly, a hot-blooded gay man would notice the attractiveness of another if there was breath in his body. There was nothing wrong with that.

I had planned on bringing it up as soon as our friends left, but then jealousy surfaced during our dinner conversation. I was ashamed of my reaction to hearing Paul's name, even though I realized it was a human reaction that most people would feel. I wasn't most people. I'd been through too much bullshit to let petty jealousy get in the way of my happiness. No matter how much I tried to reason with my heart, the damn thing still hurt in my chest. It appeared that I still had a long way to go before I wouldn't feel inadequate compared to Gabe's past lovers.

I didn't like feeling the way that I did, and I wanted to postpone being alone with Gabe for the first time since we started dating. A sure-fire way of doing that was to play Monopoly with them. Look, my friends and Gabe had wonderful qualities but being business savvy wasn't among them. It was like taking candy from a baby, but I went easier on them to drag out their misery and buy myself some more time before I had to act like a mature adult. It was so brutal that my sexy detective preferred to take his time in jail rather than play against me. Gabe assured me that he wasn't placed in general population during his three turns.

"Have mercy!" Chaz threw down the remaining $7 to his name. As frustrated as he sounded, the smile on his face warmed my heart. It was amazing how much better he looked after a good meal, dessert, and the company of people who loved him.

"That's what *he* said," Gabe replied, nodding in my direction. Chaz and Meredith snorted at his joke. Gabe sent me a playful wink before he removed his game piece from the board and tossed it into the box. "I'm out."

Meredith double tapped her fist against the dining room table. "Me too." She looked at her watch and remarked how late it was. "At least we're off tomorrow."

"Some of us are working," Gabe reminded her.

"True," she replied with a grimace. "I'm sorry we stayed so late."

"It's ten o'clock, Mere. Even geezers like me can stay up that late and still function the next day."

"I'm so glad you woke me up, so I didn't sleep through dinner," Chaz told Meredith. "I would've gladly missed out on the Monopoly, but not time with my best friends." Chaz hugged each one of us tight enough that I wondered if something else was going on with him. I had to accept his reasoning or risk an argument.

After our friends had left, I had a difficult choice to make: talk or fuck? As a man, I would always lean toward fucking over talking, but I was smart enough to know that sometimes what we needed wasn't always what we wanted. I decided to do things on my terms. I ran a hot bath because the water would help us both relax and we'd be conveniently naked for when it was time to get sexy with my man.

Instead of sitting between his legs like I normally did, I straddled Gabe's lap so I could look into his soulful brown eyes. I had to mentally nudge myself to get to talking because I could easily get lost in his gaze, especially when he looked at me with so much love. I had to decide which topic I wanted to bring up first. I went with the most complicated one to get it out of the way.

"I need you to know that I trust you, Gabe. My issues with Paul are about my hang-ups and have nothing to do with you. No, I don't like that you're working together, but I understand that it doesn't change things between us."

Gabe reached up and cupped my face. "It doesn't change anything between us. First, my time on this task force is temporary. I'll only be making the trip to Cincinnati for the next week, or so, to conduct interviews, but I won't be going there indefinitely. I doubt neither Captain Reardon nor Sheriff Tucker will permit Dorchester and me to stick with the task force much longer if something doesn't break soon. Second, I don't work with Paul. He only advised our team once. I've seen him more at Vibe than at the precinct. Even if I worked closely with him daily, I'd never choose him over you. I'm not just saying that because you're naked in my lap."

"I know," I told him. "You love me."

"More than anything, Sunshine." Gabe kissed me tenderly then said, "I want to be able to help you work through the issues that hold you back. One of these days I want you to be able to tell me what made you feel this way. I know about Sampson, but you've never told me about the loser in college."

"That's heavier than what I wanted to delve into tonight," I told him, but then realized that putting it off wasn't going to help me. "Okay," I finally said. I placed my hands on his strong shoulders and blew out a calming breath.

"I didn't mean you had to do it now if you're not ready," Gabe said. Honestly, he looked as nervous to hear about my past as I felt about telling it.

"I'm not sure it'll ever be easier unless I excise it from my soul," I replied honestly. I wiggled as close as I could get to him, which prompted my body to react to my wet, naked man whose body was reacting to a wet and naked me. Gabe trailed his fingers up and down my spine soothingly. "You might've noticed that I'm on the skinny side."

"Slender," Gabe amended. "I'd even call you sleek, but never skinny. I associate unhealthy with the word skinny, and you're healthy."

"I am healthy now, but I wasn't when I went to college. I was downright skinny," I told Gabe. "I hadn't learned from my situation with Billy either, or maybe I thought hiding relationships was the norm because I fell right back into that trap. As much as Billy hurt me, Trenton was far worse."

"What's Trenton's last name?" Gabe asked. He worked his tense jaw from side to side, and I felt his fingers press a little tighter into my flesh.

"Um… I don't recall."

"That's too bad," Gabe remarked. "How could this *Trenton* be any worse than Sampson?"

"Billy hated himself, not me," I told Gabe. "Trenton wasn't ashamed or embarrassed that he was attracted to men, he was ashamed and embarrassed that he was attracted to me specifically. That, my love, is far worse."

"I hate him," Gabe said fiercely.

"Hate is a wasted emotion, but if it was possible for me to fall further in love with you than I already am, then I just did." I lowered my head to his for a quick kiss then continued the story. Gabe's heated reaction gave me the courage to talk about my past, but I wished that maybe I changed Trenton's name for his safety. Gabe was a detective after all and trained in the art of finding people.

"You're a better person than I am," Gabe responded softly.

I thought back to the times I was rude to him out of fear, and the way I resisted the feelings he brought out in me. I was downright cruel to him at times all because I was afraid of him. "Not even close, Gabe."

"We'll have to agree to disagree then." Gabe inhaled deeply and exhaled slowly. "I think I'm ready for this." The worried look in his dark eyes told me differently.

"Let me just give you the Cliff Notes version so we can get onto better ways of ending our evening." One last kiss for courage and I laid it all out for him. "I was excited to meet a guy who was obviously open about his sexuality. It was what I'd hoped for when I started college at the University of Cincinnati. I was even more excited when it was obvious Trenton returned my interest, but it took me a while to realize that nothing had changed. We were hooking up secretly, never went out together on a date, and he never showed any affection to me in public when we were together. He introduced me as a 'good friend' to his friends in classes. The only difference was that he didn't push me away or exhibit self-hatred after sex.

"It took me awhile to see what was going on because I didn't want to believe it. I finally worked up the nerve to ask Trenton why he was ashamed… of me." My voice came out shakily on the last part because it still hurt regardless of how long ago the conversation occurred or how far removed I was from the kid I used to be. "He thought I was too thin, not masculine enough, and my flamboyant personality was fun and feisty in the sack, but I was not the kind of person he saw long-term in his future."

"Ouch," Gabe said. He rubbed the skin over his heart, and it reminded me just how much he loved me. My hurt was his hurt too. "What did you do?"

"I tried to recreate myself into the person Trenton could see in his future. I was the boy version of Elle Woods from *Legally Blonde*."

"Who?" Gabe asked. After looking at him like he was from another planet, I explained to him about the movie and how I changed my physical appearance and the way I talked. I told him how I started lifting weights and taking supplements to build bulk. Like Warner in the movie, Trenton didn't take my attempts seriously. He never got past his first impression of me. "So, she realized the guy she wanted wasn't worth her time and effort in the end, right?" he asked once I finished with my comparisons.

"Yes, and she too found the man who appreciated her for the way she was, just like I did. See the similarities?" I asked.

"I do," he agreed. "Although, I suspect Elle bounced back quicker than you did."

"Yeah, well, she found her Gabe earlier in life than I did," I told him.

"I'll never be happy for the reasons your heart was guarded when we met, but I'll never be sorry it was waiting for me either." It still amazed me that this man loved me the way he did. "I'm the lucky one."

"You have a way with words, Detective Smooth Talker." I fought off my typical inclination to cover up the emotions he made me feel with snark or sex. "But *I'm* the lucky one." Okay, so I wasn't where I needed to be quite yet.

"We going to fight over who's the luckiest or are we going to celebrate that we've found one another?"

"I'm all for a party," I replied happily.

"Not that kind of celebration," Gabe said huskily before he attacked my neck with his lips, tongue, and teeth. "I was thinking something more private for just the two of us. It involves twisted sheets and naked bodies."

Sex would never solve any issues we had, individually or as a couple, but it was surely amazing to experience once we talked through the things that bothered us. I had never experienced anything close to the way Gabe made me feel when he took me in his arms and kissed me or when he slid deep inside my welcoming body. More than the physical contact, I craved the look in his eyes when I held him inside the most intimate parts of me.

That night, I felt our bond even stronger because I had given Gabe another piece from my past for safe keeping. My trust buoyed him while I reveled in the fact that he truly loved me despite my quirks, or perhaps because of them. The growly purrs that escaped his throat and the look of complete devotion in his eyes made me feel desired and cherished, things only Gabe could do for me.

I loved feeling the power surge through his strong, large body when we became one. The differences in our physique and strength were substantial, but being with Gabe never made me feel weak. In fact, knowing that I was the one who made him shake with need made me feel like I was ten feet tall and knowing that he gave his big, beautiful heart to me made me feel bulletproof.

Gabe took his time loving me that night, making sure I knew how much he cherished me. If his actions hadn't been enough to get his message across, Gabe's words after we had made love were proof that I had found the one for me. "Sunshine, please tell me that Tweedle Dick and Tweedle Douche are the only two assholes from your past because I'm not sure my heart or my restraint can handle more."

First, I laughed my ass off because—holy fuck, Gabe was starting to sound too much like me. It reminded me of the article I read about same-sex couples starting to look and act alike. I had mentioned it to Gabe once before, and he scoffed at it, but it seemed to me he was just a few snarky phrases away from wearing skinny jeans. The idea of Gabe cramming his junk into the tight fabric made me laugh even harder until tears ran down my cheeks.

"Okay, I might sound a lot like you sometimes, but I'm not wearing fucking skinny jeans," Gabe groused, reading my mind.

"Colored streak in your hair?" I asked.

"Nope."

"Hair gel?" I asked.

"Nada." I could feel Gabe's chest vibrate with laughter beneath my cheek.

"Colorful jock straps?" I waggled my brows in the dark even though he couldn't see them.

"Not under dress pants. Too obvious," Gabe replied, catching me by surprise. The idea of Gabe in a jock was mouthwatering.

"Hmm, I can teach you to work my pole," I offered.

"Now we're talking." I could tell by the drop in his voice that he wasn't referring to my pole in the attic studio. It wasn't the first time that Gabe suggested he was versatile.

I had never topped before, but that didn't stop me from replying with the kind of brash cockiness that I showed to the world. "Not sure you're ready for the thrills I would bring you."

"There's only one way to find out," Gabe said sleepily before he dropped a kiss on the top of my head.

I narrowed my eyes in the dark over the challenge he

unknowingly issued. My mind immediately went to making big plans while my guy drifted off to sleep. I could either chew my bottom lip off with worry over my possible inadequacies or I could make it a night Gabe would never forget. I knew the choice that old Josh would've made, but I was no longer that guy. I ate meatloaf on a Wednesday if I felt like it, I found the words in a word search puzzle out of order, I shared a life and a home with a man I loved, and if he wanted to be fucked, then I would do it!

FOUR

Gabe

"I KNEW YOU'D BE IN EARLY," ADRIAN SAID WHEN HE FOUND ME AT my desk at six thirty the next morning. "Find anything yet?"

"Not much," I replied. "It's like the guy didn't exist until a few years ago. There was no property ownership, federal tax or employment information available until 2014 when he surfaced in Louisiana."

"What do you think it means?" Adrian asked, clearly as puzzled as I was.

"Well, it could be that Jonathon Silver isn't his legal name," I told my partner. "Maybe he's a criminal with a new name, perhaps he's living in the Witness Protection Program with a new identity, or he's former CIA or one of the other alphabet agencies. The only thing I can find attached to him is a company called Gemelos Properties Inc., which just happens to be the name of the company who purchased Vibe. Gemelos is Spanish for twins."

"Too much of a coincidence," Adrian replied. "Sibling rivalry? Jealousy?"

"We won't know until we get more information about Jonathon Silver's background. I'm dying to know when Nate found out about his twin and what his reaction was. Maybe Jonathon was jealous of Nate's success and decided to take it for himself," I told Adrian.

"Damn, I wish I was working this case with you," he replied.

"I wish you were too, partner." I felt dread creeping in as I thought about the week ahead and hoped that the interviews revealed new leads. Adrian and I made an excellent team, and I missed working with him. He was the good cop to my bad, and we had one hell of a track record together. "You can bet I'll be asking your feedback on what I find out."

My temporary partner, Detective John Dorchester with the Carter County Sheriff's Department, showed up about thirty minutes later. Adrian and I were split up when it was determined that the man responsible for bringing the largest amount of drugs into our county was also Josh's ex. Billy also stalked and harassed Josh while trying to make it look like Nate's killer had shifted his attention to Josh. The captain decided it would be best if I worked on Nate's homicide case while Adrian worked on wrapping the loose ends locally when the DEA took Billy Sampson off our hands.

Adrian and I were both assigned temporary partners. John Dorchester was cool and funny while Adrian's partner, David Whitworth, was uptight and asshole-ish. Luckily for Adrian, his time to work with Detective Stick In His Ass Sideways was over.

"Good morning, fellas," Dorchester said, tossing the green apple that would be his breakfast in the air. "What's going on?" His apple hit the floor along with his jaw when Adrian and I told him what we learned over the weekend.

"Shit! This could be the break we needed," Dorchester replied excitedly.

"It could, but right now it just leads to more questions," I told him then explained how Silver just appeared in 2014 out of nowhere.

Dorchester blew out a sharp whistle before saying, "This is some complicated shit."

"We'll find out just how complicated when we re-interview Nate's attorney and former silent business partner this afternoon," I told him.

"I want all the details later," Adrian said to us as we were leaving. The slight pout in his voice made me smile.

"You got it, partner," I hollered over my shoulder.

During the ride to Cincinnati, we speculated about Jonathon Silver's identity and the timing of his appearance in Nate's life and questioned if it had something to do with his death. Most of it was legitimate discussion about questions to ask, but things started to go awry as we got closer to the city.

"I bet aliens abducted him as a baby," Dorchester gave as the reason for Silver's lack of documented existence. "Only Nate was left behind."

"We may need a judge to unseal the adoption paperwork," I said suddenly. "If we know the birth mom's identity then maybe we can locate her or people she knew well who can tell us why the babies went to different homes."

"Fine, be practical," Dorchester groused from the passenger seat.

The task force had already gathered by the time we arrived. I passed out a copy of Jonathon Silver's driver license to everyone in the room. Their surprise was clearly etched on their faces and in the way they all started asking questions at once. I held up my hand to silence them.

"Here's what happened and here's what I know right now." Then I told them about my dinner and what my research turned up. "You can't tell me that Turner's attorney didn't know about Silver's existence, especially if he inherited Nate's fortune. He was either protecting the guy or is afraid of him. Today we're going to learn which one it is."

"Have you been able to connect him to Owen Smithson?" Detective Weston Jade asked, referring to the guy who had sent the threatening emails and photos to Nate. The CPD had traced the IP address used in the emails, and it led them to Owen, who unfortunately was found dead.

"I have not attempted that yet this morning. I'll assign that task to you, Detective," I told him. I looked around the room and asked, "Are there any more questions before we start our interviews?" No one had any, so I assigned interviews, times, and locations. I looked at Dorchester and said, "We're going to take a little field trip before our interviews this afternoon."

"Oh goody," he said, skipping beside me. "Can I buy a souvenir?"

"Depends on how well you play good cop," I replied.

It was nothing more than a hunch that had me driving to Vibe at such an early hour. The club closed at two in the morning so finding anyone there at nine was a stretch. I knew my gut had been right when I saw the sleek, black sedan parked around the back of the club near the employee entrance.

"That car is nearly identical to Nate's," Dorchester observed out loud. I suspected that black was probably the most common color on all luxury sedans, but that car appeared to be the exact year, make, and model as the one Nate was driving when he died. "I mean, Nate's car is still in the impound lot, so this clearly isn't it, but…" Dorchester let his words trail off.

"It looks like someone is trying to step into his brother's shoes," I said.

"Yeah, it certainly looks that way," Dorchester agreed. "Wonder if he's wearing his clothes and sleeping in his bed too?"

The thought creeped me out, but I wouldn't classify anything out of the realm of possibilities in the case—well, except the alien abduction angle. "Let's go find out, Mulder," I said to Dorchester.

"Smartass," he mumbled under his breath as he exited the car. "I guess that makes you Scully." He laughed much harder at his joke than I did.

I knocked loudly on the metal door marked as Employee's Only several times and grew frustrated when they went unanswered. I had been in Nate's office twice and knew damn well how close it was to the door I was banging on. Silver either wasn't in the office and didn't hear me or heard me and ignored me. It also could've meant that he met with foul play like his brother. I tested the handle and was surprised to find the door unlocked. I looked over at Dorchester and saw that he was just as surprised.

"That's probably not a good sign," he said, stating the obvious. Dorchester and I automatically reached for our guns. I moved to the left side of the door and gave him a nod when I was ready, and he pulled open the door with his free hand.

"Police," I yelled loudly down the long hallway that led to Nate's office and the rear of the bar. In the hallway, there were two glossy black doors directly across from one another. I knew one was Nate's office but had no clue what was behind the other one. "Mr. Silver," I yelled as we approached the two doors. "Are you in there, sir?" There was no response.

I kept my gun aimed in front of me in my right hand and grabbed the door handle for Nate's office with my left. I looked over my shoulder and saw that Dorchester had done the same. "One, two, three…" We pushed the doors open and entered the rooms at the same time.

The lights were on inside the office, but no one was there. I was about to see if Dorchester had found Silver when a secret panel behind Nate's desk opened, and Jonathon Silver walked out buck naked, toweling his hair as if he'd just come out of the shower and completely unaware that I was in the room.

"Mr. Silver," I said firmly.

He jerked to a stop and yanked his towel off his head, but made no move to cover his dick from my view. "Well, this is a surprise, Detective Wyatt."

"You know who I am?" I asked.

"Of course, I know who you are. You're the man who rejected my brother when he turned to you for help," he said bitterly. "Do you mind putting your gun away?"

"Do you mind putting *yours* away?" Dorchester asked as he entered the room.

Jonathon Silver chuckled as he wrapped the towel around his waist and knotted it. "Does my nudity offend your sensibilities, Detective Dorchester?" Silver asked him.

"How do you know my name?" Dorchester asked him. "Better yet, why don't you explain to us how we don't know about you? I find it odd that you've made no attempt to get involved and assist us with the investigation to find your brother's killer. Does that sound odd to you, Gabe?" Dorchester asked me.

"I'd move heaven and earth if it were my brother," I replied, which was the truth. I still reviewed Dylan's case file and checked if any new leads popped up twenty years later.

"And you think that makes me look guilty?" Silver asked. "Put yourself in my shoes and see how you'd feel. My brother—identical twin to be exact—is killed after reaching out to the good detective here twice and the Cincinnati Police Department once. Can you maybe see how I don't have any faith in you to catch whoever was harassing Nate?"

I could see how he felt that way, but that would only motivate me to get in their faces more, not less. "Put yourself in our shoes, Mr. Silver," I said, mimicking the words he'd used. "We had a man who claimed he was threatened but wouldn't cooperate when we tried to help him through legal channels. What exactly could we have done differently?"

"More than what you did." Silver shook with anger. "I know all about the new task force, which is too little too late in my opinion, and those who are on it. I'm staying vigilant even when those who should are not."

He sounded like some sitcom vigilante. "Mr. Silver, you weren't so vigilant when you left the back door unlocked."

"Ah, that's how you got in," he said. "I guess I need to have a longer chat with Alexander—well, perhaps an actual chat that includes words and not body language next time. Don't be too mad at him, Detectives, because I promise he wasn't capable of much thought when he left." Silver had deepened the timbre of his voice, and his words were filled with sexual innuendo, leaving no doubt in our minds what, or who, Alexander had been doing in the club at the early hour.

Silver pulled the towel off his waist and dropped it to the floor before he reached for his clothes from his desk chair. "If you want to talk to me, then you can do it in the presence of my attorney. It's the same attorney Nate used, so your task force should be familiar with him." He took his sweet time pulling on his underwear.

"Rick Spizer?" Dorchester asked, nonplussed by Silver's actions.

"The one and only," Silver replied.

"That's great news," I told him. "We have an appointment with him at noon so why don't you join him at the precinct?" Jonathon Silver narrowed his crystal blue eyes in speculation. If he refused, he would look guiltier and if he agreed he would have to answer questions or have his mouthpiece decline or interject on his behalf, which would also make him look guilty. "This is your moment to step up and prove that you want to help catch the man who killed your brother, as you claim."

"I won't be baited by you, Detective. I don't owe you a fucking thing," he replied hotly, "but I will be there at noon."

"Thank you," I told him.

"I'm not doing it for you; I'm doing it for Nate."

"We'll see you at noon," I told him. "Be sure to bring your alibi information with you for the night that your brother died."

Dorchester and I were almost to his office door when he spoke up. "Detective Wyatt, am I identical to my brother in *every* way?" His words shocked me, but I kept walking instead of responding to his crude question. I could hear his dark laughter ringing through the hallway as if it was chasing me out of the building.

"So, you and Nate, huh?" Dorchester asked once we were back in the spring sunlight.

"Once," was my response. "We were never a couple or anything like that. In fact, a year passed between our two meetings."

"You're investigating the death of a former hookup while working with another. That's got to be some interesting 'how was your day, dear' dinner conversation. Unless Josh doesn't know," Dorchester added.

"How'd you know about Paul?" I asked him after picking my chin up off the damn pavement. I didn't like that my personal life connected to this case, but I knew that my objectivity was uncompromised.

"I'm a detective," he replied. "I'm paid to read body language and stuff. I'm not sure if the other team members are as astute, but I saw the way your eyes widened slightly and your body stiffened. Paul's a smooth customer, but he had similar reactions as you. The first impression wasn't enough to convince me, but then he offered to show you to the bathroom when you asked for directions. Most guys would've told you to turn right outside the conference room and then left at the end of the hallway." Dorchester laughed. "You didn't answer my question about Josh."

I unlocked my car with the key fob. "He knows."

"And?"

I thought back to the conversation I had with Josh the previous night. I knew by his body language and words that he didn't like the situation, but he trusted me. I smiled when I thought about how much faith Josh had in me. "He trusts me," I told Dorchester.

"As he should," he replied. "I have to ask something, and I promise your answer stays between us."

"What?" I asked uncertainly.

"I'm coming at this from a purely scientific angle," Dorchester said seriously. "Are they identical *everywhere*?"

I noticed Jonathon Silver's cock, of course; I was a gay man after all. Although I knew the answer to Dorchester's question, I wasn't about to answer it. I pinned him with a disbelieving glare instead.

"Your silence speaks for itself," he said smugly. "I guess I know why Nate's stalker was so hung up on the size of his dick in that email."

I had temporarily forgotten about the exact wording in that email due to the discovery of Silver's existence, but Dorchester was right. Dorchester had never seen the email or the pictures, or he'd have known the answer to his one question. Commenting on the size of Nate's dick and being remorseful that it was wasted on him wasn't something a brother would say to another, especially one who was equally as endowed. That didn't necessarily mean that Silver was in the clear; hell, he could've said those things intentionally so that he could avoid scrutiny. Smoke and mirrors.

"Unless they had a twincest thing going on," Dorchester commented.

"Gross," I replied. "This case just keeps getting weirder every single day."

"Do you have the feeling that we haven't even scratched the surface of weird yet?" he asked.

"I do," I replied, which was why I was eager to get back to the police station to do more digging into Jonathon Silver's property company. I didn't want to be caught off guard more than I had already been.

FIVE

Josh

IT WAS BY PURE COINCIDENCE THAT I TALKED CHAZ INTO COMING with me to take Diva for her booster shots. I didn't have an ulterior motive for the invite at all. *Wink. Wink.* I didn't think it was coincidence though that Chaz dressed up a little more than he normally would for a visit to the veterinarian either, but I didn't remark on it. I was becoming one of those annoying friends that everyone groans when they see them coming. You know the type— the one that has fallen madly in love and wants everyone else to feel the same things too. So, yeah, I totally twisted Chaz's arm to come along with me and used his guilt against him to get my way. It wasn't like Diva needed an extra hand because she was a shameful slut when it came to Dr. Dimples. It was embarrassing the way she purred the second he walked into the room.

"Is that a new cologne?" I asked him, although I knew the answer. *Okay, maybe I couldn't just let it go by without a mention.* I glanced over and saw a pink flush creeping across his cheeks. I saw him fiddling with the buttons on his shirtsleeves. I couldn't remember the last time I saw Chaz wear something other than a T-shirt or long-sleeved T-shirt.

"It was a birthday gift from my mom," Chaz said softly. His birthday was eight months prior, and I'd never smelled it on him before or heard him mention it.

"Well, it smells nice," I told him. "New shirt?" *Why stop when I was on a roll?*

"It was a birthday gift from my grandmother," he replied, squirming in his seat. He was such a bad liar, but I chose not to call him on it.

"Well, Grandma Gertie has great taste." She totally did not have good taste and another reason I knew he was holding out on me. Again. I remember very well the hideous things she bought him in the past. I nearly lost my cool when I recalled the knitted sweater she made him during his *Teenage Mutant Ninja Turtles* phase. It was the most disgusting color green I'd ever seen and had sea turtles all over it; as if that was anywhere close. His mother made him wear it to school where it had an unfortunate accident with ketchup and mustard at lunch and couldn't be saved. That sweater was so ugly that no one asked how Chaz got his hands on those two condiments on sausage and pancake day.

"That combination of blues and grays makes your pretty blue eyes pop. I'll have to ask Grannie where she got it so I can see if they have any that would look good on me."

"Macy's," Chaz said quickly as if he didn't want me to call her. "She left the tag on it."

"So, who bought you the brown leather half boots?" I asked. "Don't tell me, let me guess. Hmm… Your aunt Sandra."

"Hanging around that detective has rubbed off on you. Can't get nothing past you," Chaz said sarcastically.

I wanted to come back at him with a snarky reply about Gabe rubbing off on me every chance he got, but I didn't. It was obvious to me that Chaz was going through something that he didn't want to discuss. He gave the excuse about the video games, and I thought there might be a little bit of truth there, but I suspected that something else was going on.

"You look and smell very nice," I told him. It was good to see some color on his cheeks; even if it was because he was slightly embarrassed over dressing up to see Dr. Dimples.

"Thank you."

Diva softly growled her displeasure from inside her cat carrier on Chaz's lap. "I'm not sure Diva agrees, but you know how fickle she can be. Don't take her opinion to heart," I told him. "She just wants me to speed up so she can get to rubbing her head against her favorite vet's dimpled chin." I saw Chaz squirm in his seat and I knew he was thinking about rubbing a certain head of his against the good doctor's square chin.

Alyssa smiled brightly at us from behind her desk when we entered the waiting room. "Well don't you just look adorable this morning, Chaz."

"Uh… thank you," he muttered. "I'll take Diva and have a seat while you fill out the paperwork," Chaz told me.

"Better yet," said Dr. Delicious as he stepped out of his office, "why don't you and Diva come with me. I'll get started with her checkup while Josh fills out the paperwork."

"Uh…"

"Come on, now. I don't bite." Kyle's sultry, seductive voice made me blink several times and lose focus on what I had begun to write on the paperwork Alyssa handed me. What the hell was going on here? Was Dr. Dreamboat stepping up his game?

"Uh…" Jesus, Chaz was starting to sound like a broken record. I did what any good friend would do. I subtly kicked him in the back of his leg to break him from his trance. "Okay."

I smiled as I watched Chaz follow Kyle back to an exam room. I thought they would make the most adorable couple. Alyssa cleared her throat, pulling my attention back to her.

"That's a new form, and perhaps I should go over it with you," she said to me. I looked at the form and noted that it was a new format, but it asked the same questions that were on the old one. She gave me a conspiring wink when I returned my eyes to hers. "It could take a while."

Alyssa went over every line on the form as I completed it, which added an extra ten minutes to the process. I had expected to see Kyle halfway through his exam of Diva by the time I got back to the room, but instead, I saw Diva twining herself around Kyle's legs trying to get his attention while he held Chaz's bleeding finger in his hand.

"Well, at least we know the little vixen is well-vaccinated," Kyle said as he examined Chaz.

"What happened?" I asked.

"Your little slutty cat bit me when I didn't hand her to Dr. Dimples quick enough," Chaz said petulantly. Kyle stood up a little straighter and blinked at Chaz several times before a wide smile spread across his face that showed why he earned the nickname. Unfortunately for Chaz, Kyle didn't know we called him that until just then. Poor Chaz turned an unnatural shade of white when he realized what he'd said.

"Dr. Dimples, huh?" Kyle asked. "I like it. Maybe I should change my avatar name to that."

"Chaz plays *World of Warcraft* too," I told him. "He's really good at it." I had no fucking clue if he was good or not, but that didn't stop me. "Plays a lot at night and makes a lot of friends around the world." I was starting to ramble, and Chaz was looking at me with bulging eyes that pleaded for me to shut the fuck up, but I didn't know how once I was on a roll. "I think he's met a guy online and just doesn't want me to know about it. He worries I'll make fun of him or something."

"Josh," Chaz growled.

"I would never!" I clutched my heart dramatically and blinked my eyes innocently. "We never know when we'll find the other half of our soul. Sometimes they're standing right in front of you all along."

Chaz and Kyle didn't hear a word I was saying though because they were too busy staring into each other's eyes. I was about to start patting my own back when Alyssa burst into the room.

"Dr. Vaughn," she said breathlessly, "Beth Handerneski called and said their bull got loose. They tracked him down and lured him back in the trailer, but not before he cut himself pretty bad on a fence. They want to know if you can come out and take a look at him."

Kyle broke eye contact with Chaz and looked at his reception-ist. "Tell them I'll be out there as soon as I finish up here." When Alyssa left the room, Kyle was back to doctor mode. *That's some damn bullshit right there.* "Come here, pretty girl," Kyle cooed to Diva. He picked the cat up, and she purred loudly as she butted her head against his chin. Kyle talked to her the entire time he exam-ined my shameless cat. He gave her ears an extra scratch before he handed my feline over to me. "I'll let Molly give her the booster so that Diva doesn't get mad at me." His comment made me laugh. "I better get out to the Handerneski's farm and look at Tank. I'll see you guys around." He stopped in front of Chaz and said, "Maybe I'll find you online, and we can play together." *Oh, that sounded a little naughty!* Kyle left the room without waiting to hear a response from Chaz.

Once we were alone in the exam room, a hard shiver worked its way through Chaz's body as if Kyle had asked him to play with his joystick. I was glad to see I wasn't the only one who thought so. "I'm going to kill you," Chaz said when he could finally talk again.

"Gabe won't let you," I said smugly.

"He'll help me when he finds out what you just did," Chaz said, sounding wounded.

"What? I told Kyle that you like to play *World of Warcraft* too. Did I lie?" I asked.

"You insinuated much more than that, and you know it. What the hell was that 'sometimes they're standing right in front of you all along' bullshit?"

"It wasn't bullshit," I replied. "Gabe had been right in front of me all along." Well, we lived in the same damn town anyway, which was the same as Kyle and Chaz. Besides, maybe they had already connected online and didn't even know it. That damn Tank had to get loose and ruin it. Lucky for him I loved all of God's creatures, or I'd turn him into meatloaf.

"Just because it happened to you doesn't mean it will happen for me. You really embarrassed me, Jazz," Chaz said softly. "I know you're just trying to help, but please stop it. There's no way a guy like that wants a guy like me."

My best friend was beautiful in every possible way, and I wished he could see what I saw in him. I let out a soft sigh and apologized. "I won't do it again," I added. The look in his blue eyes told me that he didn't believe me for a second, but he didn't argue.

Molly came in and gave my cat her booster shot so that Kyle could remain in Diva's good graces. Chaz was oddly silent on the way home, and I worried that I had gone too far. I pulled into his driveway and looked over at him after I put my car in park. Chaz was staring off into the distance as if lost in thought. A large grin split his face, and I looked through the windshield to see what made him smile, but didn't see anything.

"Care to let me in on the secret?" I asked him.

Chaz jerked in his seat as if he forgot I was even with him. "Uh, I just had a thought."

"And?"

"Strategy really," he clarified. "For, um… my game."

"A strategy for your game can make you smile that big?" I asked doubtfully.

"I just figured out the solution to a problematic part of the game, so, yeah," Chaz replied. "No time like the present to get to it. I wish I could say it's been fun today, but that would be a fucking lie." He handed Diva's cat carrier to me so that he could get out. "See you tomorrow," he said absently before he shut the door. I could tell his mind had already gone back to his *strategy*.

Buddy was anxiously awaiting our return as if he was worried about Diva. The two had become friends rather quickly, but only after Buddy let her know he wouldn't give into her demanding behavior. Buddy was licking the side of Diva's face in greeting when I left them to reunite in the living room so I could change the sheets on my bed and set up a romantic scene with fresh linen and candles throughout the room.

I had just removed the comforter from my bed when movement across the alleyway caught my eye. A white moving van was backing into the driveway of the home that had belonged to my friend Bianca, who was murdered the year before. In fact, her case was the one that first brought Gabe to my door. Her house sat empty since she was killed, except for when my creepy ex-boyfriend squatted there to spy on Gabe and me, but it appeared the vacancy was coming to an end.

I watched as two tall men exited the van and walked around to the back to open the large sliding door. Their uniforms were the same color as the moving company logo painted boldly on the side of the truck. My creative brain immediately started to imagine who might be moving in. A sexy single guy for my Meredith? A young family with children whose laughter would echo throughout the streets during the spring and summer months?

One of the guys walked up the back steps to the door that opened into the kitchen. He disappeared inside for a few minutes then reappeared when the garage door opened from inside. I forgot all about my task and stood there gawking at the activity going on across the alley. I decided to guess who was moving in based on the furniture they unloaded.

The first item was a large ornately carved wooden headboard that took two of them to carry. Okay, that alone didn't give much away. Next thing I saw was a gigantic flat screen TV that told me a man was moving in. But was he alone? I went to the kitchen and made a cup of coffee when the movers didn't return to the van right away. I wasn't gone long, but when I returned, I saw that there was a sleek black Mini Cooper with white racing stripes on the hood parked in the driveway next to the moving truck. I had serious stripe envy and wondered if Princess would look cute with a set of silver ones.

My musings were interrupted when a tall, slender man walked out of the garage. I squinted my eyes and leaned closer to the window to get a better look. He appeared to be wearing a pair of AG jeans that cost as much as an hour in my salon chair. His shirt was a dove gray, long-sleeved T-shirt that bore the Hermes logo on it. I would've bet money that Gucci made the black leather biker boots he wore on his feet. Just who was this stylish man and what was he doing in Blissville?

The wind kicked up and blew his longish locks of dark brown hair away from his face making it look like a model shoot. It was hard to tell from where I stood, but I thought I saw strands of caramel highlighted hair when the sun came out from behind the clouds. I was willing to bet those highlights weren't natural either. The man tilted his head back as if he was worshiping the early spring sun.

Suddenly, as if he felt my intense gaze focused on him, he lowered his head and looked in my direction. He was too far away to be certain, but it felt like our eyes locked regardless of the distance between us.

My heart raced suddenly while an inexplicable fear washed over me. I took a step back from the window and pulled the curtains closed, severing my connection with the man. I wasn't sure how I knew it, but the stranger's appearance in our neighborhood wasn't an accident. I couldn't be sure of what it meant, but I was certain I'd be the first to find out.

SIX

Gabe

THE INTERVIEWS WITH THE CLUB EMPLOYEES DIDN'T TURN UP ANY new leads. According to them, Nate hadn't acted strangely leading up to his death, none of them were aware of any illegal activity occurring at the club, and none of them knew that Jonathon Silver existed until he bought the nightclub. On the surface, the interviews looked like a complete waste of time, but I wasn't a surface guy.

"Did you notice how similar their answers are to one another?" I asked Dorchester and Weston. "As if they rehearsed what they were going to say before coming in."

"I thought so too," Weston replied.

"That may be," Dorchester answered, "but their answers are nearly identical to the ones they gave the first time around. Typically, if they weren't honest they would've deviated from their original answers."

"Unless they were afraid for their lives," I replied.

"True," Dorchester and Weston agreed.

The interviews wrapped up early enough that I had time to think about my line of questioning for both Silver and his attorney. Admittedly, the original interview questions for the attorney, Rick Spizer, were pretty basic. It wasn't that I expected to get a big confession that he helped cover up Nate's illegal activity from him, but I hoped that I could at least rattle him enough to give us something.

The two men arrived fifteen minutes early, but I made them wait. I wanted them annoyed when the interview began in hopes that they'd let something fly. It worked well in some cases, but I wasn't holding my breath with these two. One was a well-educated attorney, and the other was... I didn't yet know, but I had already seen that he didn't rattle easily.

"We're going to question you first, Mr. Spizer," I told the attorney as I led him to the first available interview room. "Then you can be present when we talk to Mr. Silver as he requested."

"Fine," Spizer said. Jonathon Silver said nothing as he followed Weston to another interview room down the hall.

I went through the routine of identifying myself and Dorchester for the recording before asking Spizer to state his full name and relation to Nate Turner. "Did Nate Turner tell you he was being harassed and threatened?" I asked, jumping right into the fire once he finished identifying himself for the recording.

"No," Spizer replied calmly.

"Did Nate Turner involve you in covering up any illegal activities for him?"

"No." Spizer's tone remained steady.

"When did you learn that Jonathon Silver existed?" Dorchester asked.

I saw a slight crack in the attorney's calm. He had to walk a fine line because he represented both the brother who died and the one who was sitting inside an interview room down the hall. He was limited to what he could say without a court order, which no judge would sign off on with the little evidence we found up to that point. I didn't want to make an enemy of this guy, so I went easy on him.

"I'm not asking you to break confidentiality ethics, counselor. I'm simply asking when you became aware that Nate Turner had a twin brother, not how you found out," I told him.

"It was June of last year, so around nine months," he said after a short pause.

"A few months before Nate began receiving threats to his life," I remarked. Spizer opened his mouth to argue, but I held up my hand to stop him. "Save your comments and defense for when I interview him. Let's start with why you didn't feel the need to tell the police about Silver during your first interview."

"No one asked," Spizer fired back. "I only answered the questions they asked."

"Counselor, Detective Jade asked for names of people who might give more information about what was going on in Nate's life, and you said that you couldn't provide any. Now, I'm not accusing you of lying, but I feel like you deliberately mislead the investigators."

"I didn't mention Jonathon because he tragically lost the brother he'd just found and was in a state of shock." His answer was asinine.

"Mr. Spizer, let me be frank with you right now. Your actions don't look like those of an attorney representing a client. If that had been the case, you would've notified the police that Nate Turner had a long-lost brother and would've asked for some time to let him adjust to the news before the interview or you would've made yourself available when he was questioned. You may not have a high opinion of police in general, but we are trained on how to handle bereaved family members."

It was obvious by the way he stiffened in his chair that he was offended by my admonishment. He was in for a real treat if he thought that was bad. I asked a few more questions that received "no" or "I don't know" answers before I ended the interview. I hadn't expected to get much out of Spizer anyway, but I at least found out how long he'd known about Jonathon Silver.

The three of us walked to the interview room where Silver was waiting for us, sipping coffee from the disposable cup like he didn't have a care in the world. I went through the same routine as I did with Spizer, but went a step further. Even though he wasn't under arrest, I read Jonathon Silver his Miranda Rights and watched him closely to gauge his reaction. His eyes narrowed, and his jaw tightened hard enough that I expected to hear his teeth crack, which told me he wasn't happy at all.

"Thank you for coming in today," I said once I was ready to begin. "Can you please state your full name for the recording and relationship to the victim, Nathaniel Turner." I saw Silver flinch slightly when I said his brother's name. The reaction was so minuscule that I would've missed it had I not been trained to look for it.

"Jonathon David Silver and Nathaniel Turner is… *was* my brother." His words faltered a bit toward the end. Earlier that morning in his office, Silver exhibited anger and arrogance, neither of which were present a few hours later. He was more soft-spoken and subdued. Was it genuine or an act in front of the attorney?

"Can you tell us who might've wanted to kill your brother?" I asked.

"No," he said softly. "He told me about the threats, of course, but he said he didn't know why he was receiving them."

"Did you believe him?" Dorchester asked from beside me.

Silver released a long frustrated sigh. "Honestly? No. Nate was a very private man and getting to know him had been hard. He was totally shocked to learn he had a twin brother and that he didn't really know the parents who raised him, so you can imagine that he had some serious trust issues."

"What do you mean that he didn't know his adoptive parents very well?" I asked. Silver made it sound like they were shady in some way.

"They never told him about me so he began to wonder what other secrets they might've been hiding," Silver replied.

"Are you implying that him digging into their background had something to do with the threats?" Dorchester asked.

Silver shrugged and said, "The timing works."

"As does your appearance in his life," I told Nate's brother. "It's pretty easy to deflect guilt on the dealings of a deceased couple." I turned to Spizer, who had reportedly been the family attorney for decades. "Could there be any truth to what Silver said?"

"Not that I'm aware of, Detective. I wasn't Charles and Marie's attorney at the time of Nate's adoption. I found out about Jonathon from Nate," Spizer replied. "I can attest that Nate was angry and bitter that he'd gone his entire life without knowing about Jonathon."

"How'd you find out about Nate?" I asked Jonathon.

"Nate was given up for adoption, but I was not. Our birth mom raised me, and she told me about Nate before she died." He swallowed hard, and I could tell it was still an emotional thing for him to discuss. It appeared to be the first honest reaction I'd gotten out of him. "The details about the adoption are irrelevant to Nate's death, and I prefer not to speak about them."

"I take it that you are the beneficiary of your brother's estate," I commented.

"Yes," Silver answered between gritted teeth, clearly not liking where my line of questioning was going.

"Can you tell us where you were between the years of your birth and 2014 when you magically appeared in Louisiana?" I asked.

"Don't answer that," Spizer informed his client. "Detective, that's completely irrelevant and none of your business."

"I don't agree, counselor." I leaned forward and pinned Silver with a damning glare. "Your client surfaces out of nowhere with no past to speak of, and his wealthy brother gets killed within months. Now he owns his brother's business, drives an identical car, and has access to his fortune. Do you live in his house too? Sleep in his bed?" I asked Silver.

"That's enough, Detective!" Spizer said firmly.

Silver didn't move, not even to blink when I threw accusations at him. I knew damn well that I was looking at a man who'd been trained to hide his reactions. CIA? Elite Special Forces? Did he kill his brother to get access to his wealth or had his past actions possibly gotten Nate killed?

"You're barking up the wrong tree," Silver finally said after a long silence. "I was ecstatic to find my brother, and I had no reason to hurt him."

"Nate's homicide was very personal," I told him. "Someone stalked him, threatened him, ran his car off the road, and put a bullet in his head. We're talking about a trained killer who leaves behind no evidence. Someone knows something, and they better start talking before whoever killed Nate decides to start eliminating risks."

"Is this an example of how you deal with bereaved family members after a loss, Detective?" Spizer asked. "If so, I'm not at all impressed." The attorney put his hand on his client's shoulder then said, "We're done here, Jonathon."

"Just one more thing," I demanded. Both men halted from rising from the chairs and looked at me. "Where were you the night of January twenty-second?" I asked Silver.

"You don't have to answer that," Spizer told his client.

"It's okay, Rick," Silver said, patting Rick's arm before he reached inside his suit jacket and pulled out a piece of paper. "These men can attest to my whereabouts that night and morning." The wink he gave me said they hadn't been playing poker all night long.

I looked at the list and was surprised to see the names of four men and their phone numbers. Yeah, my mind went there, and I wondered if he entertained them individually or all at the same time. The dark chuckle that rumbled from his chest told me it was the latter.

"What can I say? I have a very healthy appetite."

Both men rose to their feet and started to exit the room. "I'll let you know if I have any more questions," I said to their retreating backs. Neither man responded in any way.

"What do you think?" Dorchester asked me once I shut the recording equipment off.

"I don't know what to think," I replied honestly. "We need to find out more about Nate's adoptive parents and the details of the adoption. Maybe what he suggested has merit. We can't afford to ignore any avenue if we want justice." Silver's tone had turned chilly when he mentioned Nate's adoptive parents. It said to me that he knew—or at least suspected—more than he let on. His unwillingness to talk about his childhood or the reason his mom gave up one child and not the other was bizarre.

Dorchester looked at his watch and said, "At least we're down to our final interview for the day." I could tell he was as ready to head back home as I was.

Marlon Bandowe appeared right on time. He dressed like a man who was as conservative as he was reported to be and looked extremely nervous. I introduced myself and Dorchester and saw how badly his hand shook when I extended my hand to him in greeting. He greatly resembled a timid mouse.

"Have a seat, Mr. Bandowe," I said. "Thank you for coming in today. This meeting should be brief."

"Thank you, Detective Wyatt. This whole thing has been completely unsettling." I found it odd that he referred to the slaying of his former partner as unsettling. We were talking about death, not an ill-prepared meal.

"Forgive me for saying so, but you and Nate Turner seem like improbable business partners," I told the man, which earned a small smile.

"I imagine so," he said. "Our families were great friends, and we grew up together. I knew the man my entire life, so I didn't hesitate when he asked me to be a silent partner in his club."

"See here's the thing I don't understand about that," I told Bandowe. "Nate Turner had plenty of money, so why did he need your startup capital?"

"Well, he… uh…"

"Was his money tied up in a trust at the time?" Dorchester asked while the man was still stuttering out an answer.

"Not that I'm aware of, but I didn't ask him," Bandowe replied.

"That doesn't make sense either," I said, leaning forward so I could enjoy watching the man squirm. "I've read many articles about your 'Christian family values' and your stance on issues involving LGBTQ equality. You're not an ally to the LGBTQ community, yet you finance and are part owner of a gay nightclub."

"It was a good business deal," he said defensively. "I kept my personal beliefs out of the business dealings."

"I call bullshit," Dorchester said.

"Believe what you want, but it's true," Bandowe replied.

If this guy was telling the truth, then he was a real jerk. He privately took money from the LGBTQ community while he worked against them publicly. It was my experience that the more a straight man railed against homosexuality, the higher the odds were that he too was gay. Sometimes I just had to throw out a random net and hope to catch a break.

"When did your sexual relationship with Nate Turner end?" I asked.

Bandowe's body tightened and bowed like an invisible string was pulling on him. All color leached from his face until his skin took on an unhealthy pallor.

"Breathe, Mr. Bandowe, then answer my question. Honestly," I added.

The man closed his eyes briefly and swallowed hard. "It didn't end," he said in a voice so soft I barely heard him. His eyes filled with tears and his body began to shake. "Nate and I have had a relationship on and off since high school. I could never give him what he wanted from me, and we would break up for a while, but we always found our way back to one another. He had his conquests when we were apart, and I tried to fill my loneliness by making myself into something that I wasn't. I hadn't realized how much he meant to me until he was gone. He'll never know how much I loved him." I felt sympathy for the man right then.

"What do you know about his brother?" Dorchester asked.

"Not much," Bandowe said with a shrug. "He appeared in Nate's life last summer and rocked his world. He started questioning everything he knew about his parents when he discovered that he had a twin brother."

"Why didn't you mention Nate having a brother to police during your first interview?" I asked.

"The cops asked me about our business dealings, not about anything personal. I would've told them about Jonathon had they asked, but they didn't," the man said. "I got the impression that the cops thought something illegal was going on inside the club and Nate died as a result. I don't agree."

"Can you tell me if Nate had any other business dealings besides the club?"

"The last time we were together he mentioned something about investing in a casino deal, but no specifics of with who, when, or where. His comment was so innocuous that it slipped my mind until you asked me that question," Bandowe replied. I sat up straighter in my chair because that was the first time anyone mentioned the prospect of a casino. "Are there any other questions, Detectives? If not, I have another meeting to attend."

I looked at Dorchester, who shook his head that he didn't have any questions. "You're free to go," I told him. I slid him my business card and asked him to call me if he thought of anything else or if news of the casino reached his ears.

Dorchester and I met with the task force to discuss what we'd learned and I assigned duties for the next day before we headed back home.

"Casinos can be a cutthroat business," he said once we were on the road. "Things got ugly in Carter County a short time back when there was a discussion of building a casino there."

"I didn't hear about that," I told him. "When was this?"

"I'm going to say about four years ago, so probably before you moved here," he replied.

"What happened?"

"Developers felt that Carter County was the perfect spot to build a casino due to the proximity to several highways and because it was about an hour away from three major cities—Dayton, Cincinnati, and Columbus. The religious groups didn't agree and talked about how gambling destroyed families and brought in prostitution and other crimes to an area. The county commissioners didn't approve the casino, so the developers collected enough signatures on the petition to get it on a statewide ballot."

"The entire state got to decide if you guys got a casino built in your county?" I asked. "That sounds underhanded to me. 'You don't want us to build in your county so we'll find another way' probably wasn't well received."

"No, it wasn't," Dorchester replied. "It was a hotly contested issue, and the measure failed on election night."

"You think it's possible that talk has started back up?" I asked.

"Anything's possible," he replied.

"Were there any local people in Blissville or the surrounding county who did support a casino?" I asked. If so, chances were high they'd been contacted again.

"There were a few that I can recall. Your mayor and a few county commissioners were for it," Dorchester told me.

I wasn't surprised to hear that Rocky Beaumont supported the casino initiative. The man hated my guts, and there was no way that I could get him to talk to me. Rocky threatened to sue us if we leaked his affair with County Commissioner Jack Wallace. I love how he thought I had the time or inclination to out his stupid ass. It seemed that Rocky didn't mind being known as a player when it came to the ladies, but not when it came to men. "Was Jack Wallace one of the commissioners?" I asked Dorchester. I figured if Rocky was for it then maybe his boyfriend was too.

"He was, how'd you know?" he asked.

"Just a guess." Jack Wallace wasn't a big fan of mine either, but I figured I had a better chance of getting him to talk to me. "We'll want to have a chat with Jack to see if there have been any murmurs of building the casino again."

"Good idea. We'll do that in the morning before we head to Cincinnati," Dorchester replied.

I dropped him off at his car and headed home. I loved Monday nights because Josh was off and we got to spend a nice quiet evening together. I had plenty of ideas on how to make the best of our night too. As I drove down the street, I noticed a tall man standing on Bianca's porch drinking from a coffee cup. It looked like her landlord had finally found someone to rent the place. Damn, I guessed that meant no more lovemaking with the curtains open so that I could see Josh in the moonlight.

SEVEN

Josh

THE EERIE FEELING I GOT AFTER OBSERVING THE NEW NEIGHBOR stuck with me for the rest of the afternoon. His presence felt foreboding, and that made no sense to me at all. I had already been attacked and stalked, so what else could be left? I didn't let my mind linger on an answer to my question. Instead, I kept myself busy preparing for my big night.

I had the bedroom looking sexy and romantic, I manscaped my boys for their big night, got some pointers from watching gay porn, and I planned a delicious dinner. Gabe had yet to eat my homemade ravioli stuffed with ricotta and herbs. I added a salad, bread sticks, and cheesecake to make it memorable in case my bedroom skills sucked and not in a good way. I knew he was going to love at least one of my surprises.

Gabe texted me once he dropped John off at his car and what little calm I'd found evaporated. I told myself I was being ridiculous because Gabe loved me and he wouldn't laugh or ridicule me. I also knew he was a pleaser and would never tell me if something I did wasn't good for him. Gabe was the most amazing lover I'd ever had, and I wanted to be the same for him in every way.

By the time Gabe got home, and I'm talking the trip probably lasted a whopping seven minutes, I had downed a huge glass of red wine on an empty stomach. I was a lightweight drinker in the best of circumstances and that day wasn't one of them. A wave of dizziness hit me hard, and I leaned against the kitchen counter for stability, but I convinced myself I was striking a sexy pose.

"Hey, Sunshine," Gabe said, coming through the door. "How was your day?"

"Pretty damn good, but it's about to get great," I said in what I hoped was a seductive voice. I even added a suggestive wink in case I didn't get my message across.

Gabe's brow furrowed as he assessed the situation by raking his observant eyes over my body before he turned them to my surroundings. I knew the minute his eyes latched onto the half-empty, open wine bottle and empty glass on the counter. "Hitting the bottle already?" He came to me then and cupped my face in his warm, large hands.

"Your hands are as warm as your heart," I told him. *Sweet baby Jesus, I sounded so fucking sappy.*

"Sunshine, what's wrong?" Gabe brushed his thumbs over my cheekbones, and the concern in his dark eyes brought tears to mine.

I blinked away the tears and attempted to blind him with a

smile. "Nothing is wrong. Everything is right, and I'm afraid of ruining it. You see, tonight is the night I'm going to be all up in your ass." There were hand gestures that might've confused Gabe as to exactly what I had in mind. Fisting sure as fuck wasn't one of them.

"Ah," he replied. "You're nervous."

"No," I said, shaking my head as vigorously as his hands allowed. "I'm going to rock your world, Gabriel Wyatt."

"Sunshine, it doesn't give a guy warm and fuzzy feelings to know that his lover needs to get drunk to work up his courage to have sex with him," Gabe said humorously, which was in direct contrast to the chastising words. "And, baby, you rocked my world the minute you came into it, so I have no doubt that this will be any different."

"Not drunk," I corrected him. "It was just one glass of wine, but I drank it too fast on an empty stomach," I explained. "Okay, I'm a little nervous; a little tipsy too."

Gabe released me and walked to the fridge. He selected a block of cheese and some grapes from inside, then removed a box of crackers from the cabinet and pulled a knife out of the butcher block. I watched as he sliced the cheese to make a snack for me. "Come sit with me," he said once he piled everything onto a plate.

I followed him into the living room and sat on his lap rather than beside him on the couch. I ran my hands through his silky dark hair and thought to myself that he needed another trim. I wasn't tipsy enough to suggest it out loud because he already had a haircut phobia and the last thing he needed was to think of me coming at him with scissors in my inebriated state.

We talked about mundane things like the weather and how his drive to and from Cincinnati went while we snacked on cheese, crackers, and grapes. I saw Gabe's determination to return to our original topic once we emptied the plate. I did feel better after my stomach absorbed some of the liquor sloshing around inside.

"Why don't you tell me what's bothering you so that I can put your fears to rest," he told me.

"The economy, global warming, waiting on my newest Andrew Christians to arrive, and…" The stern look he gave me silenced the rest of my typical smartass response. "I think it should be obvious what worries me."

"It's not obvious to me, so you're going to have to spell it out." It appeared that he wasn't going to make it easy for me.

"Alright, fine." I took a deep breath for courage and said, "I'm worried that I'm going to suck and not in a good way. What if I only last ten seconds?"

Instead of making light of my concerns, Gabe said, "It'll be the best ten seconds of my life." When I looked at him in disbelief, he asked, "Do you want to know why?"

"Uh, yeah."

"It's very simple, Josh." Things always got really serious when he used my name. "It'll be because you're inside me. There has never been another living person who's touched my soul as you have, and there's no doubt in my mind that you'll light my world on fire once you're inside me."

I was just about to make a snarky comment about Gabe comparing sex with me to a case of raging hemorrhoids, but I wanted to prove that I was beyond that knee-jerk response stage in our relationship. The wall I had built with my acerbic tongue to protect my heart didn't crumble overnight nor did I lose my initial reaction when emotions built inside me until I felt like I might explode from the pressure. Savage started singing lines from Katie Perry's "Firework" just when I opened my mouth to say something mature and adult-ish. Gabe and I both burst into laughter over Savage's uncanny timing. I swore that the bird was more perceptive than humans.

"You were going to say," Gabe prompted me.

"I honestly don't remember, but I know it was going to be amazing and impress you by how much I've grown since we started dating." I leaned forward and brushed my nose against Gabe's.

"You have absolutely nothing to worry about," Gabe replied. "Everything you do is amazing, and the way you move your body is criminal." Then my man kissed me with purpose, and I forgot to be worried.

"You don't want dinner first?" I asked when he lifted me from his lap and rose to his feet.

"Nope, that will only allow you time to get worked up all over again," Gabe told me. "I want to feel you inside me, and I want it right now."

"So demanding," I said, but I couldn't wipe the smile off my face. I turned and headed for the bedroom but stopped when Gabe didn't follow. I looked over my shoulder and said, "I'm not carrying your big ass to the bedroom." That got him moving.

Gabe chased after me with a roar and caught me before I reached the bed. He scooped me up and tossed me on the bed like I weighed nothing because to him I probably didn't. He followed me down to the bed fully dressed. We made out like horny kids until the whys and hows of what we were about to do faded, and until every breath I took was shared with Gabe, every beat of my heart matched his, and my only thought was how incredible it would be to know him in every possible way.

My heart raced even though my hands moved slowly. My body demanded that I take what Gabe so lovingly offered, but my heart urged me to savor the gift. Instinct and the desire to please overrode the fear of not being enough. I remembered the way Gabe reacted to the prostate massage I gave him down in the spa room of my salon. We had gone weeks without talking after I hurt him by refusing to have dinner with him. I had missed Gabe so damn much and couldn't resist the pull of him any longer, especially knowing that he was in my salon; wearing nothing but a thin white sheet and a smile. He had secured my promise to have dinner with him before his massage appointment with Josi. She had found me in the salon when she was finished and told me he'd fallen asleep. Josi had offered to wake him, but I told her to let him sleep.

I had intended for him to get up and get dressed when I woke him, but that wasn't what happened. Instead, I gave him the happiest of happy ending hand jobs. His reaction had encouraged me to rub the oil over his puckered entrance and push inside when he spread his legs wider in invitation. Seeing such a physically strong man shake and come apart for me was the most powerful experience I'd ever known. I channeled the magic of that moment once Gabe and I were finally naked on our bed.

Gabe closed his eyes and arched his neck, pushing his head into the pillow when I slid my slicked finger inside his tight passage and teased his prostate. I couldn't resist nibbling his Adam's apple that was so sexily on display. "Fuck, that feels so good." Gabe raised his arms over his head and gripped the pillow tight with both hands. "I want you inside me," he pleaded huskily.

I recalled the times I had begged for the same and Gabe drew out my torture until I could only utter single syllable words and whimpers. It was only fair that I did the same to him. Every moan, every groan, and every plea for more emboldened my hands and mouth until no doubt remained by the time I rolled the condom on my dick.

"Eyes on me," I told Gabe just as he'd instructed me many times. I pushed inside him once his seductive brown eyes were on me. "Jesus, Gabe," I said when his tight heat enveloped me. I was once again worried that my inexperience would show when I lasted a whole two seconds in the saddle so to speak. Hotter than his ass's grip on my cock was the look in his eyes.

Gabe released the pillow with one hand, cupped the back of my neck, and pulled my mouth down to his. I poured my heart and soul into our kiss while I rocked slowly in and out of him. A wave of heat washed over my body and sweat beaded all over my skin while Gabe moved his legs restlessly against my hips, waist, and upper thighs. I could tell he didn't care for the slow pace and suspected that he wanted to take control.

Gabe fisted his hand in my hair and yanked my head back from his lips. "Fuck me like you mean it, Josh." His eyes were wild with desperation to come. I loved that Gabe wasn't afraid to show me what he was feeling and thinking. There was no guess work with my man. He grabbed my ass with both hands and began thrusting up to meet my downward strokes. "Need you."

"Detective Bossy Bottom," I whispered against his lips before I captured them in another soul-scorching kiss.

I told myself I only gave in to his demands because it was what I needed too, but the truth was I couldn't ignore Gabe's desires. I dug my knees deeper in the mattress and rode him harder, aiming my dick at his prostate. We filled our bedroom with the sounds of panting between kisses, groans, and flesh slapping together. Gabe released my ass with one hand to reach between our bodies to jack his dick in rhythm with my thrusts.

Gabe's body tensed, and his ass squeezed my cock tighter the closer he came to shooting his load. I needed him to come fast because I was right there and I wanted him to go first or at least blow together. Gabe tore his mouth from mine and shouted jubilantly as jets of cum spurted all over his ripped abdomen and chest. I fucked him until my orgasm hit hard enough to shatter me then I collapsed on top of him while his ass milked every drop from my sac and I filled the condom.

It seemed like it took hours for me to regain enough strength to pull out of him and roll off to his side. "Wow," I said. "I'm pretty damn good at this too. You came hard." I ran my finger through the cooling cum on his chest.

"No finger painting with my spunk," Gabe said, rolling away from me. "Come shower with me and tell me about your day."

I told him about Chaz and Dr. Dimple's *almost* moment during Diva's appointment, which caused Gabe to roll his eyes.

"You're not going to give this up, are you?" he asked while he rinsed shampoo out of his hair.

"Nope," I answered honestly. "I've watched those two circle each other for a while now, and it's time someone put an end to the madness."

"And you're the man for the job?" Gabe asked.

"I'm the man for every job," I replied smugly.

"Just tread carefully, Sunshine. Chaz is your best friend, and you don't want to ruin your relationship due to well-meaning meddling."

"I got this under control," I promised Gabe. "How was your day? Make any progress that you can't talk about?"

"A little maybe," he replied. "What do you know about the proposed casino a few years back?"

"Well, it was a big fucking deal," I told him. "It was nearly a fifty-fifty split of those who opposed and approved it. The people who were for it wanted the jobs for our area and the ones against it worried that it would bring a lot of crime and destroy families. There were a lot of heated debates. Husband versus wife and religion over prosperity kind of discussions."

"Anyone mad enough to kill over it?" Gabe asked. "Who was the strongest proponent for the casino and who hated it the most?"

I gave his question a lot of thought. Tempers ran high when it was a county issue, but became downright fevered when it went statewide. Regardless of our individual feelings about the casino, we collectively hated that the entire state of Ohio got to decide if the casino was built practically in our back yards.

"The strongest supporter was the landowner of the property the casino investors wanted to buy. I heard rumors that they offered him ten million dollars, so I guess you could say he had ten million reasons to be angry when it didn't happen," I told Gabe.

"And who hated the casino the most?" he asked.

"That would be your boss and Sheriff Tucker. They said that crime would go through the roof and destroy our safe community,"

I replied, earning a snort from Gabe. I could tell he was thinking about the rising body count in the past year.

He got quiet for a few minutes, and I knew he was processing and analyzing what I'd said. I didn't mind when Gabe checked out to think because he always came back to me. Like always, his eyes focused on me when he finished, and his smile was a beautiful reminder that I was his universe.

EIGHT

Gabe

THERE WERE TIMES THAT JOSH PROJECTED SUCH CONFIDENCE THAT I could temporarily forget how mightily he'd been damaged by careless cowards who weren't brave enough to love all that he had to offer. Then scenes like the previous night happened and I was reminded how close I came to being one of those fucking morons. Had I not discounted him outright when I first saw him because he didn't fit my typical ideal mold of a man? People say that you don't know what you're missing if you've never had it, but I think at least a part of me always knew I was missing him.

Josh getting tipsy before he could fuck me was an eye opener. I teased him to lighten the mood as he would do for me, but truthfully there was nothing funny about the situation. Okay, his attempt at smoldering looks and lecherous winks were, but not the reason behind them. Josh was naturally sexy and didn't need enhancements of any kind to make me want him. I promised myself that I would make him realize that one day. In the meantime, I did all that I could to ease his concerns by being truthful. He had rocked my world in many ways the moment I met him.

Sex—making love—had never felt so good or right as when I was with him and feeling Josh inside me was incredible. I'd had good sex, and even great sex, but being joined with Josh was… magical. I held onto that feeling and those moments whenever my day wasn't going so great or when I really wanted to grab a douche by the collar and shake him, like when I visited Jack Wallace with Detective Dorchester the next morning. The receptionist gave me the stink eye the minute I walked in and went to Jack's office to let him know I was there without being told.

"Wow, your reputation precedes you," Dorchester said. "It doesn't seem like she cares for your bad cop routine."

"We've gone a few rounds before," I told him. "Wait until you see the reception I get from the commissioner."

"I can't wait," he said gleefully while rubbing his hands together. We weren't kept waiting for long, and Dorchester let out a low whistle when he saw the deep scowl on Wallace's face when his eyes landed on me once we entered his office. "You weren't kidding." I shrugged my shoulders.

"Hello again, Commissioner Wallace," I said in an attempt at being somewhat friendly.

"State your business and get the hell out," Wallace replied.

I looked over at Dorchester, expecting to see a huge grin on his face. Instead, he stood ramrod straight and narrowed his eyes at

Jack Wallace as if he was public enemy number one. "It'd be wise if you showed the respect due to us, sir."

Wallace snorted and rolled his eyes. "Respect is earned," he told Dorchester. "Who the hell are you, anyway?"

"I'm Detective John Dorchester with the CCSD. Detective Wyatt and I are investigating the homicide of Nate Turner from January twenty-second of this year," Dorchester said in his no-nonsense voice. He was always so jovial in my presence that I was surprised to witness that side of him.

"The investigation has brought you to *my* door?" Wallace asked in surprise. He looked at me and said, "I suppose you blame me for global warming and the reason we can't have world peace, Detective Wyatt."

"Nah," I said dismissively. "We're not here to question you in an official capacity, Commissioner Wallace. We'd like to know from you if there's been any renewed interest in building a casino in our county."

"The casino?" he asked in surprise.

"I was told that you initially supported the project, and I have to ask you if you've been approached by anyone from the casino consortium," I answered.

"No." He looked and sounded genuinely surprised.

"Do you know who in town the consortium would approach first if they were looking to propose the casino again?" I followed up.

"Well, Rocky and I were the two biggest allies in town, but besides us, I would say the landowner, Lawrence Robertson," Wallace answered. "He had the most to gain and lose from the entire ordeal. His land was the one McCarren Consortium Inc. had a boner for."

"Do you know if McCarren Consortium built a casino elsewhere after the initiative failed?" Dorchester asked.

"Aren't you the investigators?" Wallace fired back.

His condescending attitude went all through me. I had let

Dorchester take the lead with the bad cop shit, but it was time for me to take it back. I leaned forward and placed both hands on the commissioner's desk. "Why don't you focus on being a good and honest person and not lecture me on how to do my job."

He glanced back and forth between Dorchester and me, wondering if I had told him about Wallace's secret life. It wasn't long ago that Adrian and I had learned about Jack's affair with the mayor. Jack told us he wanted the truth to be told and live openly with Rocky, but Rocky didn't return his feelings. Jack cheating on his wife pissed me off, but it wasn't my place to out the man.

"Okay, then," Dorchester said, clearly confused about the undertones of anger passing between the commissioner and me. "Let us know if you hear anything, Commissioner." He laid his business card on Wallace's desk before he left.

"That guy really pisses me off," I groused.

"You two have a lot of history?" Dorchester asked.

"Just one run-in, but trust me when I say that it was enough to leave a bad taste in both our mouths," I replied. "Still, I think Jack would tell us if he knew something important. What do you think about taking a ride out to Robertson's place and having a talk with him? If his property was the ideal location then, it would still be that way now. It's possible the land has even increased in value."

"Sounds like a plan to me," Dorchester said.

"Tell me what you know about Lawrence Robertson, other than he owns the land the consortium wanted to buy," I said once Dorchester gave me directions to Robertson's farm.

"Well, he's an enigma," Dorchester told me. "He's a fourth-generation farmer, he's never married, and to look at him, you'd never know he was worth billions."

"Plain dresser?"

"He looks like he can't afford soap and his clothes look like they haven't been washed in two decades," Dorchester said solemnly. "He lives all alone in that big old family farmhouse and doesn't socialize with anyone. You'll see him at the grocery store occasionally or the bank, but that's it."

"I wonder what makes a guy live in solitude like that?" I asked him. I had lived as a bachelor for quite a few years, but I still got out and socialized. I couldn't imagine how lonely that life must be for him. Josh was vibrant and full of life, like my personal ray of sunshine, and I couldn't fathom living without the joys he brought to my life. "Why would he be so keen on selling his land? And to a casino of all things!"

"Keep in mind that this is pure speculation on my part," Dorchester said. I nodded my understanding, and he continued. "He has no children to leave the farm to, but he has two nephews from his younger brother, Ken, who died in Vietnam—both brothers served, but only one returned. Rumor has it that he doesn't like the two nephews at all. They moved away for college and never showed any interest in the farm. They tried to get him to sell the farm to a real estate developer who wanted to build a subdivision years ago—back before the casino was interested in the land."

"How is that any different than selling the land to the casino?" I asked.

"Both nephews worked for the developer and probably would've been rewarded handsomely had the deal gone through," Dorchester replied. "Ole Lawrence wasn't about to let them profit off the land they turned their backs on. I reckon he wanted to be in control of what happened to the land rather than let his nephews get it through his estate or something."

"It's reasonable then that he'd strike up the conversation with McCarren Consortium again, especially if he's tired of farming on his own," I replied.

Lawrence Robertson lived in an extremely rural part of the county. His house was one of just a few on the road. The long driveway was a quarter of a mile long; it added to the seclusion and loneliness of the property. The old home stood tall among the barns and trees, but its haggard and worn appearance clearly showed that it had weathered at least ten decades. The closer we got to the structures the more obvious the neglect became.

"This used to be such a beautiful place," Dorchester said sadly as I pulled to a stop next to the farmhouse. "Damn, some of the barns look like they're about to cave in at any moment."

"How likely is it that the man has a shotgun aimed at us when we exit the car and approach the house?" I asked him. Many people shied away from crowds, but the level of anti-socialness that Dorchester described often meant that other underlying issues were present. The last thing I wanted was to get shot by a paranoid man.

"Likely," Dorchester replied. "We'll just have to make our presence known." We slowly got out of the car, and Dorchester hollered, "Mr. Robertson, we're not here looking for any trouble. I'm Detective John Dorchester with the sheriff's department, and I brought Detective Gabriel Wyatt from the Blissville Police Department with me. We just want to ask you a few questions about McCarren Consortium Inc." We took a few steps closer to the front porch. "We don't even have to come inside; we can chat on the front porch, sir."

We had continued walking slowly as John identified us and the reason we were present on his property. The total lack of noise of any kind stuck out to me. The wind was nonexistent, there were no birds chirping in the trees, and no creaking coming from inside the house to indicate the sole occupant was home and moving around. Maybe he wasn't home or... "Fuck!" I exclaimed when the putrid smell of decaying flesh reached my nose.

Dorchester was a step ahead of me. "Dispatch, I'm going to need the county coroner," he said then rattled off Robertson's address. "Detective Wyatt and I stopped by to ask Lawrence Robertson a few questions, and I can tell by the smell that there's a DB inside. We haven't made it inside the house to identify whether it's Mr. Robertson yet." Once Dorchester finished his call, he looked over at me and asked, "Are you ready?"

Death is never easy to stumble upon, but it's worse once the decaying process had started. "Let's do it." The door was locked when I tested it, so I lifted my leg and kicked it hard near the doorknob, so I could knock the lock loose from where it engaged with the doorframe. The stench that rolled out of the gaping door was enough to make me gag. People that told you to just breathe through your mouth had never been in a similar situation, or they would've known that wouldn't help. I walked over to the far end of the front porch and sucked some fresh air into my lungs.

"I've got Vick's VapoRub in my trunk," I told Dorchester after my stomach had settled down. It was a trick I had learned during my time with the MPD where DBs were a more common occurrence.

John and I smeared the ointment beneath our nostrils, stepped into blue booties, and slid our hands into black latex gloves before we entered the premises. We found Mr. Robertson dead at his kitchen table. It looked like he had been reading the newspaper and drinking coffee when he died. If not for the bullet hole in his skull, it would've looked like he had a heart attack. There was no weapon in sight, no casing on the kitchen floor anywhere, and I saw where someone had dug the bullet out of the wall where it landed after exiting Robertson's head.

"This looks eerily similar to Nate Turner's and Owen Smithson's death," Dorchester said. Both the club owner and the man who had sent him the harassing emails were killed the same way. The killer left behind no trace evidence for us to collect by removing the bullet fragment and shell casings from all three scenes.

"Call Detective Jade and let him know that we're not going to make it to Cincinnati today," I told Dorchester as I began taking pictures with my phone. I would delete them later once they'd been uploaded to my computer and tagged as evidence. The sheriff's department would take official crime scene photos, but I wanted my initial findings documented. "Let them know the latest development and get them to dig into McCarren. Does the man want this land enough to kill for it?"

Dorchester made the call then we waited for the coroner to arrive before we touched anything. An odd thought struck me while I was looking around the kitchen. The room was old and outdated, but it was spotless except for the victim at the kitchen table. It was in direct contrast from the dilapidated exterior of the home. I looked in the living room we entered moments before and noticed it was in the same condition. The furniture was shabby looking, but there was no sign of the dust or clutter I would've expected from a man who was practically a hermit.

"Do you find it odd how clean this house is?" I asked Dorchester. "Doesn't that seem atypical of a non-conforming, anti-social existence?" I expected to see walls of news clippings about conspiracies or alien sightings.

"Now that you mention it," he replied. "It's a cleaner house than I'd expect a bachelor to live in, but he's former military, and they tend to keep that tidiness with them for their entire lives."

It was possible that Robertson kept his house tidy. "Or, he had hired help," I commented.

"It's not public knowledge if that's the case, but that's what you'd expect from a very private man," he replied.

The county coroner showed up and took his photographs of the kitchen and the victim before he transported the body to the county morgue. A few other members of the sheriff's department joined us, and we combed the house looking for clues. The rest of the house was as tidy as the living room and kitchen except for one spare bedroom that Robertson used for storage. Inside, there were boxes and boxes of old newspapers and personal files filled with paperwork. It was going to take us forever to go through the files to see if they contained anything pertinent to our investigation.

The deputies who showed up to assist us carted the boxes to their vehicles and took them back to the sheriff's office to store until we had a chance to look at them. While searching the living room,

I found Mr. Robertson's checkbook in the drawer of the end table next to the threadbare couch. I found a weekly entry in his register for an Alice Davenport.

"You know her?" I asked Dorchester.

"She cleans houses for a living," he replied, confirming my earlier suspicion. He raised a brow and tilted his head slightly to the right. "I've heard about your history with housekeepers, so maybe I should take the lead when we talk to her." I appreciated Dorchester's attempt at humor, but I didn't think anything could put a smile on my face that day. I was wrong. My cellphone vibrated with a text from Josh.

I love you.

I found myself smiling amidst the cloak of sorrow and despair that clung to the air around me. I repeated those same words back to Josh in a text. Word must've reached Josh already, and he must've heard I was on the scene. I felt his lightness and warmth surround my heart, and it grounded me.

"Let's go find Alice Davenport," I told Dorchester. "I'll let you take the lead just to be safe."

NINE

Josh

WORD OF BAD NEWS TRAVELED FASTER THAN THE SPEED OF LIGHT in a small town. I had known that my whole life—or soon as I was old enough to realize that my mom would know that I was sent to the principal's office before I even reached his office—and yet it still managed to catch me by surprise at times. There were probably only three houses on that long stretch of the rural route that Lawrence Robertson lived and one of the residents just happened to have an appointment at my salon that day.

"I saw a coroner's van at Lawrence Robertson's house while I was heading to town," Sheila Jones said from Heather's chair. "Bless his heart; I hope he didn't suffer too terribly because Lord knows he suffered enough during his lifetime." To the best of my knowledge, no one truly knew the man, and it felt like Sheila's words were more like posturing than a genuine remark.

Lawrence Robertson reminded me of the next-door neighbor to Kevin in the first *Home Alone* movie. He had a solemn, almost scary countenance about him. As a child, I was afraid of him, and I thought his house belonged in an episode of *Scooby Doo*, but as an adult, I got more of a lonely vibe from him instead of spooky. I decided to tune out the gossip about the death of a sad man to focus on the contrary head of hair I was working.

"Probably a heart attack or a stroke," another client remarked.

"It could've been," Sheila answered, "but I'm not sure why Josh's boyfriend would've been on the scene if it had been natural causes."

That got my attention and my sadness over Mr. Robertson dying alone transferred to my good-looking man who had to deal with the ugliest aspects of life daily. The urge to reach out to him was strong, but I shelved it until I finished with my client. I sent him a brief text during the few minutes between clients so he'd know I was thinking about him. I hadn't expected a quick reply, but I received one. *I love you!* There was no way in hell I'd ever grow tired of hearing those words come from his mouth or seeing them in a text.

Just that little contact with him was enough to help me push my sadness away and get back to work. I had a long day ahead of me, and a sad Josh created sad-looking hair, and that would never do. I pulled myself up by my Andrew Christians, though not hard enough to give myself a wedgie, planted a smile on my face, and greeted my next client.

My day hummed along like a well-oiled machine with little disruption to my carefully crafted control until *he* walked into my salon. The wind had kicked up just as he opened the door, blowing his long locks around his head like he was shooting a shampoo commercial or vying to be the next book cover model sensation like that dude plastered all over the bodice-rippers my mom used to read when I was growing up. I got my first boner looking at his chiseled chest and square jaw while imagining how silky his hair would feel as I brushed it. *What was that model's name? Fabio!*

Fabio 2.0, as I thought of him, approached Chaz with a winsome smile on his face. He extended his hand toward Chaz, who simply stared at the man for a few awkward seconds before he snapped out of it and shook his hand. I had never wished to be a woman before, but I surely could've used a pair of "mama's ears" right then to hear what they were discussing. Then I saw Chaz turn his attention to the computer as he looked through the calendar to book the new neighbor an appointment. I secretly hoped that Chaz wasn't booking the client under my name, but I had a sneaky feeling I wouldn't be so lucky. There was something about the guy, a vibe he gave off or something, that made me uncomfortable.

I wasn't the only one looking at the newcomer; every eye in the room was on him. He must've felt our laser-like focus on him because he turned away from Chaz and looked around the room that had suddenly grown quiet beneath his attention. He smiled uncomfortably at the attention he received and offered a small wave to the crowd. *Welcome to small town America, buddy!*

"I need a big cock!" Savage's loud squawk broke the awkward lull that had descended upon us. Fabio's eyes widened until I thought they'd pop from their sockets.

"Dirty Bird," I yelled back at Savage automatically.

"Dirty Bird," he repeated.

"I think I'm going to like living here," the stranger said. I couldn't tell what color eyes the man had, other than they were light, and focused on me. I wasn't on the market for anything he had to offer me, and I'd gladly let him know at my first opportunity.

"It's unforgettable," Chaz replied then handed the stranger an appointment card. "We'll see you soon."

"I'm looking forward to it," the man said to Chaz without looking away from me.

The entire exchange was weird and unsettling, so I returned my focus back to my client. The chatting and gossiping resumed as soon as Fabio 2.0 left. "Do you have any Easter plans?" I asked Mrs. Adams.

"The children and grandchildren will be coming over after church for dinner and an Easter egg hunt," she replied. I honestly tried to pay attention as she prattled on about the food she planned on making for the event, but I couldn't stop wondering what Fabio's purpose was going to be in my life. I didn't believe in coincidence and the man showing up at my salon the day after he moved in next door reeked of something more than happenstance.

I thought I nodded and made the appropriate comments to Mrs. Adams during our mostly one-sided conversation until Meredith told me otherwise during our short afternoon lunch break in the kitchenette where we scarfed our carryout food from the diner that Chaz kindly picked up for us.

"She's talking about serving fried frog legs, and you made these yum sounds in your throat like you couldn't wait to jump all over that," Meredith said smugly. "Seems to me you were a little distracted by the visitor to the salon."

"I don't like that guy," I said emphatically.

"What did he ever do to you?" Chaz asked, clearly confused by my attitude. It was one that they hadn't seen since I fell hard for Gabe.

"Seriously, sugar. Where's the hostility coming from?" Meredith asked.

"It's just a feeling I had when I watched him move in yesterday." I closed my eyes and tried to pull up the exact emotions that washed over me, but the only one I could grab onto was fear. I was afraid of the stranger even though I didn't know why. "I just feel like this guy is bad news. Please tell me he didn't book an appointment with me," I told Chaz.

Chaz grimaced then said, "Um... I can tell you what you want to hear or I can tell you the truth. Which is it?" he asked. Meredith laughed while I groaned.

"How soon?" I asked, referring to the remark that Chaz made to the man about seeing him soon.

Chaz's shoulders hunched up and he cringed before answering. "Next week."

"How?" I demanded. I was always booked up for nearly two months in advance.

"Mrs. Melanski had to reschedule because she's having a procedure on her bunions," Chaz answered.

"Dude! Don't say the word bunion while I'm eating," Meredith told our friend.

"You just said it," Chaz replied saucily.

"No, I just repeated it and only after I held off the urge to throw up in my mouth," she retorted.

"Kids, can we please focus here?" I asked, raising my voice so they could hear me over their bickering.

"Ohhh, I love it when Jazz goes all *daddy* on us," Chaz said excitedly to Meredith.

"Me too. I notice he's getting better at it now that Gabe's in his life. I bet they role play," Meredith mock-whispered to Chaz behind her hand.

"I think you're onto something, doll. Notice how that bird screams 'Big Daddy' all the time now. Jazz blames that on Gabe, and we thought it was because he was teaching him new words. Oh, Gabe was, alright, but not in the way we first thought." Meredith leaned forward, propped her elbow on the table, and rested her chin in her palm. "Come on, sugar; you can tell us the truth. You're the 'Big Daddy,' aren't you?"

Chaz and Meredith burst into laughter as if that was the funniest thing they'd ever heard. Had I been in a better mood, I might've laughed along with them. The private joke was on them anyway because I had tapped that sexy ass and owned it the previous night. I felt damn proud of myself that I could please my man the way I did. They, however, would never know that because it wasn't something I'd share with them. What Gabe and I had was too special to blab about like some lame-ass locker room story swap. Their laughter faded and the smiles slid off their faces when they realized I wasn't joining in. I could see the concern that they'd offended me written on their faces.

"I'm not upset," I told them. "Not with you, anyway. It's that new guy, Fabio." That got them laughing again.

"That's a good one," Meredith replied. She started mimicking the model's lines from his famous butter commercials.

"Emory has similar looks to Fabio but his hair is darker, and he'd need to gain about thirty or forty pounds of muscle to reach Fabio's bulk," Chaz added with a snort.

"Emory? Is that his name?" I asked

"Emory Jackson," Chaz answered. "You know, he has this weird way of looking at you like he sees inside your mind."

"Yes!" I exclaimed. "That's what I felt when he caught me being nosey when he moved in yesterday. It felt like he was looking into my soul from so far away."

"Just how long were you creeping on the guy?" Meredith asked. I could only shrug because I wasn't sure how long I stood there trying to guess who was moving in. "Is it possible you gave him the wrong idea with the amount of attention you bestowed upon him?"

"I don't think so," I replied, but I guessed it was possible.

"You'll just have to set him straight if he gets out of line," Meredith said sternly.

Chaz snorted and added, "Or let Detective Big Guns do it." I pinned Chaz with a look that said only I got to call Gabe cutesy names.

Break time ended and we went back to the main salon area. For the first time in months, I felt like my life was spiraling out of control. I took stock of all the amazing things I had in my life and told myself I was absolutely ridiculous to fret. *What kind of trouble could Emory Jackson possibly cause for us?* A delivery man came through the salon door before I could answer myself, and I had to admit it was a welcome distraction from my thoughts, but not because the guy had any interest in me. Nope! He only wanted to give his package to Meredith.

My heart felt lighter when his big blue eyes locked on Meredith, who tried her damnedest to act like she didn't know he was there. Usually, Chaz handled all the deliveries for us, but this guy walked right past him and headed straight for Mere. I couldn't keep the smile off my face as Meredith carried on with styling her client's hair like she didn't know he was standing a foot away from her with his heart in his hands.

"Excuse me, miss," he said softly. Thank God, the poor guy got past his stuttering whenever he was near her.

Meredith let out a resigned sigh and turned to face the guy. She pointed her comb in Chaz's direction and said, "He signs for our deliveries." She'd told him that every time he delivered to our salon.

"Yes, but this package is just for you," he told her. He set the package on her counter but made no attempt to leave afterward.

I'm not proud of the snort that slipped out until I saw the irritation on Meredith's face when she glared at me. I wasn't the only one intrigued by the interaction between Meredith and Delivery Dude. Her client watched the byplay raptly with shrewd speculation glistening in her dark, intelligent eyes. It was too bad for Meredith that her client happened to be her mother when Dewey Eyes showed up.

Mama Richmond turned her salon chair around and looked the guy up and down. "Who's your friend, darling girl?"

"He's not my friend, Mama," Meredith said between gritted teeth.

"What's your name, handsome?" Willa asked, even though she could see his embroidered name on the chest of his uniform. It was hard to miss with the way his shirt clung to his muscular torso.

"My name is Harley, ma'am," he said politely. "Harley Sutherland."

"Respectful," Willa said. She extended her hand to him and said, "I'm Willa Richmond and this one's," she hooked her thumb in Meredith's direction, "mother."

"I was going to guess older sister perhaps," Harley said when he shook her hand. "You don't look old enough to be Miss Richmond's mother." Oh, the guy was laying it on thick.

Willa giggled and covered her hand over her heart. "A charmer too. Snatch him up," she said to Meredith in her no-nonsense voice.

"Mama, I don't think this is the time or place…"

"You're not getting any younger," Willa told her. "So, Harley, do you like children?"

"I adore kids," he replied with a smile. "I have two nieces and three nephews. I'm their favorite person on the planet."

"You hear that?" Willa asked her. "He loves kids."

"Mama." Meredith put so much pleading in that single word.

"Child, don't even act like you weren't expecting that package today at work instead of home. You've been tracking the progress on your phone app thingamabob and don't think I didn't notice that you wore that powder blue top that everyone says looks so good with your complexion." Harley beamed with joy at the prospect of Meredith wearing a special shirt for him.

"And you," Willa said, returning her attention back to Harley. "Are you serious about wanting to date my daughter? Are you one of those asshat white boys who doesn't want their white friends and family to know that they're dating a black girl?" Willa wanted to know. "She's had enough of that bullshit. So, if you're not man enough to want to show her off on your arm then walk away right now."

"I'd be honored to have her on my arm," Harley said, looking into Meredith's eyes.

"She doesn't have any plans on Saturday. What about you?" Willa asked Harley.

"Mother!"

"Hush, child. If you're not going to look out for your fairytale love, then I sure as hell will."

"My nephew has a birthday party at one, but I'll be able to go out afterward. How does seven sound?" Harley asked Meredith.

"Seven is good," Willa responded when Meredith stood silently staring back at Harley. "Girl, have you lost your mind? Give the man your phone number so you two can work out the details. I can't be responsible for all of it." Willa harrumphed and turned her chair back around. I caught her eye in the mirror, and she shot me a playful wink.

Meredith gave her number to Harley, and he entered it in his phone. I could tell she was nervous by the way she tucked her hair behind her ears. She glanced over at me, and I gave her a reassuring smile. Our pasts were so similar that it was almost comical. Meredith's easy smiles and contagious joy made it easy to forget how badly she'd been hurt in the past. I had my happily ever after and it was past time she found hers too.

Harley pushed a few more buttons on his phone then looked up at her with a huge smile on his face when Meredith's phone chimed with an incoming text. "Now you have my number too. Is it okay if I call you tonight?"

Meredith caught her mother's eyes in the mirror and asked, "Mama, is it okay if he calls me tonight?"

"So much sass," Willa said, but couldn't keep the smile off her face. "Do you like that in a woman, Harley?"

"Yes, ma'am. I do," Harley replied.

Meredith rolled her eyes then turned to face her suitor. "You can call me tonight."

"Great," Harley said, walking backward. "Is eight okay?"

"Eight is perfect," Meredith replied and gave him a genuine smile for the first time.

The poor guy tripped over his own two feet and nearly fell on his ass. He blushed profusely and hastened his exit out the door. I had a good feeling about the guy and figured I might be seeing him at my dinner table on Sunday nights before too long. *Now if I could just wrangle Chaz and Kyle together...*

TEN

Gabe

DORCHESTER MADE A FEW PHONE CALLS AND TRACKED ALICE Davenport to a house in town she was cleaning. She met us on the porch when we arrived. Alice had tears streaking down her face, and she wrung her hands nervously. It was obvious word had reached her before we showed up. What's that saying about how news travels? Something like news travels fast and bad news travels faster.

"Is he really gone?" she asked in a grief-stricken voice.

"I'm sorry to say that he is, Alice," Dorchester said softly. "I know this comes as a real shock, but we need to ask you a few questions."

"Um, okay," she sniffed. "Mr. Robertson didn't tell me he was feeling bad. Do you think it was a heart attack or a stroke? Did he suffer?"

"Alice," Dorchester paused to search for the right words, "what I'm about to tell you will be a shock, but I'm asking that you keep it to yourself until the sheriff's department releases the information." Alice nodded slowly. "Mr. Robertson didn't die of natural causes; someone killed him." Even though he tried to warn her, she jumped back in shock and covered her mouth with her hands. "We saw that he paid you to clean his house once a week in his checkbook register. It looks like you cleaned his house two days ago, is that right?"

Alice removed her hands so she could speak to us. "Yes, that's right. I cleaned his house and cooked him a few meals to eat through the week like I've always done."

"Did he talk to you about any trouble he'd been having or mention that anyone was angry at him?" I asked her.

"No," Alice said, shaking her head.

"Was he acting differently?" I inquired.

"He seemed like himself, quiet and solemn. He didn't say or do anything different than he normally did," Alice replied after giving my question some thought. "He was such a private man, you know," she said to Dorchester. "He had a truly kind heart. He did so many generous things that he never told people about because he didn't want the attention."

"Such as?" Dorchester asked.

"He was the one who paid to have the historic covered bridge restored," Alice said. "He gave a lot of money to the county hospital each year privately. He helped me out a few times when I hit a financial snaggle." Her voice broke, and she sobbed for a few minutes. "Who would want to hurt him? He never bothered anyone."

Dorchester reached out slowly and patted her back awkwardly. "Did he ever say anything about his nephews?"

Alice wiped the tears from her face and sniffed a few times before she could respond. "All he said about them recently was that they thought he was crazy. He said that he'd show them crazy." That indicated to me that he was determined to do something to prove that he was still in charge of his life and wasn't giving in to their schemes.

"Do you know if Mr. Robertson worked with an attorney?" I asked Alice.

"His attorney is—was," she corrected herself, "Rylan Broadman in Goodville. Lawrence didn't trust any of the local attorneys. He also has a safety deposit box at Blissville Bank and Trust that you should know about." Alice seemed to know quite a bit about Lawrence Robertson, so perhaps he wasn't as lonely as people thought. She obviously cared about him and respected the kind of person he was.

"I'm truly sorry for your loss, Alice. Thank you for making time to answer our questions," I said appreciatively. "Will you please give one of us a call if you think of anything else?" She accepted our cards silently and nodded her head as the tears continued to fall from her face. "Do you want us to call someone for you?"

"I'll be fine," she said, sounding the exact opposite. "Tell your mama I said hello, John."

"Will do, Alice. You take care now," he said warmly.

We waited for Alice to return inside the house before we got back in my car. "Let's talk game plan," I told Dorchester. "There are a lot of boxes to go through and just two of us. We need to update both my captain and your sheriff..."

"Preferably not at the same time," Dorchester interjected wryly. Those two men in the same room was a recipe for disaster. It was extremely uncomfortable, and you had a feeling that you were one incendiary comment away from a massive explosion that would burn everyone in the room, perhaps the entire county too.

"Agreed," I replied. "I'm hoping they let us borrow our partners for a day or two once they realize that Robertson's homicide connects to Turner's. We could use extra sets of hands and eyes."

"Definitely." Dorchester snorted and added, "Hopefully our partners won't kill each other in the process." Adrian couldn't stand Detective Whitworth, and I was sure the feeling was mutual. Their time working together hadn't lasted much beyond a week, Adrian said it felt like a year.

"I think they can manage if we're there as a buffer," I replied, but I wasn't so sure.

"It's worth a shot," he said, pulling out his cellphone. I listened to his side of the conversation with Sheriff Tucker and could tell that he wasn't getting any arguments out of the man. "Tucker's on board," he said after he hung up.

I placed a call to Captain Reardon, but I got his voicemail. It wasn't until I pulled into the sheriff's department parking lot that he returned my call. He agreed to send Adrian over to help me and asked me to keep him updated every step of the way.

Dorchester, Whitworth, and I began sorting what must have been decades' worth of boxes. "I bet the historical society would like to have some of these articles," Whitworth said. "I think he saved every newspaper Blissville Daily News published. Hell, some of these are older than he was."

"Looks that way," Adrian said from the doorway. "Hell, I was looking forward to working with my partner again, but I'm not so sure now."

"Awww, I missed you too, buddy. Like a toothache," Whitworth said snidely under his breath, but loud enough for us all to hear.

"I was hesitant because of the dozens of dusty, musty boxes, Whitworth, but yeah, you're a pain in the ass just the same," Adrian told him.

Dorchester and I exchanged looks that said, "Here we go." The awkwardness dissipated when Adrian came over and shook

Dorchester's hand and slapped me on the back.

"Rough day, partner? You doing okay?" Adrian asked me.

"Better than Mr. Robertson," I replied flatly. "Thanks for coming so quickly."

"I'm glad I can help. Where do you want me to start?"

Dorchester grinned broadly and handed Adrian a box jammed so full it was nearly overflowing. "The top documents in this box are dated around the year the casino was first pitched. See if you can find anything about the original deal inside. We're looking for names of the players involved or anyone who threatened him. Gabe and I will pay a visit to Robertson's attorney tomorrow, but I'd like to have some solid details before we start asking questions."

There were three boxes that appeared to have the most recent clippings in them, so Whitworth, Dorchester, and I each took a box and began digging through them. I found some bank statements in my box that told me that Mr. Robertson was not a poor individual. As mistrusting as he was, the amount of money he had in deposits in two county banks was staggering; all the account balances well exceeded the limits protected by FDIC insurance.

"Does anyone else think it's weird that Robertson would leave millions of dollars unprotected in two banks?" I asked.

"How many millions are we talking?" Adrian asked.

"Three million that I can find," I replied. "It's hard to say what might be in Robertson's safe deposit box."

"It's not that unusual," Whitworth replied. "Investments like mutual funds, stocks, and bonds aren't protected by the FDIC, just bank accounts and certificates of deposits. He might've been old school and trusted low-interest returns more than riskier investment vessels that had an opportunity to make more money. It would be a risk either way unless he wanted to divide his money between several banks. Hell, he would've needed twelve different banks." Okay, so maybe Whitworth did add value to the team.

"We'll copy the bank records then hand them over to his

attorney for his estate," Dorchester commented. "Maybe we'll get lucky and find a paper trail that leads back to our killer."

"That's how it works on television," Adrian remarked with a snort. "Hey, what's this?" he asked suddenly, pulling a small 3 X 5 notebook out of the box. "Guys, I think this is the kind of thing we need. They're the notes he made after meeting with the consortium. Check this out!"

2/5/13

Met with ML and RS regarding casino. He offered me ten million dollars. I insisted on meeting DM in person before I'd accept an offer. I want him to look me in the eye, shake my hand, and I want guarantees. I want them from him, not his lackeys.

2/12/13

Met the man himself. DM is friendlier than I thought. He brought RS and that weasel ML back with him. He's sneakier and more deadly than an old dog's fart. DM agreed to terms. Putting it in writing for lawyers to review.

2/20/13

Meeting with DM, ML, and our attorneys to review and sign paperwork. Those little asshole nephews aren't getting shit when I die.

3/25/13

Meeting with county commissioners set for April 1st. Hope the joke isn't on me.

4/1/13

The casino was shot down in a 5-4 vote. DM said he has a way of getting around it. We'll get enough signatures on a petition to get the issue on the ballot.

7/5/13

400,000 signatures were needed. We got 800,000. Casino goes on the ballot.

11/4/13

Casino initiative failed. Only 37 % voted to build it.

11/5/13

DM retracted offer for the land.

"That's the last entry in this notebook," Adrian said.

"DM is Drew McCarren, CEO of McCarren Consortium Inc.," I told Adrian. "I don't know who the other initials belong to though. We need to find out. Let's see if we can find a recent notebook in these boxes. If not, we'll check his house again for it," I said.

We searched through the most recent boxes and didn't find another notebook, so Dorchester and I planned to return to Robertson's house first thing the following morning before we met with Robertson's attorney and head to Cincinnati to update the task force. I felt it was crucial to figure out who the other players were on Drew McCarren's team.

We put everything back in the boxes, tagged them in as evidence, and the four of us packed them down in the storage room in the basement of the building. Once we finished, Dorchester called the law office of Rylan Broadman and notified him of his client's death and scheduled to meet him at ten in the morning on the following day. That would put us in Cincinnati around noon to meet with the rest of the task force and discuss the next steps in the case.

I felt like I had done all that I could that day, but I couldn't say I was going home with a sense of accomplishment. Instead, my heart felt heavy with the responsibility of tying the Turner and Robertson cases together. In my heart, I knew they were connected. The casino was the only common denominator that made sense. I knew that by solving their cases, I'd bring closure to Owen Smithson's family too.

I unlocked the rear of the salon and stepped inside the kitchenette. From inside the salon came the happy sounds of music playing through the speakers and a lot of chatter going on. It was precisely what I needed right then, so I did something I rarely did. I entered Josh's space and just watched him work. Seeing him talking and smiling with his client as he straightened her hair lifted my spirits.

"Big Daddy's home!" Savage announced loud enough for everyone to hear.

Everyone turned their heads and looked at me, but I only had eyes for one person. Josh's smile from seeing me slid from his face because I probably wore the strain of the day on mine. Worry clouded his pretty hazel eyes, and I just couldn't handle being the reason he lost the sparkle in his eyes. I went to him, realizing that every eye in the salon was on the two of us. I hooked my finger in his apron strings that he had to wrap around his slender frame twice before tying and tugged him to me.

"I'm happy to see you, Sunshine." I dropped a sweet kiss on his forehead that lingered for a few seconds. "I feel so much better now."

"Well, I don't," Josh said sassily, but the sparkle I adored so much had returned. "Now I'll be thinking about you being upstairs while I'm trying to work."

"Not sorry," I fired right back.

"Lucky for you, it's an early night for me," Josh said. I knew I was dismissed when he turned back to his client.

I waved at Chaz and dropped a quick kiss on Meredith's cheek before I grabbed Savage's cage and headed upstairs. Buddy met me exuberantly while Diva worked really hard to pretend like she was ignoring me. I had heard how much she loved Kyle and I felt the irrational desire to win her over until she liked me more, which was why I gave her a few extra kitty treats before I grabbed a cold beer and headed toward the bathroom.

My skin had begun to itch from my need to get clean. I knew

that the stench of death and decay clung to my clothes, skin, and hair. I shouldn't have touched Josh until I washed the misery away, but I couldn't resist his goodness and light. I turned the temperature hotter than I normally liked, but not as hot as Josh preferred, to scald the day off my mind, body, and soul. I sipped the cold beer while I let the hot water beat down on my tense shoulders and neck for several long minutes.

Once the beer was gone, I set the empty bottle on the shelf and began scrubbing my body hard. I didn't think that one pass with the washcloth was enough and kept scrubbing until my skin was red and felt like thousands of little needles poked me from head to toe. It was then that I realized the tingling sensation was from the water turning cold. Josh's hot water tank was a fairly big one, which meant I was in the shower longer than I had realized.

I shut off the water and ran a towel over my body before I stepped over the edge of the tub and onto the fluffy rug there. Josh was sitting on the vanity waiting for me with a cold bottle of beer and a welcoming smile. There was only one thing that was going to make me feel better, and it wasn't the beer. I took the bottle from his hand and set it on the vanity beside him then stepped between Josh's parted legs and lifted him so that he wrapped them around my waist.

"You could've gotten in the shower with me instead of waiting out here," I told him.

"I thought you might need some alone time after the day you've had," Josh replied.

"What I need is you." I captured his mouth in a kiss that was hot enough to heat my chilled flesh.

Josh pulled back from our kiss after long minutes. "You have me, Gabe. You'll always have me."

I carried Josh to our room and placed him on the center of the bed before I stripped his clothes off. His touch and his kiss restored my peace and reminded me of everything good I had in the world.

When I slid inside him, it was the purest love I had ever felt. Every kiss, every sigh, and every whispered word of love from his mouth patched the holes that the cruelty of life tore out of my soul that morning.

I loved him with my hands, my body, and my mouth. I didn't stop until our trembling bodies clung together as our orgasms powered through us. I rolled to my side and pulled him with me so I could hold him tight to me instead of squishing him into the mattress. I ran my fingers through his hair while he placed little kisses on my neck.

"What do you feel like eating for dinner?" he asked.

"Let's just have pizza delivered," I replied. I didn't feel like cooking nor did I feel like turning loose of Josh long enough for him to whip up magic in the kitchen. After the day I had, the only person I wanted to see was him, and the only sounds I wanted to hear was his voice or the television. I needed to embrace the beautiful moments with Josh because I was reminded in the ugliest way that morning of how fragile life truly was.

ELEVEN

Josh

GABE'S WORDS AND TOUCH ERADICATED THE UNEASY FEELINGS I had once *Emory* showed up at my salon. It was so easy to forget that the real world even existed when I was in his arms, but reality often found a way to make her presence known and knocked me back down to earth. *Not this night*, I vowed. I didn't know what Gabe found at Mr. Robertson's house, but I knew it had to be awful.

Gabe held me tight to him for so long that he drifted off to sleep. I didn't want to move and wake him, but I was starving, and his after-sex snoozes could last a while. I pressed a final kiss to his neck and slowly maneuvered out of his arms until I stood next to the bed looking down at him. The deeply grooved worry lines in his forehead from earlier were gone, and his mouth looked relaxed instead of tight with tension. I just hoped they stayed gone when he woke from his little nap.

I quietly pulled on a pair of sweats and a T-shirt before I tiptoed out of the room. "Don't you dare leave off your mushrooms," Gabe said drowsily just as I was about to pull the bedroom door closed.

"Triple mushrooms it is," I said saucily before shutting the door. Mushrooms were still a hotly contested issue between us. The truth was that I didn't always want mushrooms on my pizza, but Gabe thought I left them off because of him anytime that I didn't order them.

I retrieved my cellphone from where I left it and called Marty's Pizzeria to place my order. "Hello, Josh," Marty said when he answered. "You want your usual?"

"Not tonight, Marty," I answered. "I'd like a large sausage and green pepper with extra cheese."

"No mushrooms, huh kid?" he asked.

Damn, was he on Gabe's payroll? "I'll take an order of fried mushrooms and mozzarella sticks instead."

"Be there in about thirty minutes," Marty said then hung up the phone.

I let Jazzy out of his cage to play and run through his tunnels while I watched from the couch with Buddy. Diva—never one to be left out—jumped on the back of the couch and proceeded to bathe her paws loudly. I looked at her over my shoulder, and her pale blue eyes dared me to complain. That ornery cat wouldn't hesitate to swat my ears with her paw.

"Come give me some tongue!" Savage squawked from his cage.

"Not right now, Dirty Bird!"

"Dirty Bird!"

I flipped the television on and started watching an episode of my favorite home improvement show while I waited for the pizza delivery guy to show up. The doorbell for the back door rang a little earlier than I expected, but I didn't give it much thought. I grabbed my wallet and headed downstairs. I opened the door without looking to see who it was and regretted it immediately. Seriously, what kind of heinous act needed to be committed against me before I'd learn my lesson? Apparently attempted murder and stalking weren't enough to do the trick.

"Oh, it's you," I said flatly. No one would volunteer me for the neighborhood welcoming committee. What I really wanted to say was, "What the fuck do you want?"

"Hello to you, too." Emory "Fabio" Jackson wore a humorous smile plastered on his face. As if the dude commanded the wind, it kicked up as it had earlier in the day to send his hair floating artfully around his head. "I wanted to introduce myself formally," he said, pushing the bottle of wine that sported a big red bow toward me.

I looked at the bottle suspiciously then back at him. "I don't drink," I lied.

"Oh." His cheeks pinkened with embarrassment in the fading April sunlight. I almost felt bad for lying to him. The truth was, I irrationally didn't want anything from him inside my house. "Your boyfriend perhaps?"

"He's not my boyfriend."

"Oh?" Was that hopefulness I heard in his voice?

How did he even know about Gabe anyway? He'd only lived next to me for a day. I had closed the damn bedroom curtains, so I was sure he hadn't seen us getting naked. I reasoned that he would've had several chances to see Gabe coming and going from our home and calmed myself. "That's much too tame of a word for what Gabe is to me," I told him. "He's more of a beer man, anyway. Thank you for thinking of us, though. Mrs. Hastings across the way loves that kind of wine. She's the beige house with burgundy shutters." I pointed to her house just in case my message wasn't clear.

"Uh, okay," he said slowly. I expected him to turn and walk back down the steps, but apparently, Emory was a glutton for punishment. "My name is Emory Jackson," he said, extending his hand toward me.

I wasn't proud of the way I scrutinized his hand. I wanted to tell him I was a germaphobe, but one lie was bad enough. I hesitantly shook his hand and was pleased when nothing weird happened. "Josh Roman," I replied. "My boyfriend," for lack of a better word, "is Gabriel Wyatt. He's a detective with the Blissville PD with a big gun. Real big." I was blabbering at that point because I just wanted the guy to go away and didn't know how to make it happen without coming right out and saying it.

"Sunshine, are you touting my attributes to the pizza delivery guy again?" Gabe asked as he came down the stairs. I opened the door wider so Gabe could see who was on our back porch. "Oh, hey, you're the new guy who moved in next door," Gabe said with a friendly smile. "Gabriel Wyatt," he said, extending his hand.

"Emory Jackson," I said for our new neighbor. Both men looked at me oddly when they heard the hint of irritation in my voice. I really needed to learn how to be subtle.

"Look, Sunshine, he brought your favorite wine," Gabe said, unknowingly betraying me.

Emory narrowed his eyes in confusion over why I lied to him about not drinking. I had no explanations for why I didn't like him; I just didn't. "Sunshine, huh?"

"Yep," Gabe said, proud of the name he'd given me.

"I just bet he's a ball of fire," Emory commented. His eyes widened when he realized how his statement sounded. "I-I didn't mean sexually."

"Why the hell not?" I demanded. "You don't think I can burn shit down?" Who was this guy who pushed himself in my space not once, but twice, and insulted me? "I burn hotter than you could possibly handle."

"Take it easy there, Stud Muffin," Gabe said good-naturedly. "He wasn't insulting your sexual prowess. I think our new neighbor just meant you're a feisty guy."

I pinned Emory with a death glare and said, "I am feisty. All the time and everywhere."

"I think I made the wrong impression here," Emory said. He pushed the bottle of wine toward Gabe, who graciously accepted his offering. "I'm hoping not to make an ass of myself the next time we run into each other." Next time he'd be in my chair, so if he got out of line, I'd change him from Fabio to Justin Bieber so fast his head would spin.

"You're fine," Gabe assured him. "We're all good."

Emory looked at me for several awkward moments. "No, but we will be in time," he said before he turned and walked down the steps of the back porch. "Nice shirt, by the way."

I looked down and saw I had put on one of the graphic tees that Gabe bought me. That one had a large blow dryer on the front and read: Want a blow job?

"What the fuck did he mean by that?" I asked when he was at the end of our driveway. I clearly wasn't referring to his comment about my shirt.

"Why don't you tell me," Gabe said, watching the strange man across the alleyway that bisected our properties. The pizza delivery guy pulled in just as I opened my mouth to answer him. "Save that for when we're back upstairs. I have a feeling it's a long story."

"It's not a long story," I told Gabe once we were upstairs on the couch with a plate of pizza on our laps. I told Gabe about me lusting after the racing stripes on his car and trying to guess who was moving in based on the furniture that the movers carried inside the house. "The man looked up at my window like he knew to look for me. It was like he was looking inside my brain."

"Just how long were you watching the guy?" Gabe asked,

pinning me with a narrowed gaze. "People know when they're being watched. You know this from the time Billy slashed your tires. You once told me that you could feel him watching you."

"I could feel his malevolence," I told Gabe. "That's not what this was. I was just checking out the new neighbor and had no ill will toward him."

"Were you lusting after the guy?" Gabe actually sounded jealous.

"You can't seriously be worried about Fabio," I said. "Babe, believe me when I say that I'm not attracted to him."

"Then what are you so worried about?" he wanted to know.

"He turned up in my salon to schedule an appointment with me today. Chaz said he asked for me specifically. He's been here for less than twenty-four hours and already knew who I was. Doesn't that sound suspicious to you?"

"Not in this town," Gabe remarked. "All it took was him having a cup of coffee at The Brew this morning and asking for a good place to get his hair cut."

"Cut," I snorted. "Do you think those highlights are natural?" I asked Gabe.

"Uh, I didn't notice his hair," Gabe replied, a bit snidely.

"What does that mean?" I asked Gabe, feeling my ire coming on.

Gabe set his plate on the table and turned to me. I saw emotions I never wanted to see in his eyes: insecurity and dread. "What I noticed was that he only had eyes for you." True, but it didn't feel sexual to me. It was something far more unsettling to me, although I couldn't quite name what it was.

"It doesn't matter, Gabe, because he can't have me. I belong to you." I picked his plate up off the coffee table and handed it to him. "Eat your dinner. Skipping meals is the last thing you need to do while under this much stress." I shook my head in disbelief that Gabe could entertain that my heart would ever belong to someone else after he held it in his hand.

"I don't think I like him," Gabe said.

"I know that I don't like him, which was why I told him I didn't drink when he tried to hand me the bottle of wine. How'd he know my favorite wine, anyway? Who the fuck in town would've told him that?" I asked.

"Good point since you drive into the next town to buy it." Gabe narrowed his eyes. "It's possible that it was a lucky guess, but I think I need to do a little digging in to our new neighbor."

"I agree," I said. "I can't shake the feeling that Fabio's brought something bad to town with him."

"I'll see what I can find out," Gabe promised.

I felt guilty that he would even waste a minute of his work day looking at that guy when the internet was a hotbed of information. After we had finished eating, I pulled up my internet browser on my tablet and typed his name in the search box.

I didn't go into the search with a lot of expectations, but what I found shocked the hell out of me. There was a wide variety of photos of the man along with articles about his psychic abilities. "I don't believe it," I said.

"What?" Gabe asked when he returned after stacking our plates in the dishwasher. I turned my tablet around for him to see. Gabe took it out of my hands and began clicking things. "Well, what do we have here?" he asked.

"I wouldn't know because you took my tablet," I reminded him.

Gabe hooked his arm around my neck and pulled until my head rested against his chest and I could see what he was reading. "The guy has been on several of those cold case shows, and a few psychic investigation shows too. This article is from last year. 'Psychic Emory Jackson led police to a location in the woods where he claimed Tira Strebor, age twenty-two, had been buried by her killer. After authorities had recovered Ms. Strebor's remains, Mr. Jackson was investigated and later cleared of any wrongdoing. He was out of the country at the time of Ms. Strebor's abduction.' Here's an article about how they solved her abduction and murder with his help," Gabe said.

"Do you believe in that stuff?" I asked Gabe.

"There have been plenty of documented cases where psychics have provided clues that have helped solve cases," he told me. "I think for every legitimate psychic there are fifty more that are frauds. It's not an impressive ratio." Gabe thumbed through the articles written about Emory's involvement with police investigations. Some of them included photographs of the guy on the scene with law enforcement while others were clearly posed for effect.

"I don't think his appearance in our town is necessarily a good thing," I told Gabe, convinced that my trepidation was warranted.

Gabe had found an article that was titled: *Psychic's Abilities Started After Death of Husband.* I'd nestled in closer and listened as Gabe read the article out loud. In January 2012, Emory and his husband, River Jackson, were involved in a single-car accident after coming home from celebrating River's birthday with some friends. They were five miles from home when River hit a patch of black ice on a bridge and lost control of his car. Emory hadn't been wearing a seatbelt and was ejected from the car before it went over the side of the bridge and plunged into the frigid water below. Emory came out of his coma a week later and learned of his husband's death. He said his abilities began a few months later and it felt like his late husband was working through him to help people in need.

"That's really sad," I said somberly. I couldn't imagine waking up to find that Gabe was taken from me. Hell, just the thought had tears stinging the back of my eyes.

"I can't even imagine," Gabe added. I knew he was thinking the same thing by the way he pulled me even tighter against his side. "Damn, how does a guy get up the next day after learning something like that?"

"I guess he believes there's something more he has left to

accomplish or he wants to honor his husband's memory," I replied. "It sure as hell wouldn't be easy." That same ominous feeling I'd felt before permeated my body and left me cold, so much so that my teeth began to chatter in the warm comfort of my home. I closed my eyes and willed the fear away. Once I had myself together, I looked up at Gabe and asked, "What do you think it means that he's in Blissville? We don't have any unsolved cases, do we?" I asked.

Gabe appeared to be contemplating his answer as he stretched his neck by moving his head from left to right. The wrinkled forehead and frown he wore on his mouth didn't alleviate any of the uncertainty I felt. "I guess we'll find out when he reveals his purpose to us," he said. "I can tell you one motherfucking thing his visions didn't reveal, and that was you in *his* bed. You're *my* Sunshine."

"Damn straight," I replied.

"Not even close," Gabe shot back, causing me to almost choke on my drink of beer.

"Ass," I said.

"Pirate," he replied like we were playing a word association game.

"Ass Pirate! Ass Pirate!" Savage squawked.

"Look what you did," Gabe and I said at the same time.

"Me?" I asked. "You're the one teaching him horrible language."

"Oh, okay. Savage just happened to teach himself the word cumguzzler then," Gabe said accusingly.

"He came to me preprogrammed with that one," I said defensively. "I refuse to take the blame for his salty language. Dirty Bird!"

"Ass Pirate!" Savage shot back, not following the program at all.

Gabe and I couldn't help but bust out into laughter over the outrageousness of the situation. It was just what we needed to pull ourselves out of the somber mood we'd found ourselves in after reading about Emory's situation. I turned on a new episode of our favorite couple fixing up houses for home buyers, and we enjoyed the rest of the evening. The world was filled with uncertainty, but there was no reason to waste precious moments on borrowing trouble before it arrived.

TWELVE

Gabe

I picked up Dorchester from the sheriff's department the next morning because we needed Robertson's house keys from the evidence locker. His house showed no signs of forced entry, so we locked the house up after we were through the day before and logged the keys in as evidence. A house fire call came over the radio while we were en route to Robertson's house to look for another notebook that might contain notes about recent meetings. A farmer on a different road saw the plumes of black smoke and called 911.

"I don't fucking believe it," Dorchester exclaimed. "Did you recognize that address?"

"Sure did." I flipped on my lights and siren so we could get there quicker. "This can't be a coincidence," I told Dorchester.

"Why'd the guy wait until after we discovered the body to torch the place? Why not torch the place with Robertson inside? There would've been a high probability that we ruled that the fire caused Robertson's death," Dorchester said.

"Maybe he wanted us to know he killed Robertson," I remarked. "The fire could be his attempt to make sure we don't find anything else. Maybe word got around that we carted off a bunch of boxes and he didn't want us coming back to find anything else."

When we arrived on the scene just a few minutes later, angry red and orange flames completely engulfed the old farmhouse. Acrid smoke filled the air and thick, black smoke billowed from the two-story structure. The firefighters had brought in water tankers, but nothing was going to save Robertson's place. You could hear the fire roaring, wood splintering, and objects falling inside. The firemen battled the flames as best they could, but the old, somber house gave a loud, shuddering groan and collapsed in on itself.

I approached the man shouting out orders to the men scrambling to prevent the fire from spreading to the nearby barns. "Lieutenant, I know this is premature to ask but do you have any idea if this fire was accidental?"

"I can't say which accelerant they specifically used right now, but I can promise you this was not an accidental fire. Sure, the house and the timber is dry, but it still burned too hot and too fast. The fire marshal and his arson dog will investigate once we put the fire out." A call came over his radio about additional tankers on their way to assist from neighboring townships. "Excuse me, fellas," he said then walked away to respond to dispatch.

Dorchester and I were only going to be in the way. Whatever evidence we had hoped to find had gone up in flames. Our only hope was that Robertson put his latest notes—if they existed—in his safe deposit box or gave them to his lawyer.

"Let's go see Rylan Broadman," Dorchester said. "We'll get there a little early, but you can show him your bad cop if he gets lippy."

Goodville was eighteen miles north of us, and it took thirty minutes to get to Broadman's office. Instead of getting stink-eye from the receptionist that we were an hour early, she offered us a cup of coffee while we waited for the attorney to finish his call.

"We were so sorry to hear about Mr. Robertson's passing," she said sadly. "He was a sweet man." I found it interesting that every person we talked to seemed to have a different impression of the man, although the receptionist's comments were very similar to Alice Davenport's.

We accepted a cup of coffee and had a seat in the reception area, which looked more like someone's comfortable living room. The print and floral stripe fabric on the sofa and adjoining chairs was a little fussier than I would've picked, but it worked well with the classically styled furniture. I sat down in an armchair and looked through the magazines on the polished mahogany coffee table while Dorchester read the newspaper.

I had just chosen the latest Sports Illustrated magazine when a deep voice said, "Come on back, Detectives."

I rose to my feet and faced the man who spoke. He didn't look anything like I associated with an attorney. Instead of an expensive three-piece suit, he wore a pair of khakis, loafers, and a pale blue polo shirt. I noticed the calluses on Rylan Broadman's hands when we introduced ourselves, which told me that sitting at a desk wasn't all that he did each day.

When we got to his office, I noticed a collection of antique tractor toys on shelves and several aerial photos of a large farm hanging on his walls. "Family farm?" I asked.

"Yes. Fifth generation farmer," he said proudly.

"Lovely place," Dorchester said, admiring the black and white photos of an antebellum style mini-mansion that also hung on the wall.

"Thank you. It's a lovely feeling to live in the same house as your family did dating back to almost the civil war era," Rylan remarked and gestured for us to have a seat. His office was masculine and professional, but a welcoming place nonetheless. It felt more like someone's home office rather than a professional one, but I could see where most people would prefer his type of environment. "Man, I hated to hear about Lawrence," he said once we sat in the chairs across from his desk. "He was a good man."

We broke the news to him that his client hadn't died of natural causes because it wasn't public knowledge yet. His reaction was as startled and genuine as Alice's the previous day. We started off with the basic questions, like how long Robertson had been a client and what kind of services he provided him. We learned that Rylan had taken the practice over from his grandfather when he retired just like Kyle had taken over his grandfather's veterinary practice. It seemed to be a common circumstance in smaller communities. Rylan told us that all of Robertson's holdings—land and money— were in a trust and he became the trustee upon Robertson's death.

"Were you his attorney of record during his negotiations with McCarren Consortium?" Dorchester asked. We knew that he had been from the notes that Robertson made so the question was thrown out there to see if we could trust the man to be straightforward with us.

"I was," Rylan said nodding.

"How upset was Robertson when it didn't go through? That was a lot of money," I remarked.

"It wasn't about money for Lawrence," Rylan told us. "It was about being in control of what happened to his land long after he died." He smirked a bit and added, "And, to make sure his nephews didn't get any money off the land they wanted no part of until it was convenient for them."

"Can we have the names of his nephews please?" I asked. "We'd like to interview them."

"Sure," Rylan said, opening a file. "Scott and Mark Robertson. They both live and work in Cincinnati for Greg Sharpe Homes. You probably already know this, but Scott and Mark pitched the idea of selling the land to Greg Sharpe so he could build a new subdivision on the land."

"Was Mr. Robertson open to that idea until he learned that his nephews would profit from the sale?" I asked.

"He was," Broadman confirmed. "He was adamant that they would never own or profit from the land and even had McCarren add clauses to prevent it from happening."

"McCarren was okay with that?" I asked, unable to keep the surprise from my voice.

"I was surprised also," Broadman admitted. "Honestly, he seemed eager to help Lawrence thwart his nephews. There were other surprising clauses that he agreed to."

"Such as?" Dorchester asked.

"Lawrence wanted a guarantee that a certain percentage of profit was put back into the county schools, library, and hospitals. He also had asked for money to be given to local law enforcement to purchase modernized equipment. Lawrence just felt that the county would benefit more from the casino than another housing development."

"It would've brought thousands of jobs to the community," Dorchester said.

"Yes," Broadman agreed. "It's all water under the bridge now. I'm surprised you brought it up."

"We're not convinced it is water under the bridge," I said then explained to him that we thought the casino talk might've started back up again. "Had he mentioned it to you?"

"No," Broadman said in surprise, "but he did schedule an appointment with me for next week. I thought maybe he wanted to discuss trust business, but my receptionist, Lucy, said he evaded the reason for his appointment."

"Can you tell us the names of the men you met with during the land sale negotiations?" Dorchester asked.

"Sure, I can," he said confidently then proceeded to rattle them off the top of his head. "Drew McCarren was present a few times with his lawyer, Rick Spizer, and then there was Michael Larkin and Tommy Thompson. Michael was the development guy, and Tommy was the money man." I sat up straighter when I heard that McCarren had the same attorney as Nate and Jonathon.

"How did the negotiations go?" I asked. "Were there any tense moments or disagreements over the terms?"

"There was only one heated moment in the beginning," Broadman told us. "Apparently, Drew McCarren doesn't usually get involved in the actual negotiations because he has a team for that. Lawrence wanted to be able to look McCarren in the eye and assess if he was a man of his word. Larkin was pissed because he felt like Lawrence doubted his character. Larkin implied that Lawrence's demand for an in-person meeting with McCarren would be a deal breaker, but it seemed to have the reverse effect. McCarren appeared to be very honest with Lawrence."

"You didn't get an underhanded or sneaky vibe from any of them at any time?" Dorchester asked.

"Honestly, no. It was going to be a circumstance where both parties seemed to come out ahead in the deal."

"One last question," I told him, "and then we'll let you get back to your day. Alice mentioned that the nephews were making noise about Mr. Robertson being unfit to handle his affairs. Is that true?"

"Lawrence did tell me that, but there was never any evidence to substantiate his claim. He couldn't tell me of a single incident where one, or both, threatened him in any way."

"Odd," I remarked. I wondered if perhaps Robertson was paranoid when it came to his nephews. I rose to my feet, and Dorchester did too. We pulled cards out from our jacket pockets and handed them to Broadman. "Please let us know if anything comes up."

"The safe deposit box," Dorchester mentioned to me then looked at Broadman. "Does the box need to be audited by the county clerk before we can look through the contents?"

"Lawrence had a trust, so there will be no probate. The contents belong to the trust, and I'm the trustee, so you won't need a warrant to search the box. I'll check with the bank to see if they'll accept my permission in writing or if I need to be present."

"We'd like to get in there today, or tomorrow at the latest," Dorchester told him.

"That won't be a problem, Detectives. I'll rearrange my schedule if needed," Broadman assured us.

I'd dealt with lawyers hundreds of times during my career, and I could honestly say that none of them had been as helpful as Rylan. "Thank you for your assistance. We look forward to hearing from you," I said, shaking the man's hand once more.

There wasn't anything local left for us to look at so we headed to Cincinnati to update the task force on what we learned. We ordered in lunch and gathered together in the large conference room we'd taken over.

"This is what we've got so far," I said, addressing the task force after lunch. I told them about Bandowe telling us that Nate mentioned investing in a casino and how Dorchester told me about the failed attempt to build a casino in Carter County in 2013. "Since Nate was killed in Carter County, I started to question if Nate's death could be related to resumed talks of building a casino. It seemed like a long shot until we found the landowner shot dead in his home yesterday."

"Let me guess, he was shot with a forty-five, and both the casing and bullet are missing," Jade said.

"The M.E. hasn't provided the caliber of the bullet, but the entrance and exit wounds look consistent with a forty-five to me.

You're right about the casing and the bullet, though; neither were found at the crime scene. It would appear to be the same person who killed Nate Turner and Owen Smithson. We need physical evidence and a name instead of supposition and guesses." I blew out a breath in frustration.

"There are two trains of thought here," Dorchester said, speaking up. "They might've been killed to prevent the casino from going up, or maybe they were killed by a competing casino who didn't want attention drawn away from them. We're not ruling anything else out, but these seem to be the most likely scenarios."

"We need to start with McCarren Consortium," I said. "He's a Cincinnati-based guy. What do you know about him?"

"Douche," Weston said in disgust. "He's another one who vice was looking at for prostitution and drugs."

"He has a reputation for being ruthless," Harris said.

"Does anyone have a contact inside the Casino Control Commission?" I asked.

"Paul does," Harris and Weston said at the same time. *Of course, Paul does.*

I rattled off the names of the guys involved in the meeting, except for McCarren's attorney. I was saving that little bombshell for last. "I need you guys to dig up everything you can on these men. I want to know about any hint of illegal activity they're suspected in." I paused for dramatic effect. "We found the one string that's connected to both Turner and McCarren." That had everyone's attention. I told them about Robertson's notes and the initials he used to identify people at the meetings. "Robertson's attorney confirmed that Rick Spizer was the attorney representing McCarren Consortium."

"Whoa," Jade said.

"That could be huge," Harris said.

"We're about to find out how huge it is," I replied. "The connection," I said to clarify, earning a lot of laughs from the team.

Dorchester divided tasks while I took my phone out and stared at it for several long moments. I dreaded the call I needed to make, but I couldn't see a way around it. We'd gotten off to a terrible start, but I had to put that behind me. I just hoped that he could too because I was certain I'd need his assistance to solve these three crimes.

My call went to voicemail. I left my contact information, stressed the importance of my call, and asked Silver to get back to me at his earliest convenience. I disconnected the call with low expectations for a prompt response, but he proved me wrong when he returned my call within fifteen minutes.

"Detective Wyatt," I said, answering the phone.

"You rang, Detective," Jonathon Silver said sleepily into the phone. It was sometimes easy to forget that some people slept while you were awake and worked while you slept.

"I'm sorry that I woke you, Mr. Silver. There's been a development in your brother's case, and I need your help."

"Are you serious?" he asked, suddenly sounding alert. "Um, give me an hour to wake up and get my crap together. Where do you want to meet me?"

"You name the place and time, and we'll meet you," I said.

"We?" Silver asked.

"Yes, you met my partner," I reminded him.

"Oh." He sounded disappointed. "I was hoping you were coming alone." I was somewhat flattered by his attention, but that was all. My heart and body belonged to a man I adored more than life.

"Not going to happen," I assured him. "Dorchester and I will meet you. When and where?" I asked him.

Silver let out a dissatisfied sigh and said, "Four o'clock in my office. I'll even wear clothes this time."

"We'll be there," I replied, ignoring the rest of his comment. I appreciated his attempt at humor to lighten the tone of the conversation, but I felt it was better to keep things very professional between us and laughing at his jokes might've given him the wrong impression.

I hung up from Silver and sent a text to Josh. *Promising break in the case. Interview will run late. Hope to be home around 6. Love you!* It was Josh's night to work late so he wouldn't even know I wasn't home, but that didn't matter. I wasn't fucking up the best thing that ever happened to me.

Dorchester came over once he finished and I updated him on our interview appointment. "Maybe he'll keep his clothes on this time," he commented.

"He said he would," I replied.

"You asked him?" Dorchester wanted to know.

"No, he volunteered after he hinted that he wanted me to come alone," I told him.

Dorchester blew out a low whistle. "What did you say?"

"I told him it wasn't going to happen."

"Looks like we need to find your other boy toy, Paul, and have a chat with him about his contacts in the Casino Control Commission," Dorchester joked. I pinned him with my bad cop glare, letting him know I didn't think he was that funny. "Okay, I was over the line. I won't do it again."

"Yeah, I won't hold my breath," I told him.

"I wouldn't either if I was you." Dorchester whistled a jaunty tune as he walked away.

My phone buzzed with an incoming text, I knew it was going to be from Josh before I even looked. *Crossing my fingers it goes well. Be safe. Love you.* Those ten words gave me energy and propelled me out the door to find Paul. I could start making some phone calls and make use of my down time while we waited to meet with Silver.

THIRTEEN

Josh

I HAD WEIRD-ASS DREAMS INVOLVING MY NEW NEIGHBOR AND didn't sleep very well. They weren't sexy dreams or anything to be ashamed of, but I didn't talk about them with Gabe. He had enough on his plate already without adding my paranoid premonitions to the mix. Included in the myriad emotions, was the guilt I felt about my new neighbor.

Even though I remained unsure of his reasons for being in town, and I in no way believed it was coincidental, it was wrong of me to blatantly lie to him. Finding out about him losing his husband and the ways he tried to right the wrongs punched me hard in the gut. Being skeptical of his presence was one thing, but being outright rude wasn't acceptable. Letting down my defenses and falling in love with Gabriel Wyatt changed how I viewed the world. Pre-Gabe, I wouldn't have felt bad about my behavior with Emory, but post-Gabe, I realized that our first impressions weren't always accurate.

I had set out on my morning run with Buddy, hoping to get the blood pumping and wake myself up for the long day ahead of me. I noticed that the lights were on inside Emory's house as I ran by and I wondered what his life was like before the accident. What did he do for a living before his world turned upside down? How long had he known his husband? Random questions kept popping up, and the inquisitive side to my personality was quickly taking over the cautious side.

I decided to stop at The Brew for a cup of strong coffee and a pastry on my way back through town. I couldn't take Buddy inside with me, but there was always someone willing to wait with him outside while I ran in for a coffee. I pretended not to see Mrs. Perkins give Buddy a bite of her strawberry cream cheese pastry.

There were a few people ahead of me in line, and I took that time to peruse the baked goodies in the display counter. My eyes caught on the large chocolate chip cookies and thought they'd make a nice welcome to the neighborhood gift. I doubted they were as good as my homemade ones, but I only gave my cookies to Gabe, literally and figuratively, otherwise I might have a mutiny on my hands.

I ordered a half dozen cookies and a lemon poppy seed muffin for myself with my coffee. "Can you put those cookies in a cute box? They're a gift," I remarked.

I accepted my goodies and turned from the counter to leave when I saw a familiar figure coming through the door. It was all I could do not to groan out loud at being in the same room as Rocky Beaumont. I had never forgiven the way he treated Georgia, who I was proud to call my friend, even though she wasn't perfect. I had forgiven his second wife for the hateful things she said to Georgia before her death because I felt her genuine sorrow for the way she treated Georgia. We all screwed up in life and deserved a second chance. Rocky had been given plenty chances to prove that he had an ounce of decency inside him, but he never did. He was a user, a liar, and a motherfucking cheater.

I might not have groaned out loud, but my facial expression must've given me away because Rocky narrowed his eyes and scrutinized my reaction. I told myself to keep my mouth shut and not betray any of the secrets Gabe accidentally spilled about Rocky having an affair with Commissioner Wallace. I nodded politely at the mayor then walked right past him and out the door without a word.

"Thank you, Mrs. Perkins, for hanging out with Buddy."

"It was my pleasure, dear. Buddy's such a delightful boy. He reminds me of the dog I had growing up. His name was Baxter, and he was a lab and shepherd mix too." Mrs. Perkins gave Buddy's ears a good scratching before she said her goodbyes and walked in the opposite direction of my house or we would've walked with her.

Buddy sniffed the air hoping for another treat, but he knew better than to expect sugary sweets from his dads. I planned to give him one of the homemade dog cookies made from sweet potatoes that I bought from Brook's over the weekend, but only after we made a quick stop at Emory's to give him my peace offering.

"A word please, Josh," came a hissing, angry request behind me.

I turned slowly and faced Rocky Beaumont. "Mayor," I replied, not even trying to hide my contempt for the man.

Rocky closed the small distance between us and lowered his voice. "Listen to me very carefully," he said in a menacing voice, "I'll make your life a living hell if you breathe a word of what your boyfriend told you."

I stood as tall as my five-ten frame allowed, which happened to be several inches over his short, stocky build, and stared him down. Josh Roman backed down from no one, and the pissant mayor was no exception. "Gabe is a man of honor who *never* talks about his cases," I told the offensive man. Rocky didn't need to know that my man let his secret slip in a moment of weakness and it wasn't like the mayor was going to know firsthand how magic my hands were.

"You know my secret," he hissed. "I can see it in your eyes."

"A person would need to give a shit about you to want to know your secrets," I replied. "I promise you that I don't give a damn about your personal life." I stepped even closer, causing him to back up. "As for your threat, who the fuck do you think you are? Did you threaten me or my business just now? Your position as mayor in this town is basically for decoration. You don't have any real authority here, Rocky. You ride around on the back of a convertible during parades and have ribbon cutting ceremonies at businesses that the county commissioners approve or deny. All the county commissioners are my clients, or they're spouses of my clients, so don't think you'll get them to shut me down, asshole." By that time, Buddy had picked up on my anger and began growling at the reason for it.

Rocky flinched like he didn't know I owned a pair or something. "Well, I…"

"Don't threaten to malign Gabriel and me because you're a pathetic piece of shit." Subtle was not my middle name. I almost slipped and said something about not keeping it in his pants. His affair with Nadine while married to Georgia was public knowledge, but I doubted Rocky would believe that was the affair I meant. I refused to do anything that caused Gabe to look poorly in the eyes of the public he valiantly served, unlike the sniveling, scoundrel who stood before me.

"Who do you think you are, you little fa…"

"Is there a problem here?" A voice I didn't recognize interrupted Rocky before he could finish what he was going to say. I turned an irritated face on the interloper because I really wanted to hear what my mayor thought about me. My eyes widened a bit when I saw it was my new neighbor and the reason for my sleepless night. "Josh, are you okay?" Emory asked, looking between Rocky and me. His concern showed in the etched groove in his brow.

"We're fine," Rocky said, stepping back. "Thanks for clearing the air, Josh."

"Anytime you need me to straighten you out." My fake smile was met with a sneer.

"Wow, that was intense," Emory said once Rocky went back inside the coffee shop. "I'm sorry that I interrupted you, but I feared for that man's safety if he let loose the word he was about to use."

"I wouldn't have hit him no matter how badly I might've wanted to," I told him.

"I was thinking more along the lines of what your boyfriend would do to him," Emory said, adding a smile.

"Yeah, there's that," I agreed.

"Not that I don't think you can handle yourself," he amended quickly. "You were doing fine all on your own."

"I was, wasn't I?" I asked but spoke again before he could continue. "Listen, Buddy and I were on our way to your house."

"You were?"

"Yes," I said, reaching into the bag and pulling out the box of cookies I bought for him. I held the box out to him and said, "A peace offering from me for being a jerk last night."

"I'm allergic," Emory said.

"Oh, I'm sorry," I said, pulling the box back then realized by the smile on his face that I was getting played. "You don't even know what's inside," I told him.

"I know things," he said jokingly, but the smile fell off his face when I stiffened. "Did you research my name, Josh?"

"Asks the psychic," I mumbled.

"You did!" Emory blew out a frustrated breath. "Is that why

you were bringing me a… treat? You either felt bad about what happened to me, or you're afraid of what I might know. Which is it?"

I grimaced and said, "A little of both perhaps."

"That's just great." Emory threw his hands in the air and paced back and forth in front of me. "I don't need your pity, Josh," he said vehemently, never breaking stride.

"What do you need, Emory? Why are you here?" I asked, hoping to put some of my fears to rest.

He stopped then and turned to face me. The agony and despair I saw in his eyes cut me. "I wish I knew, Josh. I wish I knew." He held out his hand to me, and I looked at it in confusion. "Can I have my treat now? I think I deserve it."

"Yeah, sure," I said, pushing the box in his hand. "Regardless of the reasons, I am sorry for my behavior last night. Your presence unsettled me, and I lashed out like an immature brat."

He smiled softly and said, "Thank you. I accept your apology," he held up the bakery box, "and your peace offering."

"Great," I said, unsure of what else to say. "I guess we'll see you around the neighborhood."

"I'll see you next week at my hair appointment," he reminded me.

"That's right," I replied, suddenly feeling awkward. I wasn't sure what to say so I fell back on my old habit. "I knew those weren't natural highlights."

Emory didn't respond, he just laughed and continued inside the coffee shop. I had hoped to put the uneasiness behind me once I apologized but it didn't appear that it would happen. In fact, my nervousness had increased when he confessed he didn't know his reasons for moving to Blissville. I didn't have time to dwell on it though because I needed to get home and get ready for my day.

Meredith looked tired when she arrived like she hadn't slept well. I wasn't always the sharpest tool in the shed, but I knew damned well not to tell a woman she looked tired. Instead, I made her a cup of coffee and kissed her on her forehead and said, "Talk to me. Did he call you?"

"Yes," she said quietly, not meeting my eyes.

I slid my hand beneath her chin and lifted until her pretty, brown eyes met mine. "It didn't go well?" I prompted.

"It did." Meredith released a soft sigh and added, "It went too well."

"Too well?" I asked, making sure I understood what she said because her actions didn't match her words.

She pointed to me. "Pot," she said, then pointed at herself, "meet kettle."

"Ahhhh," I said, understanding exactly what she meant. "You like Harley and you're afraid. It's easier to believe that he can't be as good as he seems than get your hopes up only to be crushed again. Does that sound about right?" I asked.

"It does sound vaguely familiar," she admitted with a crooked smile. "Harley said all the right things, Josh, but I've been down this road before, and I am… afraid."

"I know exactly how you feel, but you're smarter than I was with Gabe. I don't know why he didn't give up on me," I admitted to Meredith.

"He was smart and could see beneath the veneer you show the world, and he thought you were worth fighting for," Meredith told me.

"Well, maybe Harley will feel the same way about you if you give him half the chance. How could he not be crazy about someone like you?" I asked. "You'll always wonder what could've been if you don't go on one date with the man."

"I'm going to give it a shot," she told me. "I'm nervous, but I'm going in with no expectations."

"That's my girl," I said, pulling her into a hug.

Chaz came in through the rear door and yelled loudly, "Group hug!" It was so good to see some life return to his face. He held his arms open wide, and Meredith and I rushed him.

It had been awhile since we'd done something as simple as a group hug and it felt right. I didn't want to be one of those people who let his friendships fade into nothingness when a new love came along. Sure, we worked together and had Sunday dinners together, but it had been awhile since the three of us did something fun together. I made a mental note to plan a date with my friends soon.

We broke up our hug and got busy setting up for the day. The rest of the staff and clients soon filed in and the day was underway before we knew it. Chaz let me know that there was a phone call for me right before my lunch break.

"Do you mind taking a message?" I asked.

Chaz smiled broadly and said, "I think you're going to want to take the call." He held out the phone toward me and did a little dance.

I rolled my eyes when I accepted the phone from him. "Hello, this is Jazz Roman."

"Hello, Jazz. This is Cindy Rollins, and I'm one of the producers with Channel Eleven News. I wondered if you had a free moment to chat about an upcoming series I'm producing."

Surprise rendered me speechless, a feat that my friends and loved ones knew was a rare occurrence. Chaz snapped his fingers in my face to snap me out of it, and I said, "Sure, now's a good time."

"Great," she said cheerfully. "Channel Eleven will be producing a wedding series that will feature a wedding gown boutique owner, a caterer, a wedding planner, a photographer, a florist, and a hair stylist and makeup artist, of course. My associate producer is one of your clients and mentioned your name. She said that you have a vivacious personality and the camera will love you."

"Me?" I asked in shock.

"Yes, you. Tabitha said that you're amazing," Cindy said. I knew that Tabitha worked for Channel Eleven News, but I never expected our connection to equal television time for me. Was that something that I even wanted? "Is it possible to schedule an interview with you in the next week or so?"

"I'm off on Mondays," I told her, not quite sure what I was getting myself into.

"That's fantastic! Can you meet me at the station at say... noon? We'll have lunch and go over some ideas."

"Noon sounds perfect," I replied, still a little numb with shock.

"Great! I'll see you then. Oh, if you don't mind, can I have your email so I can send you my contact info in case something comes up, and you need to reschedule?"

"Sure." I rattled off my email address and told her I'd see her on Monday. I handed the phone back to Chaz then turned to walk to the kitchenette to have a bite to eat.

"Oh, no you don't," Chaz said, following behind me. "What was that all about?"

I flopped down in one of the chairs at the table. "Well, it appears that Channel Eleven is interested in featuring me in a series about weddings. Tabitha recommended me," I told Chaz.

"That's awesome!" Chaz exclaimed.

"Is it?" I asked.

"Why wouldn't it be?" he questioned. "You'd be perfect for something like that."

"I don't know, Chaz. It's never been a goal of mine to be on television."

"Just see what they have to say and get a feel for how it would go. Meeting with Cindy on Monday doesn't equal a commitment to doing the show. Besides, she might not like you anyway."

"Bullshit! She's going to love me." I had no idea if she would or not, but it sounded good.

"Who wouldn't?" Chaz asked.

Plenty of people, but I didn't point that out. Besides, it was extremely flattering to be considered, even if I didn't end up accepting her offer. For once, I had something exciting happening to me that didn't involve someone trying to kill me or threatening to do so.

Word funneled in a little later about the fire at old man Robertson's house. Gabe hadn't said, and I never asked, but it seemed to me that something wicked was in the wind once more in Carter County. The excitement I felt seemed shallow in the face of something as tragic as another homicide. I tried to convince myself that I was reaching, but Gabe's text message about an interview running late convinced me that I was correct.

I loved the fact that he told me he'd be late even though he'd be home hours before I got upstairs. It showed how much he valued and respected our relationship. That was the thought I clung to for the rest of the day when fear and paranoia wanted to take over.

FOURTEEN

Gabe

I COULDN'T FIND PAUL AT THE STATION, SO I CALLED HIS CELL. HE didn't answer my call, but he returned my voicemail message about thirty minutes after I left it.

"I can't talk long," he said in a hushed voice. "What's up?"

It sounded like he was in the field and I didn't want to risk someone overhearing what he had to say. Vice work was extremely dangerous. Cops sometimes went so deep undercover that the line between reality and make believe got blurred and they forgot who they were. Only the strong made it without getting compromised or killed. It was brutally long hours where you were at the mercy of the job twenty-four hours a day, seven days a week. You couldn't have a life because who the hell wanted to be stood up by you repeatedly when the call came in, and you had to leave?

I gave Paul a quick rundown on what I learned and asked who his contact was inside the Casino Control Commission. "I'm hoping they can confirm that talks to build the casino in Carter County have resumed."

"If it's moved beyond the yapping phase then they'll know," Paul told me. "Kerry Simms is her name." He rattled off her number, and I wrote it down on a piece of paper.

"Thanks, man," I said into the phone, prepared to disconnect the call.

"Wait," Paul said suddenly.

"Yeah?"

"So, do you and your cute boyfriend ever…"

"Fuck no," I said before he finished because I knew what he was about to propose and there was no fucking way I'd share Josh with anyone.

Paul chuckled and said, "I see how it is."

"I don't think you do or you wouldn't have asked," I said through gritted teeth.

"I'll never bring it up again, Gabe," Paul said to appease me.

"See that you don't," I snarled then disconnected the call before I said too much.

Dorchester looked up from taking notes on whatever he was researching and said, "Damn, you must have serious game. They're all over you today, Wyatt." My answer to his remark was a glowering glare. "I'll shut up," he said with his hands up in a surrender gesture.

I made a call to Kerry Simms with the CCC and had to leave a message when the call went to voicemail. *Did anyone ever answer their phones anymore?* I had hoped to talk to her before I met with

Jonathon Silver, but luck didn't seem to be on my side just then. It seemed like a huge part of investigating any crime was leaving messages and waiting for people to call you back. I hoped that she'd call me promptly because driving to Columbus to force a meeting with her wasn't high on my list, but I wouldn't hesitate to do it.

Time seemed to tick by slowly until our appointment at the club. I was happy to see two things when the bartender, Alexander, showed us to Silver's office: Silver was dressed, and he was alone. I needed to see his honest reactions to the things I had to say, and I wouldn't get that if his mouthpiece was there, especially if the attorney was tied to some nasty players as I suspected.

"Thank you for seeing us on such short notice," I said to Silver and extended my hand. I was pleased that he shook my hand and let it drop without trying to be coy and sexy. I hoped that I had made myself clear to him earlier on the phone.

"It sounded urgent and I must say that I was pleased that you turned to me for help instead of accusing me of killing my brother." He held up his hand when I started to respond. "I know that you're just doing your job, Detective. I'm trained in interviewing... suspects." His words confirmed that he had most likely worked for one of the alphabet agencies. "Tell me how I can help you catch my brother's killer."

"What can you tell us about Nate's involvement in the planning of a casino?" I asked Silver.

"Nate said that he'd attended a few meetings and was definitely interested in pursuing the idea. Do you think that had something to do with my brother's death?"

"It's very likely," I replied then told him what we knew about the previous attempt to build the casino and what little we knew about Lawrence Robertson's death and how similar it was to Nate's and Owen's. "In Mr. Robertson's belongings, we found notes from the meetings he attended, and he used initials to identify the others involved. This morning, we met with his attorney who represented him at all the meetings, and he identified the names of the people who represented the casino developer."

"And?"

"There's one person we can connect to both Nate and Lawrence Robertson," Dorchester said.

"Who?" Silver demanded.

"Rick Spizer," Dorchester and I said at once.

Silver visibly flinched in shock, which told me how surprised he was about the revelation. Someone with his extensive training would've been able to hide his emotions unless it was something that struck the very heart of him, like hearing that someone he trusted might know who killed his brother.

"Rick? You think Rick was involved in killing Nate and this Robertson guy?" he asked in disbelief.

"He at least knows more than he's letting on," I told Silver. "I don't believe it's a coincidence."

"I don't either," Silver replied, but his eyes had lost focus like he was lost in thought. "Put a wire on me."

"Excuse me?" I asked.

"Put a wire on me and send me in to talk to him," Silver repeated. "I can get him to talk." *I just bet he could.*

"He's your attorney," Dorchester said. "There's a close line we're straddling if he does say something incriminating."

"Not if we have a warrant," I told Dorchester. "We'd need to find a judge we can trust, preferably one with a clerk that doesn't have a big mouth."

"Weston and Harris will know," Dorchester replied. "This is our best bet."

"I'll fire him as my attorney," Silver volunteered.

"Then he might get suspicious and refuse to speak to you," Dorchester replied. "Let us go through the official channels and make sure our I's are dotted, and T's crossed. The last thing we want to do is let someone off on a technicality."

"Okay," Silver said, but I could hear the agitation in his voice. "I don't know how I'm supposed to act like nothing is wrong when I meet with him to go over business tomorrow."

"Oh, I think you can dig deep and rely on your training for that," I told him. He didn't bother to deny it, which was as good as a confirmation I had been right.

"Is there anything else?" he asked us.

"Not at the moment," Dorchester said. "We'll be in touch soon."

We stood to leave and had almost made it to the door when Silver called out my name. "I think I was wrong about you, Detective."

"You wouldn't be the first person, Silver," I tossed over my shoulder as I walked away.

On the way home two things happened; Kerry Simms returned my call and said that there had been no conversations regarding a casino in Carter County and Rylan Broadman called and said he could meet us at the bank at ten the next morning to review the contents of the vault.

"Thank you, counselor. We'll see you there," I told him.

"It finally seems like things are moving forward," Dorchester said. "I worried that this would be another cold case collecting dust in an evidence locker."

"Not if I have anything to do with it," I replied. "I would've loved for Kerry Simms to confirm that the casino talk had reached the official stages, but that doesn't change anything about our investigation."

"True. You think the Reds stand a chance this year?" Dorchester asked, changing the subject. I was happy to have something else to discuss.

"I think it has to be an improvement over last year. Damn, we need some pitching," I commented.

"We'll have to catch a game this year," he said. "We'll bring our significant others."

"That sounds like fun. Josh isn't really into sports much, so we'll make him the DD."

"Sounds like a damn good plan to me," Dorchester said.

We chatted about sports and mundane things for the rest of the ride home. We had put our time in, we moved our case forward, and it was time to go home and be with the people we loved. I noticed that Dorchester's steps appeared to be lighter when I dropped him off at his car. I imagined I looked the same and it was amazing to me how quickly a case could change and the improvement it had on our moods. With any luck, we'd solve the case in the next few days and get back to our normal routines.

I didn't enter the salon like I had the night before, even though I wanted to. I knew Josh was aware I was home thanks to Savage screeching at the top of his birdie lungs. I stopped to give him a treat and heard the crew laughing at his antics. I was too amped up over the possibility of solving the case, and it felt like the walls of our home were closing in on me. I decided to take a jog to try to burn off my excess energy.

I changed clothes and grabbed Buddy's leash. I knew that Josh had already taken him for a run that morning, but he was young, healthy, and loved the exercise. Savage serenaded me with his filthy mouth when I walked by again.

"Dirty Bird!"

"Dirty Dog," he fired back like he was jealous of Buddy, but that was a crazy thought. Savage couldn't think and speak freely; he could only repeat what he'd heard. *Right?* Sometimes I had to wonder.

The sound of my running shoes slapping against the pavement and the steady pull of air into my lungs helped settle me. The adrenaline never left my body, but it became more productive than just making my mind spin. Of course, the increase in testosterone made me want to do other things that would have to wait until Josh got home. Sure, I could rub one out in the shower, but why would I?

Josh was in the little room off the kitchenette mixing up hair color in his little plastic bowls. I'd been a really good boy the first time through, but catching him alone in the room was a different story. I left Buddy in the kitchenette because I knew he wouldn't take off. The room was barely big enough for one person so cramming two inside was very interesting. I vividly recalled the first time I shut myself in the room with Josh and it appeared my dick did too.

"Well, hello there, Detective Sweaty Balls," he said saucily.

"God I love your mouth," I said then captured his lips in a kiss so fierce it had my insides twisted up in no time. I expected Josh to push me back and remind me that he was working or that his employees were near. Instead, he broke our kiss and put his finger over my mouth to tell me to be quiet before he dropped to his knees. "Josh," I whispered hoarsely.

Josh pulled my sweats and underwear down far enough to spring my dick free. I closed my eyes and tilted my head against the locked door when I felt his tongue flick out to tease the crown of my dick, showing me that a little sweat wasn't a turnoff for him. My hand at the back of his neck tightened to urge him to hurry up. I wanted to feel his hot mouth working my cock, and I wasn't in the mood for teasing.

"So impatient," he murmured between kisses along my shaft. "I can't rush art."

"Then you shouldn't have started anything at all," I told him. "I just wanted a kiss."

"Okay," Josh said, as he rose to his feet. "You got your kiss then."

"You're just going to leave me like this?" I hissed, pointing to my cock that was flushed red with desire and anger at being neglected.

"Yeah, I think I am." He dismissed me by turning his back to me and whipping up his little hair potions. He hummed along happily as if he had no idea of what was going to be waiting for him when he got home. I couldn't have that.

I pulled up my pants and underwear then walked up behind him until he was pinned between me and the sink. "You're going to pay for this." I reached between our bodies and ran my finger over his crack through his jeans. I was rewarded with a sharp gasp and the trembling of his body. "I'm not going to stop until you scream and beg me to let you come."

"You're so salty over a little teasing," he said nonchalantly. "This Detective Piss and Groan isn't very sexy. Bring back Detective Fuck and Moan."

"There will be plenty of fucking and moaning, Sunshine. You can count on it."

He turned around to face me wearing a smug smile. "Oh, I am."

I turned loose of him and left him to get back to work. I retrieved the dog and bird and headed upstairs to plan my attack. Initially, I planned to feed him first before I tormented him, but decided there was no fun in that at all.

Instead, I watched the clock closely as I attempted to relax while watching some TV after a quick shower. I watched out the windows as the staff left for the night and counted the minutes until I knew Josh would be coming up the stairs. I laid in wait for him and pounced the minute his feet reached the top step. I lifted him up and carried him to the dining room table where I had the lube and condom waiting. Josh laughed in delighted glee as I tore his clothes from his body.

"You've been up here naked this entire time?" he asked.

"And hard," I added. "The longer I waited, the harder I got with anticipation."

I attacked his luscious lips with my mouth and kissed him until he was boneless beneath me on the table. Only then did I begin to prepare his ass for the fucking I was going to give him. I didn't rush through it either. I wanted him to beg and plead for me. His body shook with need, but he wouldn't say the magic words that would bring him relief—not my beautiful, stubborn man.

I could see in his eyes that he was determined to hold out on me, to get the upper hand, but I wasn't about to let that happen.

I slid two oil-slicked fingers in his ass and curled them upward to massage his prostate. I kept them right there and circled them around and around until sweat popped out all over his body and he shook hard all over.

"Is there something you want to say to me, Sunshine?"

"Yes!"

I had him right where I wanted him and knew it. "There's no shame in saying what you want. Go ahead and tell me."

"I shot J.R.," he said, then grinned wickedly knowing damn well he got me with his reference to *Dallas* while I was sexing him up.

I wasn't one to give in easily or else we wouldn't have been together in that moment. I decided to switch up tactics on Josh. I pulled my fingers out of his tight clinch and began stroking my cock between his spread legs instead. His smugness faded when I continued to pleasure myself instead of rolling on the condom and fucking him.

"You're playing with me right now," he said, not believing that I'd jerk off to completion. I hoped it wasn't the case, but I was prepared to be just as coy and stubborn as him. He narrowed his eyes when he saw my wicked smile. "Okay, fine."

Josh reached down and began stroking his cock with his right hand while teasing his eager hole with two fingers of his left. His back arched off the table, but his eyes never left mine. Damn him and his ability to stay ahead of me each and every time. I had to believe that he wanted my cock even more than he wanted his fingers. Josh looked so goddamned sexy pleasuring himself in front of me. My hand felt good, and I felt the telltale signs of my orgasm building in my balls, but I wanted more.

I was just about to give in and be the one to beg when he let out a frustrated growl followed by, "Fuck me already, Gabe! Please! I'm begging, okay?"

I had the condom on in record time and pushed inside him until I was as far inside as I could get. I paused to let him adjust to my girth then I gave him the pounding his eyes and his words demanded. I pushed his legs back until his knees were almost to his chest so that he was completely open to me. I could tell by the way his balls were bouncing that he was working his cock hard.

"So fucking beautiful," I growled.

Josh's ass tightened like a vise around my cock, and he shouted my name as he came. His orgasm ignited mine, and his chute milked my balls until I had nothing left to give. I pulled out of him carefully when I was done and lowered his legs back down so I could give him a kiss.

I didn't expect to find him glaring at me, but the source of his ire was plain to see all over his face, rather it was splashed all over his face. "You came hard for me," I said before I licked his cum that had splattered over his lips. "Yum."

"It's a damn good thing I love you," he said. "Only you could get away with fucking me on the table where we eat and making me come in my own mouth."

"Well, never let it be said that I don't have skills," I said, holding out a hand to help him up.

"One of them better be that you're proficient with Clorox wipes," he said before he sauntered off toward the bathroom to get cleaned up. I loved watching the bounce of his firm ass cheeks.

"I'll even cook dinner," I hollered after him.

"After you clean the cum off the table," he fired back. "We fuck like animals, baby, but we don't live like them."

Some might call me whipped when I pulled out the wipes beneath the sink and wiped the table before I got in the shower with him, but I didn't care. I pulled him to me beneath the spray of hot water and said, "Tell me about your day, Sunshine."

"You won't believe it," Josh said with a quirky smile.

"Try me."

FIFTEEN

Josh

"It went a little something like this," I told Gabe. "I took Buddy with me for a morning run to try and wake up my sleepy brain. I'd had dreams of Fabio all night long and..."

"Whoa!" Gabe exclaimed loudly. His eyes opened wide in shock, and it was unfortunate that he'd been rinsing the soap from his hair at the time. "Fuck! My eyes!"

"Baby, I'm sorry." I worried my bottom lip between my teeth as he sputtered and cursed while getting the soap out of his eyes.

"Back the fuck up, Sunshine. Are you sorry that you confessed to dreaming about another dude or are you sorry that you burned my retinas in the process?" He shook his head slowly and asked, "You're dreaming about our new neighbor so early in our relationship? That's not good for our outlook." I couldn't tell by Gabe's cop slash poker face if he was truly upset or if he was playing me. His bloodshot eyes could've been from rage or the soap; it was hard to say which was true. Both?

"They weren't those kinds of dreams, Gabriel." The tone of my voice and the use of his first name let him know I meant business. "They were filled with fear and uncertainty. Him living next door to us increases my heart rate in ways that have nothing to do with my dick!" I elbowed him out of the way to hog the water a little more. I decided perhaps my little cock-teasing stunt below wasn't harsh enough. Had I known he had such little faith in us…

"I'm sorry, Sunshine." He wrapped his strong arms around me and nuzzled my neck.

I won't even pretend that I didn't melt into him. People can tout Disney's theme parks as the happiest places all they wanted, but Gabe's arms were my happy place. They can have the mouse; I had the man. "You're forgiven. Can I continue now?"

"Please do," Gabe said.

"So, I felt bad about how I acted toward him last night. My being uncomfortable with him was no excuse for shitty behavior. I would like to think I learned my lesson with you," I added.

"That's so mature of you, Sunshine."

"I have potential," I confidently told Gabe, then continued with my story. "I decided that I would give Emory cookies as an apology…" My words were interrupted by a loud growl emanating from Gabe's throat. "Store bought cookies that aren't half as good as mine, baby," I assured him. "I only make those chocolate chip cookies for you from now on."

"That's what I want to hear," Gabe said in a gravelly voice filled with passion. "I'll never share my cookies." The way he palmed my junk made it known he wasn't really talking about dessert.

"Yes, baby, my oven will never know any other loaf but yours," I said, pushing my ass against his groin. I cleared my throat and decided I better focus because I could tell our cookie talk was going to lead to activities that didn't include baking or talking—unless it was dirty talking.

"Damn straight," Gabe said. There was nothing straight about me but I dared not veer down that road, or I'd never get to the interesting parts of my day.

"I stopped by The Brew for a coffee and to grab a muffin and some cookies for Emory. As I was leaving, I ran into the *good* mayor, who basically threatened to…"

"Wait a fucking minute," Gabe interrupted me. "Do you want to repeat that?"

I turned in the circle of his arms and looked up into his face, which was red with fury. There was no mistaking his bristling as anything other than raw anger. "Not really," I said honestly. "Look, let's do the quick version of this so you don't stroke out. Rocky thought by the contemptuous look on my face at seeing him that you told me about his affair with Jack Wallace. He started to bluster about what he'd do if I revealed his secret. I told him that you didn't tell me anything and I didn't need another reason to hate his fucking guts…"

"You said that?" Gabe asked in shock.

"I'm paraphrasing, Gabe. Keep up here." I rolled my eyes exaggeratingly. I vowed not to mention how Rocky almost slipped up and used the three-letter F-word because I worried what he might do to the toad. "I told him he couldn't do shit to me as mayor and that all the power came from the county commissioners who wouldn't dare stand against me. They're either my clients or spouses of my clients, and they adore me," I boasted proudly. "I might've advanced on him and pointed my finger in his smashed, ugly face. I'm sure it looked like a heated argument when Emory walked up and…"

"Wait. Emory just happened to show up at the same time and place that you were getting harassed?" Gabe asked.

"You make it sound like he's some superhero or vigilante or something," I scoffed. He did claim to be psychic. *Did that mean he had a vision? Did he follow me?*

"Hey," Gabe said softly. He placed his hand beneath my chin and brushed his thumb over my lips. "I didn't mean to spook you."

"You didn't," I said, but I could tell he didn't believe me. "More than I already am," I amended. "I apologized to Emory, even though he didn't make it easy." Gabe frowned at that, so I explained about Emory saying he was allergic to the cookies, sort of like I said I didn't drink. "I did come right out and ask him what he was doing here."

"You did? What did he say?" Gabe questioned.

"He said he wished that he knew," I replied. "I could see the confliction in his eyes. He had no clue why he moved to Blissville— or at least none that he was willing to share. That only made me even more curious, but I let it go instead of pressing the issue."

"Strange," Gabe said. I could tell he had his thinking cap on again. "I'm not saying that I believe in the whole psychic phenomenon, but it's hard to argue with his success rate. He may not know the reasons why he's here, but I'd like to know what he 'saw' to prompt him to move." I thought Gabe's little air quotes were adorable.

"That makes two of us," I admitted. "Now, let's get on to the exciting part of my day."

"There's more?" Gabe asked.

"Yessss!" I did a little shimmy. "I lead an exciting life."

"Do tell," he prompted.

"I got a call from the producer of Channel Eleven News today. She wants to meet with me and discuss the possibility of me joining them for a series about weddings. They're featuring a boutique, a caterer, a wedding planner, a photographer, a florist, and a hairstylist and makeup artist. One of the executive producers of the show happens to be a client of mine."

"Sunshine, that's fucking amazing!" Gabe said happily. "Oh my God, we'll have to record the series to keep. Oh! I hope they'll have a link online because our parents will want to see it too."

"Slow down there, babe," I cautioned. "It's not a done deal, so I'm not telling anyone about it until I know it's a sure thing. I'm meeting with Cindy on Monday at noon to go over ideas and get specifics."

"Is it an interview? Are there other candidates?" he wanted to know. His happiness for my success made me smile like a goon.

"I'm not sure about other candidates, but it does feel like an interview to see if we're a good fit," I replied.

Gabe pondered that for a second and asked, "So, you get the impression the decision is up to you?"

"Yeah, I do," I admitted. "Babe, we better finish up in here before the water gets cold. My water heater is better than your old one, but it's not endless."

"True," Gabe replied.

We made quick work of washing and rinsing then shut off the shower. My stomach growled, making its displeasure of being empty known. "Food," I demanded.

I had thrown some ribs and barbecue sauce in the crockpot before I went to work that morning so Gabe's offer to cook dinner was sweet, but not needed. The ribs would be tender and delicious and exactly what I needed. Gabe and I got dressed then headed into the kitchen to finish putting the rest of dinner together.

"Listen, I need what's about to happen to stay between us, Gabe. Do you promise?" I asked seriously. He looked a little nervous but nodded his head anyway. I reached inside the refrigerator and pulled the pre-made mashed potatoes that I hid in the very back behind the milk and juice cartons. "There are times in life when you need to go with a quick fix."

Gabe's lips trembled from the restraint of holding back his laughter. "I'll take your secret to the grave, Sunshine. No one will ever know you served me instant mashed potatoes."

I slammed the package on the counter and squared myself in front of him with my hands on my hips. "I have *never* made instant potatoes in my life, Gabriel, and I sure as hell wouldn't serve them to the love of my life." I placed my hand over my heart to indicate how seriously his words wounded me. "These are made with real Idaho potatoes, milk, and butter." I pointed to the words on the packaging.

"I stand corrected," Gabe said, doing his best to look like he learned a serious lesson just then. "It's good to know that I'm the love of your life."

"Duh!" I rolled my eyes in frustration. "That's what you took from all of that? You didn't hear me say that these aren't fake potato flakes? Gabriel," I said in disappointment. "What am I going to do with you?"

"Oh, Sunshine," he replied with an evil grin. "I'll let you do *whatever* you want to me, but after you feed me." So many wicked, naughty ideas crossed my mind, but I pushed them aside because it felt like my stomach was eating itself.

Gabe heated up the mashed potatoes while I tossed a salad and baked some crescent rolls from a can. He wisely kept his mouth shut about that shortcut because he could eat eight of them all by himself if I let him.

I inspected the table to make sure it was as clean as Gabe had guaranteed. I saw no assprints, handprints, or jizz anywhere and decided it was good enough to eat on once again. It was just the two of us, and no one would think anything of it if we ate on the couch and watched television, but eating together at the table was our thing—unless it was pizza night.

"What can you tell me about your day?" I asked once Gabe had a chance to sample everything and praise its deliciousness.

"We have a promising lead," he confirmed. "There's one guy

who can be considered a common thread, so we'll see how that goes."

"I heard about the fire at Mr. Robertson's house," I told him. "I'm not asking you to tell me anything, but I'm guessing that the fire the day after his dead body was discovered wasn't an accident."

"It sure wasn't, although it will take a few days for the fire marshal to give us a detailed report." Gabe was silent for a few minutes while he chowed down some more food. "What I'm about to tell you will be public knowledge soon enough. In fact, I'm impressed the truth isn't out yet." I nodded for Gabe to continue, although I was pretty sure what he was going to tell me. "Mr. Robertson's death wasn't natural."

"I figured as much, but thank you for telling me. I'm sorry that you see such shitty things in your job. I know that somebody has to do it, and I sometimes wish that burden wasn't on your shoulders, but I'm glad we have someone as dedicated as you are looking out for us."

"Thank you, Sunshine. There are some really hard days, but coming home to you each night helps me in ways I don't think I can properly express," Gabe told me.

"You can try," I suggested. I never considered myself to be a glory hound or attention seeker, but I won't pretend that I didn't love hearing how much Gabe loved me. He was the first and only man to say those words to me, other than my father and Chaz.

"You give me a reason to smile, you make me laugh, and you remind me of good in this world. Loving you gives me a purpose to live for, something other than a job. You make me want to be a better version of myself," Gabe said tenderly.

"Wow." I wasn't sure what to say, but that didn't last long. I pointed my fork at him and said, "That right there is why no one else will ever get my chocolate chip cookies." I should've said more and reciprocated those sentiments back at him, but I was too emotional to do it just then.

After dinner, Gabe turned on a baseball game. The Reds were on the west coast taking on some team in royal blue jerseys. I couldn't tell you what the name of the team was, but I was fond of the way their asses looked in their white baseball pants. Because the game started three hours later than normal, it wasn't half over by the time we went to bed.

"Maybe you can call Emory and find out who wins," I said, as I snuggled up to Gabe beneath the sheets.

Gabe chuckled then said, "Smartass," before he kissed my forehead.

My heart still felt full from the words Gabe used earlier to express his love for me. In fact, it felt like it might explode if I didn't tell him how I felt. Telling Gabe that he was the most important person in my life and that I couldn't imagine a day without him seemed like the best way to open up a valve and release some of the pressure.

"You're an incredible man, Gabe."

"I am?" he asked.

"The best. I thought men like you only existed in fairy tales, books, and movies, but here you are," I said, placing a kiss on his chest over his heart. "You're kind, genuine, you speak from the heart, and you love with everything you have, and somehow you want to share that love with me. I am the luckiest man on this planet. So, on the days when things look bleak, and humanity has let you down again, know that I'll be here to show you that this life is worth living and there is always sunshine waiting to brighten your world after those dark clouds pass."

"Josh, that's a beautiful thing to say," he said tenderly.

"I have my moments," I said sheepishly.

"Oh, Sunshine. Every moment with you is precious and beautiful. I want you to take that knowledge into your dreams with you tonight and know that I'm here and I'm not going anywhere. I want you to have sweet dreams about a happy future with me and not turbulent ones about the man next door. Will you do that for me?" he asked.

"I'll try my best," I promised.

Sleep, when it finally came, was better than the previous night, but not filled with sunshine and fields of flowers like Gabe had wanted. I didn't want to worry him, so I did something the next morning that I had never done with him up to that point: I lied. I told him I slept great and then distracted him with a blow job in case my smile hadn't been convincing. I would need to face down whatever demons were possessing my dreams on my own. I had a feeling that I could only do that by going straight to the source of my fear—Emory.

SIXTEEN

Gabe

Good morning, Detectives," Rylan Broadman said outside the glass doors of Blissville Bank and Trust.

"Counselor," I returned.

"Morning," Dorchester replied.

Broadman opened the door, and we followed him inside the bank. I remembered how surprised I had been the first time I walked into the building after moving to Blissville to open an account. It was more opulent than any big city bank I had ever been to with the white and gold marble floors that gleamed beneath the bright overhead lights and cashier wickets made of an expensive dark wood. The office furniture throughout the building was constructed of the same high-quality wood. The sitting area furniture looked like expensive antiques that a person didn't expect to find in a bank. I had almost been afraid to sit in them for fear that my big frame and weight would break them.

"I spoke to the bank manager, Ken Divers, and he's going to give us a private room to go through and document the contents of the safe deposit box. I would need to take this step for trust purposes even if you didn't want to see what's inside," Broadman told us.

The chairs and sofas were as elegant as I recalled from the time I opened an account. My doubt in their ability to hold me had grown, as had my waistline from eating Josh's cooking the past few months. It seemed like I wasn't the only one who felt that way because Broadman and Dorchester looked them over and remained standing with me while we waited for the bank manager to meet us.

My first impression of Ken Divers was that of a man who worked endless hours and didn't take home much to show for it. I'd always heard that the only people who made money in banking were the presidents and CEOs. Ken's shirt looked a tad threadbare around the elbow when he extended his hand to Dorchester first, and then to me. I wondered if perhaps the bank could've invested more money in their employees instead of the building itself.

"Come with me, gentlemen," Divers said. We followed him down a hallway that led to a vault filled with various sizes of safe deposit boxes. "Box five twenty-nine," he said out loud as he looked for the right one. "Aha," he exclaimed when he spotted it.

Lawrence Robertson's box was the largest size the bank offered. Each safe deposit box required two keys to open it: the client's specific key and the bank's master key that fit all the boxes. The bank couldn't open the box with just their master key. If a client lost a key, the bank hired a locksmith to drill the lock to open it. Divers slid his key into place then gestured for Broadman to do the same. Broadman had told us that the bank issued two keys for each box; Robertson kept one, and he'd given the other to his attorney. The men turned their keys at the same time, and we heard an audible click when the box unlocked.

Divers opened the door, and both men grabbed a side of the box and began to pull. It was longer than I expected it to be. The height and width were about a foot, but I estimated the length of the box to be at least three feet long. I could tell by the grunts the two men made and the way their knees bent that it weighed quite a bit too.

"Jesus," Divers exclaimed. "I think we know where the missing gold from Fort Knox is hidden."

"It sure feels that way," Broadman said.

The two men carried the box inside a rather cramped room, that only had two chairs and a cheaply laminated table that was attached to the wall. The unglamorous appeal of the room was in sharp contrast to the glitz and glam of the rest of the building. It was like they ran out of money or stopped caring when they got to that part of the building.

"I guess this won't work, will it?" Ken asked.

"Not unless one of these guys sits in the other's lap," Broadman returned quickly.

"Rule number three twenty-nine: No lap dances inside the bank vault," Divers said dryly, but good-naturedly. "I like the privacy of this room, but it's too small. I tell you what," he said, "if you don't mind, I'll set you up in a conference room. We don't have any loan closings scheduled until this afternoon. Will that do?"

Broadman looked at us to get our okay. Dorchester and I nodded that it was fine by us. "Perfect, Ken. Thank you."

"You lead the way, and I'll help carry the safe deposit box," I told the manager, who gladly let me hoist the bulky box with Broadman. The fucking thing weighed even more than I thought. "Jesus!

Someone call Geraldo Rivera and tell him we found the missing loot from Al Capone's secret vault," I said excitedly. I sounded more and more like Josh every damn day, which was fine by me but I wasn't ever going to wear his skinny jeans.

"You got this, buddy," Dorchester said encouragingly.

We followed behind Divers to the conference room. "Is there anything else you need?" he asked once he flipped the lights on in the spacious room. The gleaming mahogany table was large enough to seat a professional football team around it and still have room. Divers' eyes flipped between the box and each of us. I could tell his curiosity was getting the best of him, and he wanted to know what was in that box.

"That will be all," I said, placing my hand on the doorknob as a subtle hint that he could leave.

"Oh, okay," he said, slowly backing out of the doorway. "You know where to find..." I closed the door as soon as he was clear of it, cutting off his words.

Dorchester chuckled and said, "What an asshole."

"Nah, he was just curious," I said, waving off the idea.

"I was talking about you," Dorchester told me.

We had a good chuckle then focused our attention on the safe deposit box. There was a bit of tension in the air since we weren't sure what to expect. "Let's do this," I said, reaching for the top of the box. I waited for the guys to get ready and for Dorchester to give me the okay.

Broadman opened his notebook and clicked his pen to prepare for taking notes. Dorchester had pulled out his phone and clicked on the video feature. "Detective John Dorchester with Carter County Sheriff's Department, Detective Gabriel Wyatt with the Blissville Police Department, and attorney Rylan Broadman at Blissville Bank and Trust." He rattled off the date and continued with, "We are taking inventory of the box with the permission of Rylan Broadman, who also acts as the trustee for the Lawrence Robertson Revocable

Trust. Okay, Gabe, open the box," Dorchester said.

I opened the box slowly as if I expected the thing to be booby trapped or some shit. I watched *Goonies* enough as a kid that I knew better than to just rush into a situation. Nothing exploded when it was finally opened, which was great, but the sheer number of items crammed inside the box seemed overwhelming. It looked like everything was wrapped in the plastic bags you get from the grocery store.

"We'll go with the notion that the newest items would be on top, but we won't take anything for granted. Dual control on each item with the camera on us at all times," I said, making sure we were protected from false claims that we helped ourselves to whatever might be inside, especially cash. Not only that, the video could appear as part of the evidence presented at trial and we weren't about to lose a case over the camera panning away from the box and then back or video feed that got cut and looked like it was edited. "Ready?" I asked Broadman.

"Ready," he responded.

I grabbed the first plastic bag and opened it up. "There's a stash of cash here," I said clearly for the video. "A stack of hundred dollar bills with a ten-thousand-dollar money wrapper on it. Do we count it to verify for your notes or assume it's full?" I asked Broadman.

"We count it to make sure we're accurate," he replied. "Are either of you opposed if I ask for a money counter machine?"

"Call the manager from your cellphone," I said. "I don't want to be accused of stealing anything out of the box."

"Good point," Broadman said. He called the bank manager, and we waited for a few minutes for the knock on the door.

Dorchester kept the camera firmly on the box, so it was clear that no one touched or moved the box. "I'll take over for you if your arm gets tired," I offered. It would be easy enough to move in behind him and take the phone, so he could move out from behind it and get a break.

Broadman set up the money counter right beside the box so that it was in sight of the camera. We ran the first pack of money through the machine and confirmed that there were exactly ten thousand dollars inside. We both initialed and dated the strap and set it aside. We repeated this same process with nine additional bags of cash.

"One hundred thousand dollars in cash so far," I documented for the camera. It seemed that Mr. Robertson had some emergency money on hand just in case the banks failed. It was hard telling what else we would find.

Beneath the row of money was several envelopes that appeared to be letters. Most of them were thanking Robertson for his generous benevolence to their charity or university. Alice Davenport wasn't wrong when she said that he was a generous man. The charitable amounts in that stack of letters equaled a staggering one million dollars. In my head, I said it in my Mike Myers voice from *Austin Powers*. As impressive as his donations were, it was the last letter that sent my heart pounding.

It was a letter from Michael Larkin sent in September to Robertson. "Larkin was the guy from McCarren Consortium that Robertson didn't like or trust, right?" I asked the men in the conference room with me.

"Yeah," Dorchester agreed, "what do you have?"

"It's a letter dated in September from Larkin, and it's inquiring if Robertson is interested in resuming talks about selling his land for the casino. He says he can assure him that things will turn out differently this time. He's willing to offer the same contingencies as Mr. McCarren did with the first deal." I turned and held the letter up for the video. I was sure I looked like a grinning fool because the timing was right. Nate Turner had called me mid-November about the threats he'd been receiving, and he was killed in January. We just had to figure out Nate's exact involvement.

"We'll be taking this letter as evidence, Mr. Broadman,"

Dorchester told him. "We'll be sure to get a copy back to you."

"Mr. Robertson didn't mention this to you at all? Not even in passing?" I asked the attorney. It seemed to me that Robertson had placed a lot of confidence in the younger man. It was odd that he wouldn't have told him, even if he planned on ignoring the letter.

"Not a word, which feels strange to me," Broadman replied earnestly. "But, there's the evidence that it happened. That's clearly McCarren letterhead."

The rest of the box was anticlimactic compared to the cash and the smoking gun of a letter. We replaced the items back where we found them and Dorchester filmed us putting the box back and locking it away before handing over the bank's key to Divers, who looked nervous about being on camera. He resembled a lizard by the way he kept licking his lips and stared at it with bulging eyes.

We shook Broadman's hand then headed to the sheriff's department to copy and enter the letter into evidence before we headed to Cincinnati.

The conference room buzzed with excitement when the task force learned about the letter.

"Hot damn!" Weston said loudly.

"It's about time," Harris added. "Let's get this all wrapped up in a pretty bow for the DA."

"We need to find our killer first," I told them, trying to project a little levity into the situation. Yes, we were getting somewhere, but there were a few missing pieces, and we still didn't know who pulled the trigger. "Do any of the players at McCarren have military backgrounds or connections?" I asked. Our killer knew what the fuck he was doing, which didn't necessarily equal ex-military, but sometimes special forces turned to mercenary work once they returned to civilian life.

"Other than our ghost, Jonathon Silver," Weston asked. "Let's not forget his appearance was awfully damn convenient."

"We haven't ruled him out," I explained. "It's better that he thinks we believe every word that comes out of his mouth. He'll cooperate more that way," I said with a wicked smile. "He has an alibi for the night of Nate's homicide, by the way, so let's look to see if any of the men employed by McCarren could be co-conspirators. Like Michael Larkin," I told the group.

"I've got backgrounds," Detective Allyson Drake said. It was the first time in a few weeks she'd joined us, but she was finished with her latest undercover bust and was looking to stay busy until her next assignment came in.

"You have the floor, Detective," I told her and took a seat.

Drake typed a few things on her laptop, and an image popped up on the whiteboard behind her. "This is Drew McCarren," she said. The man wasn't what I was expecting, although I couldn't pinpoint why. He had a sexy silver fox thing going for him, except his dark eyes resembled those of a shark. McCarren gave the appearance of being cold, ruthless, and dead on the inside. Drake rattled off his age, income, and a few of the things he was accused of doing, although no arrests had been made.

Detective Drake hit a key, and a different image popped up. "This is Michael Larkin, the man who Robertson disliked the most," she said. "Former Marine..."

"No such thing," Harris said, pushing back his sleeve to reveal his globe and anchor tattoo with the dates of his service. "A Marine until you die."

"Michael Larkin *is* a Marine," Drake amended. "He served for twenty-two years before he resigned. He has a degree in urban planning and development as well as an architectural degree. He's the lead man on all projects at McCarren. He's not on anyone's radar that I can see."

She went through the money guy Tommy Thompson pretty

quickly because there wasn't anything there that raised the hair on the back of our necks. When she put up a photo of Rick Spizer, I sat up a little straighter, as did everyone else in the room.

"Former Green Beret." You could feel the energy pulsating through the room when she made the announcement. He was involved somehow, and we knew it.

"Let's get on that warrant to wire Jonathon Silver and set up a meeting between the two men," I told the room.

I didn't trust Jonathon Silver, but I had no choice but to use him to try and get to the truth. I'd wire him up, send him undercover, and give him enough rope to hang himself. If he were responsible for his brother's death, I wouldn't stop until I proved it.

SEVENTEEN

Josh

My day started out similar as the day before, minus the confrontation with the mayor and my half-attempt at an apology to Emory. I seldom ran consecutive days, preferring to do yoga or work my pole in between runs to let my body recover. Not even my tried-and-true yoga helped me shake the anxiety I felt over Emory's presence in our lives.

Buddy eagerly waited in the kitchen next to his leash that hung from a hook on the wall when he saw that I was putting on my bright running clothes and shoes. That day's ensemble was lime green and navy. I liked the color combo and remarked that I'd like to have it in a pair of underwear. There was no one there to hear my comment except the pets, and they didn't look impressed.

Like the day before, I ran into Emory. He had been out running too, wearing a somber charcoal gray jogging suit and had his hair up in a man-bun. He entered the park on the outskirts of town from the opposite side that I did. I always stopped and stretched at the gazebo since it was the midway mark for my run. It seemed that we were of the same mind, or did he read my mind? I narrowed my eyes in speculation.

"I can't read your damn mind, Josh." He propped his heel on the back of the bench so that his leg was extended out in front of him. He bent over his leg and reached for his toes, stretching his hamstrings.

"You just did," I told him suspiciously.

"It didn't take psychic ability to know what you were thinking," he said, switching legs. "Did anyone ever tell you not to play poker?"

"Yes, but then I took all his money and that of his parents too." I laughed at the memory of shock on their faces.

"Good to know," Emory said with a nod of his head. He noticed that my eyes kept straying to his man-bun and chuckled. "Not a fan, huh?"

"No, although I can appreciate the necessity to get it off your neck while working up a sweat. Not that I'm thinking about the ways you work up a sweat or anything." My cheeks turned pink with embarrassment. I didn't want to give him the wrong idea.

"I didn't get the wrong idea," he said. "I knew you meant jogging and not other, um… sweaty activities."

"You did it again," I said, taking a step back from him. I'd risk pulling a muscle from not stretching properly if it meant getting away from the man because I always made an ass of myself in front of him. Some people brought out the worst in me without trying.

My mind went to Gabe, but that was a completely different situation. I was protecting my heart from getting hurt. Emory was no threat to my heart because I'd already given mine to Gabe.

Emory threw his head back and laughed hard for several long seconds. I couldn't help but notice how rusty it sounded as if he hadn't laughed in a really long time.

Maybe I should've been offended by his laughter, but instead, it made me sad. "What are you doing on Sunday?" For the life of me, I had no idea where the question came from. It was out of my mouth before I could stop it.

"Sunday? Isn't that Easter?" Emory asked.

Well, I couldn't un-speak my damn words, so I rolled with it. "Uh, yeah. Do you have plans?"

"I'll probably still be unpacking then," he said. I noticed he started to shift his weight slightly between his right and left foot. I figured it had more to do with me making him feel uncomfortable than an effort to keep his heart rate up.

"Well, I'll be serving dinner around five if you'd like to come over," I said.

Emory nodded noncommittally then looked away briefly. He bit his bottom lip and appeared to be thinking about how to react, unlike me who often shot from the hip. "I appreciate your invite, Josh. I'll think about it, okay?"

"Sure," I replied. "I don't mean to toot my own horn here, but I can pretty much guarantee that you've never had a glazed ham better than one I'll serve you."

"Oh, I'm vegan," he said.

I gasped and stood back from him like he announced he had a deadly infectious disease and I was minutes away from my insides imploding and drowning in my own blood. I checked myself because I loved animals and I could understand why people didn't want to eat them. But no bacon? Emory's lips twitched at the corners, and I realized he was playing. "You're a complete shit, Emory!"

"Man, you're so easy," he said between chuckles.

"Who told?" I demanded to know.

He clutched his stomach and laughed even harder. "So sorry," he said as he tried to catch his breath.

"If you think I'm funny then you should see my makeshift family. I can promise you a good time," I said, sounding like one of those scribbled comments on a bathroom stall.

"I'm not touching that one," Emory said, shaking his head. "No way."

"The offer is there if you want to accept it, but I won't take it out on your hair at your appointment next week should you not show up to dinner," I told him.

"Yeah well, this style—or lack thereof—is from not giving a damn. I guess you could say my looks have lost their importance to me the last few years." He smiled softly as if he tried to soften the sadness behind his words. "Can I ask you for one favor if I do show up?"

"You can ask," I told him, but I didn't commit to granting it.

"Will you please not tell anyone about my... *gift*?"

"That I can guarantee," I told him.

"Good," he said in relief. "I don't do parlor tricks. I take my abilities seriously, and I use them to help people, not hurt them." I felt like he was directing the last part toward me and not making a general statement.

"I understand. I doubt the rest of the group will whip out their phones and search your name like I did, but I do advise you make up a believable excuse as to why you moved to Blissville," I told him. "It's a nice town and all, but rarely do people move here unless it's work-related."

Emory thought about it for a few seconds then asked, "What do you think they'd find acceptable? Honestly, I'm out of my league here. I don't know why I'm in Blissville beyond the fact that I knew I was needed."

I took in Emory's appearance and air of mystery about him. "How about a writer? Maybe you moved here to do research on small towns for a series you're writing. They may not drill you down as to exactly how or why you picked Blissville, but have an answer ready if they do. My friends have an attention to detail like you won't believe."

"Oh, I believe it," he remarked. "Thanks for the advice. You know," he said after a brief pause, "it's not far off the mark. Right now, I'm just jotting things down in a journal, but I have tossed around the idea of publishing a book about my experiences."

"Can I ask you something, Emory? You can say no, but I need complete honesty if you're willing to answer my question."

"Ask away." I could tell by the look on his face that he was anticipating my question.

"Will you share with me exactly what you saw to make you move here in the house behind mine?" I asked.

"Honestly, Josh, it was a vision of a piece of mail with my name and the Blissville address on it. Nothing else. It was the oddest thing to ever occur to me. I ignored it for a few weeks until I started to see the vision daily. I knew it was time to pack up and move here to find out what was waiting for me."

"Do your visions ever help you prevent crimes or do you only help solve them after they're committed?" I asked him.

"That's two questions," Emory said, reminding me that I asked for just one.

"You're right. I apologize."

"Don't apologize, Josh. I was only teasing you." He blew out a long breath then said, "I've worked in both situations, but the majority have been the latter scenario you described." His answer didn't make me feel better, but I couldn't continue to live in an anxious state of mind.

"Well," I said, ready to end the conversation and move on with my day, "you know where I live if you feel like having company."

"Will there be an Easter egg hunt?"

"No," I said with a laugh. "Deal breaker?"

"Nah," he said good-naturedly. "I'll see you around. Perhaps on Sunday."

"See you, Emory."

We continued in opposite directions even though we were heading the same place. It seemed that we jogged at the same pace too since we turned down opposite ends of the alley that bisected our back yards at the same time. I gave a friendly wave as I hit the end of my driveway and headed inside to get ready for work.

Chaz showed up on time that day but looked like he'd had little sleep again. Meredith and I exchanged a look that said we were both keeping an eye on him. He must've caught our little exchange because he rolled his eyes and went to make a cup of coffee.

"Did you talk to any interesting people last night while playing games?" I asked him. "Did he sound like he was about six-two with black hair and bright blue eyes? Could you tell he had a way with pets?"

He stopped in the middle of the room then turned and faced me. "I know where you're going with this, Josh. I'm telling you the likelihood that I'm playing games with Dr. Dimples into the wee hours of the night are slim to none," Chaz said.

"You wish you were," Meredith said sassily. Both of them were completely unaware of who walked in the salon door in time to catch the brief exchange between them.

"Okay, maybe I do. Are you happy now? If I admit to jerking off while thinking about the good doctor will you shut up about it?" Chaz asked.

"Uh…" I said. I wasn't sure how to get him to stop talking without giving the reasons away, but I hoped my stammering and bug-eyed appearance would get it across, but it seemed like Chaz was just getting started. Kyle stood behind Chaz with his mouth hanging open and his eyes doing a rapid blinking thing that reminded me of an owl.

"So what if I want to take in every stray cat I find so that I can look at him and smell his body wash. You think I'm the only one? Please," he said exaggeratingly. "If that man knew how many people fantasized about his hunky body then he'd never leave his house."

Meredith turned to look at Chaz just then and let out a high-pitched squeak when she saw Kyle had overheard every single word that our friend had said. Me staring speechlessly at him wasn't enough to get his attention, but apparently, both of us doing it got the point across. Chaz's eyes widened in alarm when he realized what was going on.

"That Dr. Rogers is sex on a stick," Chaz said. It might've been a good recovery had his words not croaked out of him like a bullfrog and the man he mentioned not been almost a hundred years old and lived in a nursing home. The man hadn't practiced veterinary medicine for decades. I just shook my head, uncertain what to say or do. Chaz cleared his throat and swallowed hard to choke down the frog then said, "If you'll excuse me, I just remembered that I have some, um, inventory to order before the day gets away from me." As he approached Meredith and me, he whispered, "I'm just going to go dig a hole in the back yard. Call Gabe and tell him to come home and shoot me."

A slow smile spread over Kyle's face as the reality of the situation sank in. "Good morning," he said to Meredith and me. "I just stopped by to grab some hair wax. I'm almost out." Kyle walked dazedly over to the display and grabbed a bottle off the shelf.

"Honey, that's the wrong kind of wax," Meredith said, then walked over to save him from himself. "The ladies use that for other things."

"Some men too," I reminded her. Women didn't own the market on waxing.

"True," Meredith said.

"Ouch," Kyle said with a shiver. "I'll stick with hair wax, thank you."

I walked over to the register and began ringing up Kyle's purchase. I figured the quicker we got him out of the salon, the quicker we could talk Chaz down off the ledge. Poor guy. Chaz was probably going crazy while hiding in the kitchenette or my mixing room.

Knowing that, I still opened my mouth and asked, "What are you doing on Sunday?" I heard Meredith gasp but kept on trucking right along. "I'm having the dinner of the century at five, and you're welcome to join us."

Kyle tipped his head to the side a bit and leaned forward. "Us?" Kyle inquired.

"You know, the usual suspects. Meredith, Gabe, Chaz, and me. Oh," I exclaimed loud, "I also invited the new guy next door."

"You did?" Meredith asked in surprise.

"I did," I confirmed. "Emory's new to town, and it's a holiday."

"I'm not sure what I have planned yet," Kyle told me. "I usually have dinner at my folks' house…"

"Please don't feel like you need to change your traditions," I told him. "I just felt like extending the invitation. I'll make enough food for an army, and you can stop over if you wish. No pressure."

"I'll think about it," Kyle said. "Thank you, Josh. That's very nice of you."

"Nice is his middle name," Meredith said in a saccharine-sweet voice.

"I got to get going," Kyle said. "I never know who'll drop by to smell my soap."

"Body wash," I corrected. I heard Kyle chuckling as he left the salon and jogged down the porch steps. There was a definite pep to his step as he headed to his truck.

"Chaz is going to kill you," Meredith hissed, pulling my attention to her.

I rolled my eyes. "So let's not tell Chaz." I grimaced because I couldn't believe what I'd just done either. "Let's go find him and see if we can calm him down."

After a long pep talk and several hugs later, we coaxed Chaz out of the mixing room that was about the size of a coat closet. Any other time, I might've made a closet joke, but it wasn't the right moment. I needed to spend my energy coming up with a plan should Kyle accept my offer and show up for dinner on Sunday.

EIGHTEEN

Gabe

Harris called while we were on our way to Cincinnati to inform us that a judge signed off on a warrant to wire Silver for sound to meet with Spizer. I had already been in a hippy-skippy good mood before taking the call, but I tipped over to the euphoric zone on the mood meter at hearing the good news.

"We're close, Dorchester," I said. "I can feel it."

"Me too, Gabe. We're going to nail that bastard," he said emphatically.

My call to Silver's cellphone went to voicemail, but I didn't expect anything different since he most likely had only been home a few hours after closing the club. I was confident he'd call me back when he woke up and listened to my message.

In the meantime, we needed to devise a game plan for when and where the meeting between the guys would take place, and we needed to do it before the task force interviewed the members of McCarren Consortium. It made the most sense that we should go in there surprised to see him. Therefore, we had to walk a fine line and come up with questions for Silver to ask and we needed to prepare him for the interview. I needed to make it clear that we were running the show and that he was nothing more than an extension of us.

The last thing I wanted, or needed, was for him to go all vigilante and take matters into his hands and fuck it up. Call me a judgmental asshole, but Silver came across as a guy who didn't want to take instructions from another. It was too fucking bad because I was in charge. If I could've avoided sending him into the interview, I would've, but he was my best bet at catching Spizer unaware.

"Where do we want the interview to go down? Where will Spizer feel most confident, other than his office," I amended. If the man was really into bad shit, he might have equipment in his office to scramble the signal. "The club?"

"It depends on where they typically meet," Dorchester remarked. "Anything outside the norm could tip Spizer off. Although, I'm pretty confident that Silver can sell anything." I thought Dorchester was right and that it was possible that I was overthinking things.

"Let's talk strategy," I told the group. "I think our best ploy is for Silver to drop the bomb that we've connected Nate's death to the casino. We can have Silver give false information and see what Spizer does with it."

"That's a good suggestion," Harris said. "The other approach is to make it look like everyone involved with the casino is at risk of being hunted down and killed. That should rattle everyone and maybe pit them against one another."

"Great idea, Harris. That's the tactic we'll use to at least get ourselves in the door at McCarren," I said. "What else do we have?"

We continued discussing the different strategies we could use and began putting a plan A and plan B together. So much of it hinged on whatever Silver could get from Spizer. We walked a fine line, which the judge reminded us when she signed the warrant for the wire. Nate's attorney/client privileges died with him, but Spizer remained the legal counsel for others associated with Nate. We wouldn't be able to use the information he gave us about the other clients since privilege protected them. We also couldn't put him in a situation that could get him disbarred. The more I turned it over in my mind, the more I worried about the many ways it could blow up in our faces.

Silver returned my call at noon and said that he'd already had an appointment to meet with Spizer about a revitalization project he wanted to undertake. "I'm meeting him for dinner tomorrow night. Will that work or will there be too much noise?"

"Depends on the restaurant," I replied. Silver rattled off the name of the restaurant where I first saw him days ago, even though it felt like years. "That'll work," I told him. "We need to go over the questions we want you to ask and explain just how tight of a rope we're all walking."

"I won't let you down, Detective." We decided to meet him in a hotel room a few hours before he went upstairs to the fancy restaurant on the top floor. We'd have time to wire him up for sound and video, rehearse what we wanted him to ask, and how to avoid stepping on a landmine with a question we didn't want asked.

"We'll see what we get from Spizer tomorrow before we set up meetings with McCarren Consortium," I told the group. There wasn't anything else for us to do that day, so I congratulated them on a great day and sent them all home. "Let's meet here at noon tomorrow since we'll be working late."

I had several errands I wanted to run before I went home because I knew I wouldn't want to go back out once I got there. I stopped by Marabeth's first to see if she had a bath oil or something that would help Josh sleep. It was adorable how he played off sleeping well that morning, but I knew better. My guy was many wonderful things, but an actor wasn't one of them. I didn't get all pissy when he lied to me because I knew his reasons were well-meaning. Besides, it was more of an exaggeration than a lie.

Marabeth recommended a chamomile and spice bath oil that I thought Josh and I would both like. I wasn't much of a bath guy until he came into my life. I enjoyed any activity that included Josh naked against me. My next stop was Harry's Hardware. He'd been in business for forty years, and I did my part to make sure he wasn't gobbled up by the large chain home improvement stores that were close. I was pretty sure I saw some loose screws at the base of Josh's pole where it screwed into the floor in the attic. Not only that, I found the perfect trees in Josh's—our—back yard to hang my hammock.

I had grabbed what I needed and was headed to the front of the store to pay when a guy stepped out of another aisle and nearly collided with me. Emory Jackson clutched his chest and offered me a sheepish smile.

"I'm sorry, Gabe. I wasn't paying attention to where I was going." A husband and wife walked by us and gave Emory the once over. Oh, how well I remembered being the new guy in town.

"No problem, Emory. How's it going?" I asked. "You getting settled in okay?"

"It's going to be an adjustment," he admitted, "but it feels right to me. Josh's cookies and thoughtful invitation helped to make me feel welcome."

"Josh? My Josh?" I asked in surprise. "An invitation to what?"

"Um, dinner," Emory said uneasily. "On Sunday."

"Sunday dinner? This Sunday, as in Easter?" I asked in surprise.

"Is that a problem, Gabe? I don't want to cause any trouble." Emory said, backing up as if I would snap at him like a dog over a favorite toy or a steak. His reaction broke through my shock.

"No, there's no problem," I told him. "It's just that Josh's Sunday dinners are very sacred. They're very important to him, which means that you've made a good impression on him." *Perhaps better than I realized.* I wasn't going to stress about it, and I surely wouldn't ruin Josh's good deed.

"I think it's more like pity, Gabe, but I appreciate what you said. If you're sure it won't be a problem…"

"You're more than welcome to join us for dinner, Emory. I mean that." Before I could say anything else, Mrs. Miller from two doors down stopped and introduced herself to Emory. "I'll see you Sunday," I said firmly, letting him know I expected to see him there.

I stopped by Brook's Pets to pick up more of those dog treats Buddy liked so much, a tug-of-war rope, and more catnip mice for Diva because Buddy kept stealing them. Jazzy got a big red sea creature that had tunnels running through the tentacles and a huge mouth as an extra opening and exit. She was going to love that thing. I knew I would probably regret it, but I bought a multi-leveled perch with a bell at the bottom that I could suspend from the top of the cage for Savage. He could curse and ring his little bell for hours.

I checked the time after I loaded the pet toys in my trunk and noted that it was close enough to dinner time to stop at the diner and order takeout. I sent Josh a text to let him know I was bringing food home and settled in on a stool at the L-shaped countertop bar.

"Mind if I have a seat?" Kyle asked from behind me.

I twisted to look over my shoulder and offered him a smile.

"Pull up a stool," I replied.

"How's it going?" I asked.

"It's been a really interesting week thanks to your boyfriend," Kyle said then grinned.

"He told me about the vet visit with Chaz," I said. I leaned forward and lowered my voice when I asked, "Did you two really have a 'moment' like Josh said you did?" I left off the part about them staring into each other's eyes and such.

"It was… *something*," Kyle said. I grinned broadly then because it sounded awfully damn familiar to me when I met Josh.

"Something, huh?" I asked.

"Definitely." His blue eyes took on a faraway look for a few seconds then he looked back at me. "You won't believe what happened at the salon," he said. I would expect just about anything where Josh was concerned.

I listened and laughed at what happened in the salon that morning, even though I felt horrible for Chaz. Kyle must've been blind to it, but the rest of us saw how much Chaz blushed whenever Kyle was near. My ex-boyfriend seemed to have his radar honed in on Chaz too, so I was pretty sure Josh was right about the potential there. I also knew that you couldn't force it, and that they'd need to find their way at the pace that worked for them.

"Then Josh invited me to dinner and…"

"Wait! He did what? When?" I asked.

"Um, Sunday," Kyle said hesitantly, a lot like Emory had.

"This Sunday? Easter Sunday?" I asked. Kyle nodded to confirm, and my eyes narrowed in speculation. What the hell was Josh up to? He probably did feel bad about Emory being alone for the holiday, but why invite Kyle? Then it dawned on me. He was playing matchmaker. Of course, with Emory thrown in the mix, there could be trouble. What would Josh do if Kyle and Emory hit it off right in front of his best friend? Oh man, it could get ugly. "Did you accept his invitation?"

"Should I *not* accept his invitation?" Kyle inquired. "Is that going to be a problem for you or something?"

"For me? No. I have no problem with you being there. I was just surprised is all," I assured him. "Be on time," I warned him. "He runs a tight ship, my guy."

Daniella placed my carryout order on the counter in front of me. I ordered the meatloaf dinner for Josh and the cabbage roll dinner for myself. I patted Kyle on the shoulder, told him I'd see him Sunday, and went to the register to pay for my food. I gave Daniella a tip—even though we didn't eat in—because she had started back to college and could use all the help she could get.

Josh was already upstairs when I got home. "Honey, I'm home," I called out. He came out of the bedroom chewing on his lip, looking like he had been beating himself up all day long. "What have you done?" I was certain to keep the scorn out of my voice because he wasn't a child, he was my equal. "Kyle *and* Emory?"

"You know already?" Josh asked. I told him about running into Emory at the hardware store and Kyle and the diner. "And you still brought me home food?"

I set the bags of food and my purchases on the dining room table and opened my arms to him. "You shouldn't feel guilty about extending an invitation to our home to enjoy a lovely dinner."

"Yeah, but those nights are just supposed to be for the four of us," he said.

"Sunshine, it can't just be the four of us forever. Chaz and Meredith will find their soul mates like we found one another and they'll be joining us. Families are made to expand, that's just what they do." I ran my thumbs over his cheeks, and I saw the tension drain from him. "As long as you extended the invitations for the right reasons and you don't have Hallmark Movie Channel expectations, then I'm perfectly fine with what you did."

Josh snorted and rolled his eyes. "I have yet to see an LGBTQ couple featured in one of their shows, nor many people of color for that matter."

"I think you get my point, don't you?" I asked.

"Yes, dear," he said snarkily. I slapped his round bottom for his sass and began to unload the food and the loot. "What's this?" he asked, holding up the bottle of oil from Marabeth's. He read the ingredients and what it was intended to do then looked up at me. "Having trouble sleeping?"

"I thought we could both take a hot bath after dinner and the kids had a chance to play with their new toys," I suggested. "So we *both* sleep well."

Josh's eyes softened like they did when we made love. "I love your considerate heart, Gabe."

"I love you, Sunshine."

The ballgame played in the background while we had fun playing with our critters. It didn't hurt my feelings that Buddy wanted to play tug-of-war with Josh instead of me. I was busy splitting my attention between Jazzy and Diva while I tried not to regret getting Savage that ringing bell.

"Fucknugget!" *Ding. Ding. Ding.*

"Cumguzzler!" *Ding. Ding. Ding.*

"Dirty Bird!" *Ding. Ding. Ding.*

"Fire in the hole!" *Ding. Ding. Ding.*

"That's new!" Josh and I both said at the same time, followed by, "I didn't teach him that."

"Roger's boy!" *Ding. Ding. Ding.*

"That must be his previous owner," Josh said. "He's only said his name a few times in the few years that I've had him."

"Big Daddy's boy," I said to Savage.

"Big Daddy," Savage repeated back.

"Big Daddy's boy," I tried again.

It took several attempts, but he eventually said, "Big Daddy's boy" to me. It made my entire night—well, that was until Josh pressed his wet, naked body against mine. As much as I loved the bird, it was nowhere close to the way I felt for his owner.

Once I had him spread and pinned beneath me in our bed, it was his turn to yell out who owned him—heart, body and soul. After we finished making love, we both fell into a deep sleep tangled up in limbs and love.

NINETEEN

Josh

It was nice having Gabe home later in the morning, and not just because he made me breakfast. Watching him cook our omelets reminded me of the time I'd gone to his house for a physical release—or so I had convinced myself at the time—and ended up accidentally staying the night. After sex, Gabe pulled me to him to cuddle before I could bolt from the bed and get dressed. He promised to wake me up, but I wasn't smart enough to nail down the details before I closed my eyes and fell asleep against his chest. He woke me up the next morning, not in a few hours like I had intended.

I ran around his bedroom cursing him and everyone he knew while I dressed. The echoes of his laughter still bounced around in my heart. I knew then that I was crazy about him, even though I wasn't ready to acknowledge it. Once we started dating, Gabe had told me about the omelet he had planned to make me that morning, and I demanded that he show me what I had missed. Gabe didn't cook a lot, but it was always tasty when he did, especially his omelets.

It felt more like a Sunday morning than a Friday with Gabe reading the newspaper and drinking coffee after breakfast. I hoped that his sting operation didn't run too late and I tried hard not to get jealous of him meeting with a sexy guy in a hotel room and touching his naked chest while affixing a wire to his body. I hated the images that my overactive imagination created and talked myself down by reminding myself that strip searches and lingering touches weren't part of the process. It wasn't like Gabe was going to be wrapping the wire around the guy's cock. *Right?* I reminded myself that Gabe was just one of the guys on the task force and that he wouldn't be alone. Okay, then my mind headed straight to terrifying threesome images of Gabe with Jonathon Silver and Paul. *Nope! Not going there!*

"What's going on in that mind of yours, Sunshine?" Gabe asked, startling me back to reality. One corner of the paper was turned down, and he was peering at me over the top of it. "The hamsters in your brain are running so hard I could hear it over here. You might need to squirt some WD-40 on that thing too. It's starting to sound a bit squeaky."

"That'll be the sound your balls make when I... never mind." We both knew I wasn't going to withhold sex from him as a form of punishment. "You better not be implying it's rusty and squeaky from underuse." I pinned him with my best threatening glare.

"Quite the opposite. That thing never shuts down and needs a rest," Gabe reached across the table and covered my hand with one of his. "Seriously, what's bothering you?"

I wasn't about to tell him where my mind had gone because I knew my worry was unfounded. I trusted Gabe with all my heart, and I wouldn't ruin our happy morning over problems that I had to work through on my own. "I'm just worried if I have enough ham to feed all the extra guests." I had been worried about that before I worried about Gabe engaging in hot, sweaty cop porn.

"That's what put that frown on your precious face? Or maybe you're thinking about how you need to tell Chaz about Kyle coming to Easter dinner and how it's not a good idea to wait until Kyle shows up to eat," Gabe recommended.

"Chaz won't show up then," I said worriedly.

"Chaz isn't going to skip dinner with us, but he can at least show up looking rested and have his hair styled." I knew Gabe was thinking about Chaz's ruffled appearance the previous week. I thought it was adorable that he wanted Chaz to look his best. *Hmmm, had he finally joined the matchmaking bandwagon?* I still suspected there was more at play than just video games with Chaz, but I wasn't sure what the hell I could do about it. He was, in fact, a grown-ass man and could make his own decisions.

"I'll tell him," I said to Gabe, but I didn't promise when.

"Today," Gabe added firmly, not falling for my shenanigans. It was okay for him to be vague with time and make up his own rules, but apparently, I didn't have the same freedoms. Lucky for him he was so fucking sexy with his dark scowl and demanding tone of voice or I might've put up a bigger fight. Of course, it helped that he was also right.

"Fine," I said like a petulant brat. I rolled my eyes at the huge grin that spread across Gabe's face. My mind skipped past being jealous and insecure and started plotting strategies to make him suffer.

"I know that look too," Gabe said smugly. "You going to cuff me to a chair again and fuck my brains out? That'll teach me." The sarcasm rolled off his tongue so naturally, it was like he was born to snark. *Damn, that would make a great coffee cup.*

"You're one more wisecrack away from wearing skinny jeans," I told him.

"Never going to happen," he said shaking his head. "I'll stick with my relaxed fit."

Here's the thing, I had zero plans of turning Gabe into a more muscular version of me. I just liked to rile him up. Although, I did feel that a dark wash denim in a straight leg fit was a good compromise between skinny and relaxed. I thought about buying them and slipping them in his drawer to see if he noticed. I knew what would happen when I saw those sexy, long legs in that dark denim, which would cling tighter to his thighs and delicious ass than his preferred fit. I loved jeans with a button fly because I could take my time kissing each inch I revealed as I unbuttoned them slowly.

"Oh, baby, I know that look too," Gabe remarked gleefully. He looked at his watch then back at me. "How much time do you have?"

I stood quickly from my chair and replied, "Enough to give you a proper send-off and remind you who loves you." I turned and made a dash to the bedroom.

"As if there's ever a doubt," Gabe said following hot on my heels.

It was still amazing to me how much emotion and love Gabe could pack into a quick, hard fuck. It wasn't about me presenting my ass to him in the middle of our bed and making myself available just to please him. He was completely devoted to getting me off at the same time. Beyond the physical aspect, there were the kisses he placed on my neck and the loving way he caressed my chest as he told me how much he loved me and that he could never get enough of me. Never, not even when I wanted him just to use me, did Gabe ever make me feel like I wasn't valued.

I decided that days that started out with grunting, groaning, and coming were absolutely the best. I had just enough time to clean up and give my man a long, lusty kiss before I headed downstairs to start my day.

I was surprised to see Chaz was already downstairs waiting for me. Hell, he even beat Meredith in and that was no easy feat. He was sitting kind of primly in my salon chair with his legs crossed sipping a cup of coffee. The expression on his face looked like a combination of anger and admiration. "I know what you did," he said gravely.

"Oh," I said, feeling my cheeks flush with mortification. "We would've tried to be quieter if we knew you were down here already. Sorry, man."

"Not that," Chaz said in a voice that clearly stated how aggravated he was with me. "It's nice to know that someone got their morning started off the right way," he added snidely. "You know what you did." I did know what he was referring to but wasn't sure how he knew.

"Who told? Meredith?" I asked.

"Kyle called me," Chaz said flatly.

"Oh! Did he? What did he say?" I had to know. "Is he coming to dinner?"

"Josh, do you have any idea how humiliated I was by the encounter yesterday? Or, are you so blinded by your happiness that you've lost sight of how others might be feeling?" Chaz asked.

I gasped and took a step back as if he slapped me. "I did it for you," I told him. "There's just so much," I made wave motions with my hands that were meant to be vibes, "going on between the two of you and I thought that..."

"No, you did this for *you*, not me or Kyle. You weren't thinking either. You, of all people, know that these things can't be rushed or forced. You didn't see Meredith or me interfering with you and Gabe when you were trying to find your way. We encouraged you to be brave and take chances, and we even called you out on your bullshit..."

"Like you're doing now," I interjected.

"...when you needed it. We never put you in a situation where you were made to feel uncomfortable," Chaz continued as if I hadn't interrupted him.

"I'm sorry, Chaz, I truly am. I overstepped, and I'm not sure how to fix it. I can't uninvite him to dinner. Besides, it's a holiday, he shouldn't be alone."

"Kyle has his parents, three sisters, and two sets of grandparents living in this town. Do you honestly believe he has no place to eat ham and deviled eggs?"

"They won't be *my* ham and deviled eggs," I retorted.

Chaz sighed in frustration then rose to his feet. "I don't think he's coming, Josh, so you can just forget about your little matchmaking schemes. He knows you've made me feel awkward and he didn't want to ruin my dinner." The phone started ringing so he headed to his desk by the front door. "By the way, your deviled eggs had too much mustard in them last time."

Had I been wearing pearls, I would've clutched them. I staggered and stumbled like I'd been dealt a hard blow to my body. The happy cloud I floated down on was starting to dissipate beneath my feet, and I wondered how far the fall would be until I crashed to the earth. Would my heart give out first or would I know the horrendous sound of every bone in my body breaking when I hit the fiery pits of hell?

Meredith came in a few minutes later, her smile adding some warmth to break through the tension between Chaz and me. The smile slid off her face when she read the situation. "What's going on?" she asked.

"Nothing," Chaz and I replied at the same time.

"As if that doesn't give you both away." She put her hands on her hips, shook her head in disgust, and said, "Spill it." Chaz and I just stared at each other without saying a word. "Whatever it is, we need to clear the air before everyone else gets here."

I swallowed my pride and said, "I was too pushy."

"I was too sensitive," Chaz said at the same time.

We burst into laughter, which erased the tension between us. "I am very sorry. I honestly thought I was doing something helpful, but looking back I can see that I should've just kept my mouth shut." I walked over and hugged him tightly.

Chaz returned my squeeze then stepped back to look at me. "Maybe you should've, but I probably overreacted to your match-making attempts. I'm flattered that you think I would stand a chance with a man like Kyle. I know that you only had my best interests at heart and I was out of line when I said that your own happiness blinds you. It was mean, and it wasn't true."

"I'm so happy we had this Dr. Phil moment," Meredith said. She looked at Chaz then and asked, "How'd you find out? Did he confess out of guilt? Just so you know, I was giving him until Saturday to fess up to what he did before I tipped you off."

"Dr. Dimples called him," I told Meredith.

"Did he tell you while you were up all night chatting while playing games?" she asked Chaz.

"Guys, I don't know who he's met online, but it's not me, which just makes me more certain that him coming to dinner on Sunday is a mistake. Look, I'll admit that there's a definite spark of *something* there between us, but how real can it be when he's obviously inter-ested in someone else? My heart can't take being a temporary fill-in while he waits for his perfect guy to show up. Look at him and look at me," Chaz said.

My mind went into hyperdrive as soon as I heard Chaz refer to the *something* they shared. It was just like the beginning for Gabe and me and it solidified my belief that these two guys were meant to be. I just needed to find less annoying ways to try to work some magic.

"I am looking right at Charles Bailey Hamilton, and you're beautiful," Meredith said. "I fail to understand what you're talking about."

"It's not about me having low self-esteem in regards to my

looks," Chaz said. "This is about compatibility. What could a highly-educated veterinarian possibly have in common with a receptionist in a salon?"

"THE salon," I said jokingly. "Chaz, it's so much easier to find all the reasons why something won't work than it is to try to find the reasons it will. When the hell has easy equaled right?" I released a soft sigh and reached for his hands. "This isn't us telling you how to live your life, babe. This is us encouraging you to be brave and take chances, and maybe we're calling you out on your bullshit a little." Hearing me repeat his words from earlier brought a smile to his face.

"Jazz, your deviled eggs were perfect," Chaz said softly.

"Honey, I know it. And, just like Jesus, I forgive." I leaned in closer and said, "Next time you want to get back at me, choose something more believable than bad cooking."

The rest of the staff staggered in and our day got underway. I was happy that Chaz and I cleared the air and got past my boneheaded move. He had been dead-on when he said that he and Meredith never interfered with Gabe and me as we stumbled along the path to happiness. I needed to show them both the same amount of respect.

My day moved along at a quick pace, I was shocked when Sally Ann showed up for her four o'clock appointment because it felt like my day had just begun. She was beauty and happiness personified.

"Hey, honey," she said, leaning in to kiss me on the cheek.

"Hey, beautiful," I returned. "Hello, sweet Adrianna," I said to her ever-growing baby bump. Sally Ann hadn't confirmed the choice of name, but I had a strong feeling. "How're the Goode girls today?" Sally Ann smirked at the nickname I'd given them.

"Doing great," she replied. "I'm enjoying spring break at home on the couch with my legs propped up and a good book on my tablet."

"Sounds nice," Heather told her from across the salon. "What are you reading? I could use a good book."

Sally Ann's cheeks turned pink, prompting us to tease her for a few seconds about reading naughty books. "It's not naughty or inappropriate," she said. "It's just not going to be for everybody."

"It's bestiality," Marci guessed. *Whoa, girl!* Sally Ann said it wasn't naughty or inappropriate and Marci chose bestiality of all things!

Heather gasped and said, "Twincest!" *Who were these women I hired? Dayum!*

"I bet it's gay romance," Meredith said. "Those are my favorites." That got my ears perked up.

"Yes!" Sally Ann said excitedly. "The book I'm reading is from a new author. His name is C.B. Hesterson. His debut book is just fabulous. It has everything I loved in a book—angst, twists, complicated characters, and the sex scenes are hot enough to steam off wallpaper. I'm telling you, between my pregnant hormones and this guy's writing, I've worn Adrian out."

I heard Chaz coughing and sputtering at his desk. I checked to make sure he was okay, and he waived me off. "Good stuff, huh?" I asked Sally Ann.

"It's brilliant!" Sally Ann said.

"I'll have to check it out," I told her. "I can read while Gabe watches baseball."

"Do it," she said. "You're going to love it. In fact, the main character reminds me of you a little."

"Yeah? Dashing, smart, and amazing with hair?" I asked her.

"Charming, brilliant, and snarky," Sally Ann told me.

"You know what? I'm going to download and read it tonight while I wait for Gabe to come home," I told her. I knew I needed to keep my brain busy lest I wanted it to conjure up every terrible scenario that Gabe could face during his undercover operation. "He's going to have a late night."

"You're coming to our house for dinner then." Sally Ann's firm tone said she meant business and wasn't taking no for an answer.

"You can start the book later tonight or tomorrow."

"Sounds like a plan. Thank you for inviting me." I loved spending time with the Goodes and my evening suddenly looked a lot brighter.

TWENTY

Gabe

"Detective Wyatt, relax." Jonathon Silver stood up from the bed across the one I sat on in the hotel room. He looked at Dorchester, Weston, and Harris. "Is he always like this?"

"Mostly," Dorchester replied, "but he knows his shit, so maybe you should stop busting his balls and listen to him for a damn minute."

Everything I suggested had been rebuked or mocked by Silver, and it was wearing hard on my nerves. The tech team had already stopped by to hook him up and test his equipment. Not only was he wired for sound, but they also gave him a tie clip that had a tiny camera hidden among fake diamonds, or at least I thought they were fake. That part went smooth; it was the part that came afterward that seemed to rile him up. It was obvious as hell that he wanted to oversee every situation.

"Too bad you weren't this dedicated when my brother turned to you for help," he snarled. "Maybe he'd still be alive."

"Clear the room," I commanded. My team obeyed the order immediately. I slowly rose to my feet and squared off against Silver. "You have every right to be angry over the loss of your brother, but blaming me for his death isn't going to bring him back. Instead, focus your damn energy on catching his killer by listening to what I'm telling you." I pointed my finger at him and said, "If you go in there half-cocked you could destroy *everything*. Are you listening to me?"

Silver turned and paced away from me, running his fingers through his hair in agitation. He turned to face me and released his pent-up frustration in one, long breath. I saw the tension fade from his tall frame.

"I didn't *refuse* to help Nate; he refused to help *himself*. He should've been up front about everything because it was highly unlikely he didn't know why he was targeted. He might not have known who, but he might've had an idea of why. His asking me to sneak around outside of the law to find his harasser was wrong." Technically, he hinted, not asked. "He wasn't forthright with the CPD when he finally turned to them for help. We can't help someone who doesn't want it, Silver."

"I know," he said softly. "I was out of line. I'm sorry." His apology was completely unexpected, but not unwelcome. I wasn't ready to stick my neck on the line by removing him as a viable suspect, but my conviction that someone other than Silver killed Nate grew stronger each day.

"Trust me when I tell you I know how powerless you feel right now. My brother was killed in a robbery when I was fifteen. He was my hero, and I was devastated," I told Silver. "His killer was never arrested, so please believe me when I tell you that I will do every-thing *legally* within my power to solve Nate's case. I need your help to do that, which means you have to listen to what I say."

"Call the team back in. I'm ready to cooperate," Silver said.

An hour later, the team gathered around eating pizza while we waited for Spizer to show up. Silver made sure he arrived early at the restaurant so that he wasn't caught getting off the bank of elevators used by the guests of the hotel. Silver wasn't wearing an earpiece so he couldn't hear us when we discussed the situation.

"Spizer is thirty minutes late," Dorchester said. "He could be running up the billable hours, or he's not coming." As hard as we tried to keep the warrant a secret, there was always a chance a clerk tipped him off.

As if he sensed our anxiousness, Silver pulled out his cellphone from his inside suit pocket. He held the phone in front of him where we could see it before he dialed Spizer. "Rick, I've been sitting here at the restaurant for thirty minutes waiting for you. Did I get the time wrong? Give me a call, buddy."

Silver set his phone on the table and drank another glass of water while we waited some more. He checked his phone every few minutes, but there was never a call or text from Spizer. My spidey sense told me something was wrong. My suspicion was confirmed twenty minutes later when dispatch called to let me know that Spizer had been found dead in his home office. His death appeared to be a suicide.

"What?" I asked. "Give me the address and tell everyone to keep the scene clear until my team gets there. Only the M.E. goes in." The more people that were there, the more opportunities to contaminate the scene. "Who found Mr. Spizer?" I asked, drawing the attention of my team. I snapped my fingers and pointed to the screen, indicating that I wanted someone to call Silver and let him know. I wanted to have a quick chat with him before we left for Spizer's house.

"His wife did, Detective. As you can imagine, she's a mess right now. The responding officer thinks she's going to need sedation. He also said there's a suicide note that admits responsibility for the deaths of Owen Smithson, Nate Turner, and Lawrence Robertson."

"We'll be there asap, but she should go to the hospital if they think it's necessary. We can interview her in the morning."

"Yes, sir. I'll pass the message along."

I hung up and waited for Silver to get back to the room. "What's going on?" he asked as soon as he flung open the door.

"Spizer was found dead in his home," I told Silver. "We're going to head over to his house right now. I'll call you when we know more, either tonight or tomorrow."

His normally stoic mask was gone, and in its place, was shock and raw grief. "I don't believe it," Silver said. "Honestly, I thought there was another explanation for Rick's involvement instead of him killing them or hiring it done, but this can't be a coincidence. He was good to me when everyone else was skeptical of my appearance in Nate's life, including my brother."

There were no words I could say to make him feel better. If I wanted to help Silver, then I needed to get to Spizer's house and investigate his death with a dubious eye, because I had learned long ago that reality was often the opposite of our expectations.

I crossed to him and patted the grieving man on his shoulder. "I'll be in touch," I said before we left.

I wouldn't classify Spizer's house as a mansion, but it was pretty damn close. The patrol officers were waiting outside as we had requested.

"We asked Mrs. Spizer if there was anyone we could notify for her and she asked us to call her sister." The officer ripped out a piece of paper from his notepad. "Here's the sister's address and phone number in case you need to talk to Mrs. Spizer."

"Thank you, Officer."

The task force had put on protective gear before we entered the house to avoid contamination. We walked into a foyer of gleaming hardwood floors that shone beneath the crystals and lights in the chandelier. We followed the sounds of whirling cameras and murmured voices to the crime scene.

I knocked on the doorframe of the study, and all eyes turned to us. "Can we come in?" I asked. The M.E. would be running the show until the body was cleared, but I wanted to be able to see the scene with my own eyes before that happened.

"Come on in," the M.E. said. He introduced himself as Miguel Espinoza then identified the rest of the men and women in the room that were processing the scene.

"I'm not looking to get in your way, Dr. Espinoza. I'd just like to get a feel for the crime scene myself instead of looking at pictures of it."

"I understand, Detective. We're almost done here. I saw the letter on the desk beneath Spizer's head." He had slumped over in his chair the same way that Robertson had, but the trajectory of the bullet was completely wrong. Spizer put the barrel of the gun beneath his chin and pulled the trigger. He fell forward and pinned the hand holding the gun beneath his chest.

"Have you looked at the gun? Is it a forty-five?" I asked. He confirmed that it was and I asked him to compare the entrance and exit wounds to those of Owen Smithson and promised to make sure he got copies of Turner's and Robertson's autopsy files and photos. "I'd like to wrap this all up in a tidy bow, but I am going to be sure that every avenue is investigated."

I stayed out of their way and looked around the room at the photos hanging on the wall or sitting in frames on his shelf. The gilded gold, marble, and crystal wet bar that stood in the corner of the room probably cost more than my car. I took photos so that I could compare them to crime scene photos later.

It didn't take the medical examiner long to finish and remove Spizer from his office. Then I got my first look at the apparent suicide note he left addressed to his wife. Like the officer said, Spizer took responsibility for the deaths of the three men. What it didn't say was why he did it. He told her how much he loved her and apologized for ruining her life. As much as I hated to be the one to show the note to Mrs. Spizer, I needed her to confirm it was his handwriting.

A handwriting specialist would be able to determine if the note was written under duress. Some signs of fear, shame, or anguish was expected, but it would be exacerbated if someone had a gun pointed at their heads while they wrote. That was *if* we got the approval to hire an expert.

There was a picture on the corner of his desk that caught my eye. It was a picture of a boys' baseball team; the kids in the picture looked to be between the ages of ten and twelve. Something about the picture stood out to me, but I couldn't place it. I snapped a picture of it with my phone, so I could look at it later.

I wanted to believe that the cases were over and solved, but I couldn't shake the feeling that they weren't. I placed a call to Silver, but it went to his voicemail like usual. He might've gone to the club to stay busy rather than sit around and wait for me to call. I left him a message and told him he could call me whenever he wanted. I wouldn't say that I liked the man, but I'd be lying if I said I didn't feel bad for him. I didn't know his story, but I had a feeling that it probably wasn't a happy one.

Dorchester and I said very little on the way home. It seemed that we were both lost in our thoughts. I dropped him off at his house then headed home to Josh. I could tell that he wasn't home by the lights he had left on, even though his car was parked in the driveway. I wondered where he'd gone on foot so late. I looked suspiciously over at Emory's house and wondered if he'd gone over there since they'd gotten chummy. I realized I was being ridiculous and called his cellphone number.

"Hey, baby," he said into the phone. "How's it going?" I heard Adrian and Sally Ann in the background laughing about something; I knew just where I could find my guy.

"It's better now," I said into the phone. "How was your day?" I backed out of the driveway and drove the seven blocks to the Goodes' house while Josh told me about his confrontation with Chaz. "But you guys are okay now, right?" I asked.

"We sure are," Josh replied. "Do you have any idea what time you'll be home?"

"That depends." I parked the car and got out.

"On?" he asked hesitantly.

"How late we stay at Adrian and Sally Ann's before I take you home." I knocked on the front door and heard Josh gasp seconds before Buddy barked. Josh yanked open the front door and jumped me right there on the front porch. "I'm happy to see you too, Sunshine."

Josh visibly melted in front of me and I realized he had been tense with worry, probably the reason he was at the Goodes'. "Have you eaten?" he asked, ready to nurture and fuss over me. I freely admit that I liked it.

"I had a few slices of shitty pizza before everything went to hell," I told him.

"Sally Ann made a delicious chicken dish that you'll love. There's plenty leftover so I'll reheat some and make you a plate while you chat with Adrian. I'm sure you guys want to go into his office and talk shop anyway." He wasn't wrong. Josh handed me a beer and shooed me out of the kitchen. "Meet me back here in fifteen minutes."

"Yes, sir," I said over my shoulder as I followed Adrian to the smallest of the extra bedrooms where he had an office.

"Tell me what happened, partner. You're looking a little rough,"

Adrian told me.

He didn't say anything until I'd told him every detail of my night. "I don't know, Adrian. My gut tells me that this isn't over with Spizer's death. I'm not willing to just say that he was the shooter and close the cases. Something about the scene is nagging at me to keep digging."

"Then you keep digging," Adrian said.

"Dinner!" Josh's call to eat cracked me up. He ran a tight ship when it came to eating and my fifteen minutes had clearly passed.

I entered the dining room and took a seat. Sally Ann and Adrian were talking, but I had no idea what they were saying because I only had eyes for Josh. He set my plate of food on the table in front of me and moved to step away so I could eat. I snatched his wrist and tugged his arm so that he leaned down. I raised my head for a kiss, and he obliged me. The tension from the events of that night still had me strung tight, but I could feel the strain starting to fade in small increments.

"Eat, Gabe."

I dug into the delicious chicken and stuffing casserole, green beans, and mashed potatoes. It was like a miniature Thanksgiving, and it was fucking scrumptious. "We need this recipe," I said between bites.

"We?" Josh asked.

"Okay, *you* need this recipe. I could eat this at least once a week," I told Sally Ann.

"It's Adrian's favorite too," she said.

I had eaten two plates full of food before I sat back from the table. I should've been embarrassed by the amount of food I consumed, but I had been too hungry to worry about appearances. I was ready to go home, but it was rude to eat and run. Josh, sensing my weakness for good manners, pounced.

"Let's play a board game," he suggested.

"Not Monopoly," we all said.

"Fine," he said in a huff. "What else do you have?"

My cellphone rang, saving me from having to decide what game we played. I was okay with anything other than Monopoly. And poker! "I need to take this," I told them. I went out on the porch and answered Silver's call. I told him what we had learned so far and explained that the investigation would continue until we were certain it was solved.

"I appreciate the information, Detective." Silver sounded vulnerable and lost, two words I would never have associated with the man.

I blamed Josh's influence for what happened next. "What are you doing on Sunday?" I asked. *How in the hell was I going to explain this to Josh?*

TWENTY-ONE

Josh

I STOOD WITH MY HANDS ON MY HIPS AND SURVEYED THE LAYOUT of my tables. My everyday dining room table wasn't big enough to seat all the guests that were invited to dinner, so I had to improvise. I borrowed Mama Richmond's large, rectangular folding table and wooden folding chairs she used for large family gatherings. I put a tablecloth on the table to hide the unattractive, industrial gray plastic. The wooden chairs weren't so bad because they at least came with attractive cushions. My table would be used to set out the food so people could walk around it and serve themselves buffet style. I used spring flowers and vanilla candles as centerpieces and set the table with my grandmother's china.

"Kyle probably isn't coming," Gabe said as he placed Nana's real silverware next to each plate.

"If you set a plate, they will come." I put my spin on a well-known phrase from one of Gabe's favorite movies. He just shook his head and began placing the water glasses on the table. I was pleased to know that Gabe had a lot of experience with formal tables, even though I only set one three times a year—Thanksgiving, Christmas, and Easter.

"It's his loss if he chooses not to come," Gabe said. "My gain because he eats his weight in ham. I'll have leftovers for sandwiches if he's a no-show."

I had freaked out about having a ham shortage when Gabe informed me that he had invited Jonathon Silver to our home for Easter two days before my dinner. Gabe, being practical as always, suggested I just buy a ham from the supermarket like everyone else does. *Since when in the hell did I do anything like anyone else?* My hams came from our butcher in town and nowhere else. I ordered a fresh turkey for Thanksgiving and a sexy, spiral cut ham for Christmas and Easter.

Instead of whining and crying or making Gabe feel bad for being compassionate, I jumped into action the next morning. I was the first customer through the door and was prepared to do just about anything to get an extra ham. I even took a generous gift certificate for my salon that Skip could give to his wife. I knew she'd enjoy it and both of us would be heroes on the holiday.

I had just started in on my desperate plea for help when Skip laughed and waved his hands in the air to cut me off. "I order extra hams for these types of emergencies, kid. I've got you covered." Skip was still my hero, so I gave him the gift certificate so he could treat Brenda.

"Your table looks nice, Sunshine." Gabe hooked his arm around my neck and pulled me to him. "The food smells even better."

"Thank you." I rose on my tiptoes and gave him a kiss. "There will be plenty of ham for leftovers," I said. "I have to confess that I'm a little nervous about this gathering. There are a lot of newcomers, and I'm worried it will be awkward."

"I have faith in you, Sunshine." I was glad someone did.

Meredith arrived first, and I was practically bouncing on my feet to hear about her big date the night before. I had wanted to text her so many times, but Gabe took my phone away, so that I didn't ruin her night. His sexy hide and seek worked wonders to distract me the night before, then I had too much food prepping to do that morning to hound her.

"How was church service?" I asked instead of what I wanted to know.

"I didn't go," she said casually. "I just got back home in time to change to come here."

"Really?" I asked. "The date was that good?"

She laughed at my wide-eyed expression. "Our date was fine."

"Fine?" That wasn't a ringing endorsement for the guy.

"It was nice," Meredith added.

"Nice?" That was possibly worse than fine.

Meredith giggled and took pity on me. "I had a great night with Harley, sugar. I just wanted to wind you up."

"It worked," I groused. "So, did you or did you not sleep over?"

Mere pinned me with a look I'd seen her mother use a billion times when we were working on her last nerve. "Not that it's your business," she said, "but I didn't stay overnight. I need to take this slow and be sure we're on the same page before I let my heart get carried away." *As if we controlled our hearts.* "We met for coffee first to get the introductory stuff out of the way and to see if we sparked."

"And?"

"Just call me Sparky," Meredith said with a giggle. "He's sweet and funny. He crazy loves kids, and his manners were impeccable." Her voice grew softer, and her eyes lost focus as she thought back on her date.

"So, I'm assuming you advanced to the dinner phase of the evening," I said prodding her.

"Wait!" Chaz said, bursting up the stairs. "I want to hear all about it."

"There's not a lot to tell," Meredith replied. "We had dinner then went to a movie."

"Did you kiss him?" Chaz asked.

"Are you twelve?" I asked him. *I was just pissed because he beat me to it.* "Well, did you?" I asked Meredith.

"Do you kiss and tell with Gabe?" she asked, knowing full well that I didn't.

"I see your point," I replied.

"Do you?" she asked. The thing was, I had kissed and told plenty of times in my past. Gabe had been different from the very start. I got what she was saying without her saying it.

"I do."

I checked the clock and saw that it was time to get my ass in gear and put the finishing touches on my dinner. I had made the mashed potatoes early and kept them warm in a crockpot so that I could look put together and poised when my company arrived. Gabe made a wisecrack about instant potatoes that morning and nearly missed out on the amazing blow job I bestowed upon him.

Meredith filled water glasses while Chaz stared at the extra plates at the table. I could tell he was struggling internally with the pros and cons of Kyle showing up, or not. I felt horrible that I had put him in the situation. The doorbell rang downstairs which meant it was either Emory, Silver, or Kyle since everyone else had a key to the back door.

Chaz bit his lip while he waited to see who came up the steps with Gabe. Emory's soft laughter rang out from the bottom of the steps and Chaz's shoulders slumped. I had half a mind to tell him to call Kyle or ask Gabe to do it, but I had learned my lesson. He seemed to snap out of it quickly and offered a warm smile to Emory.

"It's good to see you again, Emory," Chaz said.

"You too." Emory's slight blush was cute. He turned to Meredith and said, "I don't think we've formerly met. I'm Emory Jackson." He extended his hand to Mere which she used to pull him into a hug because that was her preferred way to greet people.

"I'm Meredith Richmond," she told him, pulling out of the embrace. "I'm so happy you're joining us today."

The doorbell rang again, and I saw Chaz wipe his hands nervously on his jeans. I was so excited to hear about Meredith's date that I forgot to mention to them that Gabe invited Jonathon Silver. In fact, they didn't even know that Nate Turner had a twin brother. It wasn't my story to tell, and the last thing I wanted to do was inadvertently fuck up Gabe's case. I felt bad about not giving them a warning though until I saw the shocked expressions on their faces, then I thought it was funny. Emory turned and looked at the newcomer curiously to see what caused such a stir.

His eyes widened slightly, but the sexy man standing awkwardly next to Gabe with a bottle of wine in his hand was impressive. He wore dark jeans and an impeccably pressed, white dress shirt that was open enough to get a glimpse of dark chest hair. It was shocking how much he looked like his brother, yet there was a completely different look in his eyes. Nate had looked arrogant and entitled, Jonathon looked wary and cynical. There was a great sadness about him, and I understood why Gabe felt the need to make sure he wasn't alone that day.

Meredith and Chaz blinked a few times then closed their mouths that had fallen open in shock. They looked to me for answers then to Gabe. They were so synchronized it looked rehearsed, but it was because they were so in tune with one another. I was sure I would've been making the same face had I not already known about Jonathon.

"Guys, this is Jonathon Silver," Gabe said. "He's Nate's twin brother. Jonathon Silver, this is Meredith, Chaz, and Emory."

Chaz was the first to snap out of his surprise to cross the room and shake Jonathon's hand. Meredith hugged him and told him she was sorry for his loss, which Jonathon seemed to appreciate. Emory stepped forward slowly with his head tilted slightly as he studied Jonathon, who seemed uncomfortable with the intensity aimed in his direction.

We all watched as both men cautiously extended their hands toward one another. When their hands connected, they both narrowed their eyes suspiciously. I wondered if they felt an electrical current zinging through their bones like I did when Gabe touched me. It was something that seemed to get stronger with time, not fade. I also noticed that neither of them pulled away from the other.

Emory closed his eyes for a few seconds then jerked, breaking their connection. He opened his eyes slowly then blinked as he came back from wherever he had gone. Only Gabe and I knew about his abilities, and I wondered if he'd had a vision or something. Was Jonathon the reason why Emory moved to town? Why Blissville though when Jonathon lived in Cincinnati?

Jonathon's face was completely devoid of expression as he looked back at Emory. I would've loved to know what was going through his brain right then. Wanting to break the weirdness that had crept into the celebration, I walked over to the two men and kind of wedged myself between them. I looked over at Gabe and found him glaring at my proximity to them. I expected to hear a possessive growl from him at any moment.

"Welcome to our home," I said to Jonathon. "It's nice to meet you."

"It's nice to meet you too." He looked over at Gabe and smiled wryly. "No wonder you turned me down. Twice. Your man is adorable."

"Wait until you eat his food," Gabe said proudly like our guest had commented about something as docile as the weather and not propositioning him.

I turned away from my guests, intending to make my way to the kitchen to start carrying food to the table. I pinned Gabe with a glare that let him know I wasn't happy that he left out the parts about Slick Silver trying to steal my man. I was busy planning my retaliation tactics when his arms snaked around my waist and pulled me back against his chest.

"Don't spit in his food," Gabe whispered in my ear.

"It was your food that was in jeopardy, not his," I confessed, although I'd never do anything so tacky. I turned in his arms so that I could look up into his beautiful eyes. The thing was, I knew Gabe was a good-looking guy and when you added in his personality and character, he became devastatingly sexy. I couldn't blame Oversexed Silver, or anyone else for that matter, from wanting a piece of my man. I just didn't like being caught off guard in my home. "I'm planning more devious ways of torturing you."

"Ohhhh, the chair and cuffs again?" he asked hopefully. Someone cleared their throat, letting us know Gabe wasn't as quiet as he probably intended.

I leaned closer and pressed my lips to his ear. "Much worse, baby. Think restrained hands *and* a cock ring that won't let you come no matter how badly you ache." I couldn't get the image out of my mind once the words left my lips and I knew for sure that I'd be making a special stop to purchase a cock ring on my way home from my interview with Channel Eleven in Cincinnati.

Gabe closed his eyes briefly and whimpered softly. "Evil," he said, but his wicked smile told me how much he loved the idea. His confident gaze said he could take whatever I dished out, but we'd just have to see about that. I took his smile as a challenge; one I would not fail.

"Should we leave?" Meredith asked good-naturedly.

"Speak for yourself. I'm not leaving here until I get some of that ham."

I tore my eyes away from Gabe and turned to look at Kyle. I was so dialed into Gabe that I hadn't heard the doorbell ring. "You made it after all," I said happily.

"You sound a little too eager, Sunshine." Gabe peered at me through eyes that were narrowed into slits, as if he just learned that *I* was the one fighting them off instead of *him*.

"I hope you wore pants with an elastic waistband on them," I told Kyle. "I bought a second ham just for you."

"Yeah?" he asked hopefully. "These jeans might be a little too tight." Chaz was standing behind Kyle and doing his best not to stare at his ass, but failing miserably. "I should've worn maternity pants like Chandler on *Friends* in the Christmas episode."

"It was Joey and Thanksgiving," Chaz said suddenly, then turned bright red.

Kyle turned to face Chaz, who luckily had shifted his eyes upward in time, so Kyle didn't catch him ogling his ass. "Yeah, it was Joey at Thanksgiving."

"Let me help you get the food on the table while it's still hot," Meredith suggested. She grabbed my arm and tugged me away from Gabe. "You have some serious explaining to do. I feel like I'm in an episode of a soap opera or something."

"Yeah," Chaz hissed from behind us. "What's up with Striker Ramoray in there?" he asked, continuing with the *Friends* theme.

"Or maybe it's Nate with a brain transplant like Dr. Drake Ramoray," I replied sarcastically before I changed my voice to a pleading tone. "Come on, guys. Gabe found out about him during his investigation into Nate's death. I very well couldn't blab his secrets."

"So much for besties before testies," Chaz said with an exaggerated eye roll.

Meredith and I burst into raucous laughter, earning the stares from everyone else. We laughed until we had to lean on him for support. I was so happy to see that he hadn't lost his sense of humor due to the awkwardness of having Kyle there. Chaz began repeating some of Drake Ramoray's best lines as we carried the food to the table.

I was even happier to see the smile on Chaz's face when Kyle joined in on the fun. I glanced over at Gabe, and he winked playfully at me. I thought that maybe my scheme wasn't so harebrained after all. I puckered up my lips at him in a mock kiss, but he need not think I forgot about the bomb Silver Ramoray dropped on me.

TWENTY-TWO

Gabe

RELATIONSHIPS WERE NOT NEW TO ME, I MEAN, MY EX-BOYFRIEND had joined us for Easter dinner for Christ's sake. Believe it or not, and I was sure that Josh fell into the *or not* category, I didn't have dudes flashing their cocks at me all the damn time or propositioning me. Was I supposed to tell Josh about that stupid shit? Was he supposed to tell me every time a guy sized him up like he was thinking about trying Josh's ass on for size? I had seen it with my own eyes so he need not pretend that guys didn't find him attractive. I trusted him, and I didn't need to hear how other guys wanted him.

Josh was new to relationships and just because something didn't bother me didn't mean that it wouldn't annoy him. It wasn't my place to tell him what should or shouldn't be an issue for him, but I could assure him that it made no difference how many guys wagged their cocks in my direction. I had the one that I wanted. Although I'd been in relationships before, I had never been in one with so much at stake. Josh was my be-all and end-all, and I wouldn't risk fucking it up. So, if he wanted me to tell him every time I rejected a dude, I'd do it.

Although, I'd gladly take the punishment he was cooking up for me. He wanted to see how many times I could make him come before I busted a nut and I was *up* for that. Thankfully, Kyle showed up and provided the distraction I needed to get my mind off sex with a house full of people, two of whom were new to our little circle.

Josh and his two cohorts giggling in the kitchen made me smile, and I was happy that Chaz recovered from his initial shock at seeing that Kyle had shown up. It tickled me when Kyle and Chaz started saying lines from a TV show to one another. Maybe Josh was onto something with them.

The smells coming from the kitchen had me salivating so much that I almost missed how Emory kept glancing at Jonathon with a worried expression on his face. I wouldn't say that I put a lot of stock in psychic phenomenon, but Emory clearly believed in it. Did he see something? Was Jonathon in trouble? I wanted to ask, but it wasn't exactly the right time or place.

Josh made enough food to feed more than twice the number of people who arrived for dinner. His fancy china was pretty, but I wished the plates were bigger and held more food. Kyle elbowed his way to the ham, not caring who was in his way. I noticed that Meredith lingered around the food longer than normal and thought it was odd until I saw her glance to see where Chaz and Kyle sat.

Normally, Meredith sat across from Chaz, but it looked like she was hoping Kyle would sit across from him instead. She was wrong; Kyle sat directly next to Chaz. She did a happy little shimmy that she thought no one saw until I chuckled softly. She took her normal seat, Emory sat beside her, and Jonathon surprised me by sitting next to Emory. The seat on the other side of Kyle was empty, and I wondered if Josh had schemes to fill it on the next holiday gathering.

Meredith said grace, as she did every Sunday, and everyone dug in. God, the food my man could make was out of this world. No one had time to do any talking for the first few minutes because we were too busy shoveling food into our mouths. We acted like cavepeople, grunting our appreciation for Josh's efforts.

Emory recovered his manners first and said, "So, how did the two of you meet?" He looked at Josh and me, so I knew he was talking about us. Josh was the better storyteller, so I gestured for him to tell it.

"Once upon a time, a boorish, brute for a detective walked into a salon owned by a sweet and sensitive man." Meredith snorted, earning a brief glare from Josh. "Detective Tall, Dark, and Dickish had stopped by to ask the sweetheart questions about a crime he potentially witnessed." We all listened as Josh wildly embellished our first encounters, although I noticed he didn't mention the time he came to my house with cookies and rode me like I was his favorite carnival ride. I didn't add anything or correct him until he said, "I was trying to fight the assailant off when Gabe came to my rescue. He hollered for the man to freeze, but he kept pushing the knife closer to my chest. Gabe shot the mirror, and it pulled my would-be killer's attention off stabbing me long enough for Gabe to shoot him."

"I didn't shoot your mirror," I said to Josh.

"Sure you did," he said. "I heard it shatter seconds before you shot Oscar." It was good that Josh could finally say his name. He had refused to learn anything about the guy for months, hoping that his nightmares would fade, but it didn't help.

"Sunshine, I didn't shoot the mirror. It must've already had damage to it because it just shattered."

"That can't be right," he said, skeptically.

"Stop and think about how many gunshots you heard. The responding officers took my gun from me, and only one bullet was missing from the clip."

Josh sat in his chair and thought for a few seconds before he said, "There *was* only one shot fired. The mirror shattering was very loud, but it wasn't anything close to the noise the gun made when it went off. How the hell did the mirror just shatter?"

"I can't answer that. I just know I didn't shoot it."

"Huh," he said.

"One of your neighbors was killed?" Emory asked, going back to the case that brought us together.

"She lived in the house you're renting," Chaz said automatically then froze when he realized what he'd said.

Emory nodded somberly. "I knew something bad had happened there because I could feel the residual negative energy in the house." Emory's cheeks pinkened when his words had everyone's attention. "I'm just sensitive to stuff like that," he said.

"Tell us about yourself," Josh said to Jonathon, trying to divert attention away from Emory.

Silver was too busy staring at Emory to answer him right away. Finally, he looked at Josh and said, "Well, that's not an easy story to tell." I could tell he was searching for something that he could share.

"Another time perhaps," Josh said, saving him. "How are things going at the club?"

I could see the tension fade from Silver's frame, and he began to talk about the club. "I'm more excited about my revitalization plans for Cincinnati. I bought the club because it meant a lot to Nate, but I thought a better way to memorialize him was through improving the city he loved so much."

"Wow," Emory said softly. "That's a wonderful thing to do."

Silver winked at him and said, "I have my moments." His expression and tone of voice said that he wouldn't mind having a *moment* with Emory later. I couldn't get a read on what Emory was thinking.

The conversation turned to less emotional subjects and ended up back on the show that Kyle and Chaz could quote from memory. The funny thing was, I had no clue that Kyle loved that show so much. He was a man I spent three years with and sometimes I felt like I didn't know him. He was different with Chaz, and I liked what I saw. He laughed and teased more than I could remember him doing in the past. The Kyle I had known was more aloof and serious. Although, Kyle probably saw sides to me that he had never seen either. It was plain to see that we weren't meant to be together as a couple, but I was glad we could be friends.

There was after dinner drinks followed by coffee and dessert. Josh packed up leftovers for everyone to take home while Meredith and I cleaned up the kitchen. I expected the conversation to lag a bit as the evening grew on, but it didn't. Emory and Silver talked about the different places that they'd lived, but I noticed that neither of them talked about what they did while in those locations.

"What brought you here after living at all those fabulous places?" Chaz asked.

"I'm researching for a book that I'm planning to write," Emory told him. "I like it here, although I'm a little worried about the number of homicides in a small town." He was completely unaware that Silver's brother was one of the deaths in our county. "What did I say?" he asked when everyone grew quiet.

"My brother was one of the guys killed here," Silver told him.

"Oh damn," Emory said. "I'm so sorry, Jon." He placed his hands over Silver's.

Jon?

"It's okay, Emory." Silver smiled softly and turned his hands over to squeeze Emory's before he pulled them back. He rose from his chair and said, "I should be heading back to the city. Gabe," he said looking at me, "thank you for inviting me to dinner." He turned to Josh and said, "Dinner was magnificent. Thank you so much." His words of gratitude couldn't disguise the sadness I heard in his voice.

"Anytime," Josh told him. "Have a safe trip home."

"I'll walk you out," I said, rising to my feet.

Silver didn't say anything until we reached the back door. "You have an amazing guy waiting for you upstairs," he said. "I am sorry that I disrespected your relationship with my flirting. It won't happen again."

"Thanks," I told him. "I'll be in touch if I learn anything else." Silver nodded his head and walked out the back door.

I turned and found that Emory had come downstairs too. "Man, I feel terrible that I ran your friend off, Gabe."

"You didn't run him off," I replied. Jonathon Silver wasn't the kind of guy anyone ran off. "His loss was recent, and he's still coming to terms with things."

"Still, I didn't help matters any," Emory said.

"You can't be blamed for what you didn't know, Emory." I tipped my head to the side and debated on whether I should ask what I was thinking or let it go.

"Go ahead and ask me," he said.

"Did you have a vision or something when you shook Silver's hand?"

"Yeah, you could say that," he replied wryly. "He wasn't in danger in my vision, if that was what you were concerned about." It was what worried me, so I didn't press for more information. Besides, the telltale blush on his cheek spoke volumes. "Thank you for a lovely evening," he said. "I'll see you around the neighborhood."

"Take care, Emory."

Back upstairs, the vibe in the room was more relaxed. Someone had loaded up *Friends* on Netflix, and Chaz and Kyle were busy talking *World of Warcraft* in between reciting their favorite lines in the episode they were watching. It looked like they were getting more relaxed with each other's company. *Friends* and *World of Warcraft*; I guess relationships were built on less.

I sat down on the couch next to Josh, and he curled into my side. As much as I loved having our friends over, I hoped they wouldn't stay too late since some of us had to work the next day. Josh had his big interview for the wedding series with Channel Eleven, and I figured he wanted a good night of rest. Meredith tagged out pretty early, but Chaz and Kyle seemed unaware of the time or that they were keeping us awake. Me anyway; Josh had fallen asleep against my shoulder.

As happy as I was for them, I was ready for them to go home. Other than throwing Kyle and Chaz out, I wasn't quite sure what to do. I must've conked out too because the next thing I knew, Chaz was nudging my shoulder and waking me up.

"I'm sorry that we stayed so long," he said sheepishly. "I lost track of time."

"It happens," I told him. "Don't worry about it." I slid out from beneath Josh and laid him on the couch so I could lock up downstairs.

When I returned upstairs, he was in our room getting undressed. "Never doubt my matchmaking skills again," he said sleepily. "I know what I'm doing." He slid beneath the sheets and patted the mattress for me to climb in too.

I tossed my clothes in the hamper and slid in next to him. "Sunshine, we need to talk about this thing with Silver."

"No sweet talking your way out of your punishment," he said. He nestled closer to me, and I knew he wasn't angry.

"I'll take your punishment, but I want you to know why I didn't say anything about him or Paul's advances..."

"Paul too?" he asked, lifting his head off my chest.

"Listen, Sunshine. I didn't tell you because it didn't mean anything to me." I repeated my thoughts earlier to him about the swinging dicks; he wasn't amused.

"I guess it's okay as long as you're not swinging yours around too." I couldn't see his eyes in the darkness, but I could tell by the tone of his voice that he was rolling them. "That's why I'm going to put a ring on it."

That had my drooping eyes opening wide. Was Josh still talking about a cock ring or something more?

TWENTY-THREE

Josh

I DON'T KNOW WHY I WAS SO NERVOUS ABOUT THE INTERVIEW FOR something I wasn't sure I even wanted, but since when did I always make sense? I was a complicated person on my best day and an annoying shit on my worst. I wasn't sure what the hell to wear for my interview. Did I want to look like hip Jazz with a graphic tee and dark jeans that made my legs look a mile long, something a bit campier perhaps, or something classy like dress pants and shirt complete with suspenders and bowtie? I chewed on the corner of my thumbnail while I looked at the three different outfits I had laid across our bed.

"Don't look at me," Gabe said when I asked his opinion. "You know I'm no good at these things."

A frustrated growl escaped my throat. "I want to look professional, but cool at the same time. Are the tie and suspenders dorky?"

"Sunshine, you wouldn't look dorky in any outfit. You're one of those guys who can pull anything off." Gabe came over to the bed and stared down at my outfits. "Today is about making a good impression, right? You want to come across as a successful business owner who knows his shit, yes?" I nodded. "I'd go with this sexy bowtie and suspenders number for today. You can always wear something more casual when you're styling hair for a segment. You'd want to be comfortable and not feel hindered by clothes in that situation."

"That's a fabulous idea, Gabe," I said excitedly. He preened under my praise until I added, "I can strip down to my undies. Think of how easily I can move around then."

"No one sees that but me," he said possessively. "I wish I had time for a private showing right now." He pulled me to him for a long goodbye kiss. "Keep that outfit on so I can strip it off you when I get home. It'll be like unwrapping a birthday or Christmas gift months early."

I loved that he thought I was his personal gift. I'd leave the outfit on for him, but he wouldn't have free hands to take it off me. The suspenders he admired so much were going to pull double duty that day. "I look forward to it," I said honestly and without a hint of what I was planning.

I took my time grooming and getting dressed before I headed south to Cincinnati. I knew traffic wouldn't be too heavy during the late morning commute until I got closer to the city. I cranked up the music and sang along, not giving a shit at what the drivers in the other lanes on the interstate thought about it. I decided the day was about having fun because I already lived the life I wanted. If this worked out, great, but it wouldn't change my quality of life if it didn't.

I paid to park in a garage a block away from the large building that housed the news station. The spring weather was perfect, and the bright sunlight put some extra pep in my step. A knuckle-dragging Neanderthal made a remark as he passed me by but I didn't let his ignorance bring me down. I wasn't going to change his mind about gays nor would his opinions turn me straight. It was best to keep moving.

I was given a visitor's pass at the reception desk and instructed on where to go. At least her directions led me up an elevator to meet with Cindy instead of down to the pits of hell I had just heard from the stranger on the street. My excitement increased with every floor the elevator traveled because, if nothing else, I at least got to tour the newsroom and see what it looked like behind the scenes.

Cindy's personal assistant was waiting for me when I got off the elevator. She introduced herself as Rachel and asked me to follow her. She rattled off a bunch of facts about the news station and the building as we walked. "Here you go," she said, stopping outside a set of etched glass double doors. Rachel knocked twice then opened a door for me. "Good luck," she said.

"Thank you." I entered the room and admired the expanse of the space and the view of the city it offered, but I found the furniture and decorations to be a bit too modern for my liking. I thought it could use some rich woods to break up the black, chrome, and glass, but it wasn't my workspace. It was a little bland to be honest, which surprised me.

Cindy Rollins stood from her chair and walked around her desk with her hand extended. "It's good to meet you, Josh." She was almost as tall as Gabe and was dressed to kill. I loved the intricate way her hair was braided and how she twisted the braids into a low bun on her nape. The lavender color of her suit looked amazing with her dark coloring. Cindy's firm grip was all business, but her smile was warm and welcoming.

"It's good to meet you too," I replied. "I'm excited to be here."

"You didn't sound too convinced on the phone," she said, resuming her seat behind her desk. I changed my mind about her office decorations. The understated scheme allowed Cindy to be the focal point of the room.

"Honestly, starring in a news series wasn't something I ever planned or even thought about, but the idea has grown on me. I..." A knock on her door interrupted me.

"Come in," Cindy called out before she added, "Tabitha is joining us."

I stood and turned to greet Tabitha, and my eyes widened in shock. "Oh dear Lord, girl. What have you done?"

"*Not done* is more like it," Tabitha said, cringing while she covered her garish roots with her hands.

I turned back to face Cindy. "You called me based on *her* recommendations with her hair looking like that?" I asked. Cindy's throaty laugh over my question warmed my insides and bolstered my confidence to relax and just be... me.

"Tabitha," I said circling back to face her. "Root tip number one: never pull your hair back into a ponytail when you are weeks—possibly a month—past a root touchup. You might as well write 'Look at my roots' across your forehead when you do that."

"I know," she said. "I've been so busy lately that I haven't had the time to schedule an appointment."

"I can't have this, Tab," I told her. "We need to resolve this issue immediately. When can you see me? I'll squeeze you in."

"How about now," Cindy offered. "Did you happen to bring any supplies and equipment with you? We have some here, but..."

I held up my hand to stop her. A master never worked with someone else's tools. Luckily for Tabitha, I came prepared as hell. I had no idea what my interview would entail and brought a lot of things with me. I didn't bring hair color, but my wholesaler was in the city. All it took was a phone call, and they delivered what I needed to the station. I retrieved the rest of my items from the trunk of Princess and set up in the mock salon in the studio.

By the time I finished with the hair emergency fix that doubled as an interview, I had landed myself a segment on Channel Eleven that would begin filming after we finished the series on weddings. Cindy said the camera loved my face and she loved my personality and talent. She wanted me to film three segments each week where I gave tips on hair and makeup, provided makeovers, and tested out new products. The great part was that I could film all three segments every Monday and it wouldn't interfere with my schedule at the salon.

I was excited to see Gabe and tell him the good news, but I wasn't too excited that I forgot to stop by Kinky Kim's on the way home to get Gabe's *punishment* device. There was no way in hell he would be prepared for what I had in mind for him.

Gabe was home in the bedroom waiting for me when I got home, wearing nothing but a cocky smile. "What's in the bag?" He waggled his brows when I held it up for him to see. "Kinky Kim's, huh?" He rubbed his hands together gleefully. "Of course, I'm not sure why I'm in trouble. It's not like I took them up on their offer, or even was tempted by it, for that matter."

I set the bag at the foot of our bed and slipped my thumbs beneath my suspenders and ran them up and down the length, causing Gabe's nostrils to flare. "Baby, you're not *really* in trouble, I wouldn't be scheming to blow your mind if I was mad at you. Just maybe you tell me when stupid shit happens because it always seems to get back to me." I reminded him of running into Paul at the club. "I'm not talking about random dudes who give you the eye, but if it's guys you're working closely with…"

"Not closely," Gabe said. "Besides, Paul wanted you too."

"What?" I asked in disbelief. "Get out of here."

"Okay, but can I wait until after I see what's in the bag?" He gave me his puppy dog eyes and batted his lashes. "Seriously, I cut him off before he could finish because I knew where the dumbass was going."

"Huh," I said, perking up a bit.

"Oh, so now it's okay," Gabe said accusingly. "I will never share you, Josh."

"Who said I wanted you to?" I asked him. "It's just a little flattering. And Sneaky Silver? What's this about him flashing his cock at you?"

"He flashed Dorchester too," Gabe said, causing me to raise my brows.

"Those Cincinnati boys are kinky," I said. Gabe laughed and told me how it all played out. I couldn't help but chuckle when he told me about John telling Silver to put his gun away too. The twin brother remark wasn't as funny, but I couldn't stop my brain from wondering what the answer was to the question.

"No, they're not identical," Gabe said with a wry smile because he knew what I had been thinking.

"So, there's no way Jonathon took over Nate's identity?" I asked.

"Definitely not," Gabe said emphatically. My mind immediately began to work out the differences between their two cocks. *Length? Girth? Both?* "Cut and uncut," Gabe said, answering my unvoiced question.

"Really?" Somehow that didn't occur to me.

"According to Silver, Nate was given up for adoption, but he remained with his mom. I think there's a huge story there, but I've not pressed him because it hasn't been relevant to my case," Gabe said. "Can we start talking about our cocks now, because as far as I'm concerned, they're the only two that count." He chewed on his lip while stroking his erection. "Show me what's in the bag."

I reached inside the bag and took my time pulling out the first item. "Vanilla whipped body butter," I announced and held it up like I was one of Barker's Beauties. "I plan to lick it off your sensitive, erect nipples…"

"What about my erect cock?" Gabe asked eagerly.

"I was getting there, but you didn't let me finish," I said with mock annoyance.

"Sorry." *He wasn't.*

I pulled out the next item in the bag and held it for him to see. "Cock ring," I announced as if he didn't already know what he was seeing. "I'm going to see how far I can push you."

"Bring it on," he said arrogantly.

"I'm going to kiss you, lick you, and ride you like I never have before," I unclipped my suspenders, pulled them off my body, and held them in front of me, "all while your hands are tied so you can't touch me." I saw his smugness fade. "Lie down," I demanded.

"I wanted to strip you down," he said petulantly but did as I asked.

"Another time," I told him as I wove the suspenders through the ornate wrought iron headboard and wrapped them around both wrists until he was tied firmly to the frame but not too tight that I cut off his circulation. I removed the condoms and lube from the bedside table drawer and set them on the bed next to him with the body butter.

I slid the rubber cock ring down the length of his erection then secured his balls tightly in the second ring made to restrict them. Gabe's cock was already leaking, and he arched off the bed the second my hand touched his dick. I turned undressing into a striptease by moving seductively to music I heard in my head. Gabe's eyes glittered with unbridled lust while he yanked on his restraints. Oh, I was going to have so much fun with him.

Once I was naked, I straddled his sexy body and wiggled my

ass against his erection while I squirted body butter on his sexy, pert nipples then slowly slid down his body so that I teased his hard-on with the friction. I swirled my tongue slowly around his areola before I sucked his stiff peak in my mouth. I knew how badly he wanted to tug my hair, but I wasn't giving in. I squirted the cream down his torso and enjoyed the sweet treat on my path down to the promise land.

By the time I reached his cock, he was leaking a lot of pre-cum and he became my favorite sweet and salty treat of all time. His thigh muscles bunched and felt like stone beneath my hands; it thrilled me to know I could rev him up so much. I worked his dick slowly in and out of my mouth until his body shook from the restrained pleasure. I let his dick slip from my mouth once I reached the point where I couldn't wait for another second to feel him inside my ass. I slid the condom down his length before I oiled it generously with the lube.

I didn't stop to stretch myself that time; instead, I lowered myself on his dick until he was buried to the hilt. Once I adjusted to his size, I began my slow, torturous ride. It felt so damn good I felt tears of happiness spring to my eyes. I ran my hands up and down my torso and teased my nipples like he would have if his hands had been free. Gabe's pupils were blown, and his gorgeous brown eyes were unfocused from the lust pumping through his veins.

I reached down and stroked my cock to match the up and down rocking I was doing on his erection. It wasn't long before my body was trembling just as hard as his with the need to come. I didn't hold back; I painted his chest with my spunk. Gabe looked smug with the knowledge that he was going to get his opportunity to come soon.

"I'm not done with you yet," I warned him.

I removed the condom from his dick and tossed it aside then started to blow him again. It was more than he could take. He groaned and pleaded with me to put him out of his misery, but I knew the intensity of his orgasm was going to be worth the torture.

I slipped a lubed finger beneath his balls to tease his puckered entrance before I slid it inside him, aiming right for his prostate. I kept the pad of my finger pressed against the bundle of nerves and circled it around to give him the most stimulation while I took his cock to the back of my throat again.

I kept at his torture until I worried he would bruise himself from yanking on his restraints. I released the rubber circle from around Gabe's sac with my free hand, then massaged his swollen balls that were ripe and ready to release their load while I simultaneously worked his cock and prostate.

"Fuck me!" Gabe shouted before he came in my mouth. It was so thick, and there was so much of it that I could barely swallow it all down, but I managed. "Untie me, you little imp." There was no heat behind his words, so I let him loose and massaged his wrists. "Mind you, I'm not complaining, but what was the purpose of this exercise?"

"Hands off," I told him. "It's to remind you of what you'd lose should you ever take another guy up on his offer."

"Sunshine, I'd never hurt you like that," Gabe said. "No fucking way." Gabe pulled me down until I lay on top of him and I didn't even care I was lying on top of a puddle of my own spunk when his arms were around me. "You're my whole world, and I love you."

"I love you too, Gabe. Sometimes it still scares me, but I'm done living in fear," I told him. "I used to be afraid of people finding out that I was gay. Then I was scared that I would never find someone who would love me as I was and would be proud that I was his man." I lifted off his chest enough so I could look into his eyes. "Then you came along, and I was afraid to believe, but you wore me down, and I quit running. You made me proud of who I am, confident to stand beside you, and believe that I deserved the life that only you could give me. I'm done being afraid."

"Those are some beautiful words," he whispered hoarsely.

"You're a beautiful man," I repeated.

"You're the beautiful one," Gabe countered. "I'm going to be the one fighting them off when you get your show on the news channel."

"I didn't tell you I accepted the offer," I told him.

"You didn't have to, Sunshine. No one sticks around for four hours for an interview if they're not interested. I knew you were going to blow them away. I can't wait to hear about it, but do you mind if we get cleaned up? Your spunk is starting to dry in my chest hair, and it hurts."

"You're so high maintenance, Gabe." I pushed myself off his body and removed the rubber ring from his spent cock. "I told you I was going to put a ring on it."

"I thought maybe you had another ring in mind," he said teasingly before he got up and walked into the bathroom. "Can you guess which kind?"

I stood there in the middle of the bedroom, paralyzed by his words. My heart and my mind started to race. Were we ready for such a big step? What if.... No! I meant what I said. I was done living with doubts and fears. "How about a Ring Pop?" I hollered after him.

Gabe's laughter echoed in the bathroom. "Close, but not quite. You're a smart fella, so I'm sure you'll figure it out."

"So long as it isn't ringworm," I told him.

"Get your ass in here and quit playing around. Don't freak out either. We'll know when the time is right to 'put a ring on it.' Come tell me all about your big adventures in television."

"You won't believe it," I said as I entered the bathroom.

"Try me," he said with a smile.

TWENTY-FOUR

Gabe

SOMETIMES A MAN WAKES UP, AND HE JUST KNOWS IT'S GOING TO be a great day. He starts his day by waking up next to the man he loves after a night that physically and emotionally rocked him to his core. His first cup of coffee is perfect in every way with just the right balance between sweet and bitter. He gets a goodbye kiss that curls his toes and knows an even sweeter welcome home kiss awaits him.

Then sometimes that same man arrives at work, and his conviction is shaken. He's reminded of how motherfucking cruel the world can be when faced with a brokenhearted widow whose entire world had been ripped apart by ugliness she can't possibly comprehend. She'd been hospitalized for treatment the night she discovered her husband's body and I hadn't tried to see her again until Monday. Her sister told me she was still heavily sedated and promised to bring her into the station the next day. Dinah Spizer didn't look anything like the woman in the photo on her husband's desk. I could tell by Rick's appearance in the picture that it had been taken recently, but the woman who sat before me looked like she had aged twenty years in a few days.

After introducing ourselves, we handed her a copy of the suicide note. Her hands shook violently, and she sobbed loudly while she read what Spizer wrote.

"Rick didn't kill himself, Detective," she said pleadingly. "We didn't even own a gun. He had seen enough violence in the military and wanted nothing to do with them." She sat shredding the tissue she held between her hands. "I don't know why he's taking responsibility for these deaths, but I know he didn't kill them." There were dozens of legitimate stores he could've recently purchased the gun from without her knowledge, not to mention all the illegal options as well.

"I'm so sorry for your loss, Mrs. Spizer, but we do need to ask you some questions." She closed her eyes and tears ran down her cheeks, but she nodded for me to continue. "Can you confirm that this is your husband's handwriting?"

"Yes, but…" She stopped talking and nodded her head. "Yes."

"Had you noticed a difference in his personality recently? Had he been more withdrawn or had trouble sleeping lately?" I hated to ask those questions and cause her more pain, but I had to weigh hard facts against her unwillingness to believe her husband was capable of hurting others and taking his own life.

"Yes," she said softly between tears. "Rick had only been sleeping a few hours a night, if that, for the past few months. I asked him about it and he said his back was bothering him again. He'd grown sullen, but I had blamed it on his lack of sleep. I had no idea..." She shook her head vehemently. "He didn't do those things, Detective. I've known Rick since we were kids. He was a good person."

"Mrs. Spizer, I want you to know that we're taking this case seriously and looking at all the evidence. We're not just going to rule his death a suicide because it's quick and easy. That's not how we operate," I told her.

"Thank you," she said. "Please call me one way or the other. I'll never believe my Rick was capable of doing those things he said in his letter. I just can't."

Dorchester walked her out of the interview room to help her find her way out while I stayed behind and thought about what she said. No matter how much my heart ached over what she was going through, I had to find the truth. There was nothing about the scene that said it was a homicide made to look like a suicide. The angle and trajectory of the bullet plus the way his body and the gun fell afterward all lined up with a self-inflicted gunshot. It wasn't that the CPD wasn't listening to what she said; it was a situation where facts pointed to one thing while her feelings pointed to another. Cases didn't get solved and closed on feelings. I was starting to think that Rick Spizer did take his life over the guilt of what he had either done alone or with someone else. If he had an accomplice, I wanted to know about him or her.

Dr. Espinoza studied all four cases and determined that a .45 caliber pistol was most likely the gun used each time. We had the gun used in Spizer's death, but we couldn't be sure the other victims were killed with the same gun unless we could find the bullets removed from the other three scenes. If we recovered the bullets, a ballistics expert could compare them to see if they all had the same striations as the bullet fired from Spizer's gun.

Dorchester returned minutes later and said, "Damn, I hate those kinds of interviews. I feel terrible for that woman. To find her husband's body like that and then read the horrible things he'd confessed to doing." *But was it a confession?*

"This part of our job fucking sucks," I told Dorchester. "I felt like we twisted the knife that reality had shoved into her heart."

"Pretty much," he agreed. "What's next? None of the evidence points to anything besides suicide. His files are off limits because privilege remains intact for his clients after his death."

"We march on with our plan to interview the main players at McCarren Consortium," I told Dorchester. "I meant what I said about making sure we don't leave any loose threads." The CPD might refuse to hire an expert to analyze the handwriting on the suicide note, but talking to McCarren's employees cost them nothing.

"Let's do it," Dorchester said. "It's been a while since you dusted off your bad cop."

I followed Dorchester out of the interview room. "Are you accusing me of going soft?"

"That sounds like a personal problem and none of my business," he said cheekily. "All I meant was that we haven't had to go hard at anyone lately."

"True," I admitted. "Today is the day. Let's take a copy of the letter that Larkin sent Robertson."

It turned out that both Dorchester and I dusted off our bad cop routines for the interview. The poor receptionist looked terrified when we glowered at her and showed her our badges. "We want to talk to McCarren, Larkin, and Thompson. Now." I wasn't exactly sure what I was going to ask them because all my questions had been prepared before Spizer's death.

"J-j-just a minute," she said, holding up a finger. "M-m-mr. McCarren, there are two detectives here to see you, Mr. Larkin, and Mr. Thompson. Okay, sir. I'll call him." She hung up the phone and buzzed us through the glass door. "Follow me," she said skittishly as if she was afraid to turn her back on us.

We followed her through the private offices of a man with more money than sense. The money spent on the opulence throughout the space could've fed every starving family in America at least twice. I had a feeling that the paintings hanging on the walls were originals valued in the millions rather than a knockoff you'd find in most office buildings. It was something you'd expect to see in New York City, not a place like Cincinnati that was once referred to as Porkopolis.

"In here," she said, pulling open two black doors.

I heard the doors close soundly behind us after Dorchester and I entered McCarren's office, which was as ridiculous as the rest of the office building. I never harbored ill will toward people who were successful, but this was a man who I felt probably didn't come by it honestly, and I'd have a problem with that all day, every day.

"Gentlemen," McCarren said, attempting to be polite. "Larkin and Thompson will be here momentarily, but I can tell you that none of us will be answering a single question until our legal council arrives."

I looked at Dorchester and said, "That didn't take him long to find new representation."

"Spizer's body hasn't even made it to the funeral home yet," Dorchester remarked.

"Excuse me?" McCarren asked. "Spizer? Rick Spizer is dead?" I had to hand it to him; he sounded genuinely shocked.

"You didn't know?" I asked skeptically. It wasn't that I expected Dinah Spizer to contact his clients, but surely word had gotten around in their close circle. People of his magnitude of wealth usually kept their thumbs on the pulse of everyone and everything around them. The death of his lead counsel was no small piece of news.

"I-I have been out of town for months, Detective. I don't care for Ohio winters at my age and choose to spend them in warmer climes." He shook his head in disbelief. "How did it happen?"

"His death is still under investigation, so we're unable to release those details at this time," Dorchester told him.

We didn't have long to wait until Thompson and Larkin came through the door. They bristled and tried to look like badasses, but neither Dorchester nor I were impressed or intimidated.

"Have a seat," I told them, unwilling to waste a minute on their posturing. "We've been investigating a series of related deaths that have been traced back to the interest you've shown in building a casino in Carson County."

"Detective, I can't see how the failed initiative from years ago could be responsible for these deaths," McCarren said.

I removed the letter from the file I held in my hands and laid it on the center of the highly polished conference table. "This one letter dated September of last year could be responsible for four deaths," I told him. I saw Larkin flinch in his seat when he heard the date on the letter.

"What's the meaning of this?" McCarren demanded of Larkin. "I didn't authorize you to contact Lawrence Robertson on my behalf." He looked back at me and asked, "Is Mr. Robertson one of the people who died?"

"Yes, then his house was torched because we think someone didn't want us to know about this letter," Dorchester added.

"Damn," McCarren said sadly. "Lawrence was a good guy, a principled man of his word. I don't meet many like him anymore."

"Wait!" Larkin exclaimed. "I sent that letter because I remembered how much you wanted to build a casino there, sir. I did not kill anyone because of the letter nor did I burn anyone's house to hide it."

Thompson piped in and asked, "Why am I being questioned? My name isn't on that letter. Furthermore, shouldn't we wait for Spizer to get here?"

"He's one of the four deaths," McCarren told him. "They haven't read us our rights nor have we been accused of anything. Let's hear what the detectives have to say, and we can call a halt to it if they ask questions that make us uncomfortable." He aimed his shrewd gaze back at me. "Start from the beginning."

I told them what I knew and what I also suspected. "Spizer is connected to all but one person who is dead." We still had to work out how they pulled Owen Smithson into the equation. "Larkin, you must've mentioned the casino deal to Spizer."

"I did mention it to Rick one day at lunch while going over other corporate legal matters. I asked him if he thought Mr. McCarren would be pleased if I could get the talks going again. Rick told me that he thought so, and if not, he knew someone who might be interested in investing in the casino."

"Nate Turner," I told them. "Mr. Turner started getting death threats in November and was killed in Carson County, not too far from Robertson's house, in January. The CPD traced the IP address used to harass Turner to an Owen Smithson, who was found dead in his apartment when they went to talk to him. While investigating both of those deaths, we found out that Nate had shown interest in building a casino. The fact that he was in Carson County made us want to revisit the players involved in the original casino deal. Dorchester and I found Mr. Robertson shot dead in his kitchen."

"Fuck me," McCarren said.

"We started reviewing documents and notes that Robertson had made after his meetings with all of you. That's when we discovered that Spizer was the attorney for both McCarren Consortium and Nate Turner."

"I don't believe that Rick could be involved in something like this, Detectives. He was a good man," Thompson stated emphatically.

Larkin let out a soft sigh and said, "The only thing I can tell you is that I did send the letter to Mr. Robertson because he didn't have a phone. He was kind of a paranoid guy who believed the government was listening to every call he made. Rick asked me about the letter a few weeks, maybe a month, after I sent it and I told him that I'd had no reply from Robertson and I was going to let it drop. Perhaps Turner picked up where I left off. Maybe he decided to drive out to see Robertson in person."

What Larkin said had merit, except the time of Nate's death. When Nate was killed, we had first assumed he was seeking me out for help. Once we connected him to the casino deal, we realized that probably wasn't true. It wasn't likely that Nate was meeting with Robertson in the middle of the night, which gave credence to there being someone else involved. Was that person in the conference room with me?

"I knew nothing about any of this," Thompson said. "Larkin didn't mention any of this to me."

"He's telling the truth," Larkin said. "Besides Rick, I told no one about my idea to establish talks with Robertson again."

That meant that it wasn't likely that a rival casino consortium was behind the killing. Spizer wanting these men dead made zero sense to me and was the main reason I didn't want to close the case.

"I'm sorry that we're not able to assist you further, Detectives," McCarren said. I was sorry too because I had hoped to learn something definitive that would help us close the case. I wanted everything tied up with a pretty bow.

Dorchester and I thanked them for their time and showed ourselves out. "Let's go talk to Robertson's nephews and see if we can shake any information out of them. They're the only ones that I can think of that might be salty about Robertson selling that land to someone other than them."

We drove thirty minutes north of the city to Sharpe Development Inc. and asked to speak with Scott and Mark Robertson. We learned that Mark was in Arizona and Scott was in New York on business. Dorchester and I were frustrated that it looked like we wouldn't be making any advances in the case that day.

"Now what?" Dorchester asked after a long-suffering sigh.

"We're halfway home already," I said. "There's nothing else we can do until we uncover more evidence so we might as well head that way." And so we did.

The lure of a welcome home kiss was too much to resist after a shitty day that had started out with so much promise. Josh looked at me with surprise when I entered the salon, but then a smile spread slowly across his face when he saw the intent in my eyes. He rose on his tiptoes to meet me halfway once I reached him. I dropped two quick kisses on his plump lips and said, "Don't be too late."

I smiled when I heard whistles and catcalls ring out behind me when I left the salon. "Y'all behave," Josh told his clientele. "That man doesn't need any more encouragement from you."

"Blow me, baby," Savage said when I stopped to retrieve his cage.

Damn, it was good to be home. I didn't allow myself to dwell on the sadness of the day once Josh got home from work. We made dinner together then Josh went upstairs to work on Adrianna's painting while I watched some baseball. The game was a defensive one, which meant low scoring and boring, so I went upstairs to see what kind of progress my guy was making.

Josh truly was magical to me, regardless of what he was doing. He was so enthralled in his painting of baby zoo animals that he didn't notice I was in the room. I must've sat in the chair for hours watching him dip his brushes in the paint before brushing them on the canvas. Only when he stopped to stretch did he realize I was in the room with him.

"How long have you been sitting there?" he asked. Long enough to know he was the only one I wanted to spend my life with, but that wasn't the answer I gave him.

"Long enough to know it's time to go to bed." My tone of voice told him that sleeping wasn't what I had in mind.

"Who needs a bed," Josh said, giving me a come-and-get-it smile.

Who could resist that kind of invitation? Not me because I would never pass up the opportunity to be on the receiving end of his magic.

TWENTY-FIVE

Josh

I had gotten used to running into Emory every time I turned around, or so it seemed, but I hadn't seen hide nor hair of him once he left our home on Easter Sunday. It had only been a few days, but it seemed longer. The sadness that clung to Emory when he went home had left me feeling unsettled. I was eager to see if he was okay and knew I'd get my chance because he'd have his hide parked in my chair and his hair in my hands at his appointment.

I had a busy morning and lost track of time until I realized my chair had been vacant longer than normal. I mean, that chair saw more action than a high-priced hooker and it was only empty when I took a break or had a day off. Neither of those things was happening right then, which meant that I had a no-show. That. Never. Happened. Ever.

Annoyance, anger, and concern fought for dominance in my brain as I marched my unhappy ass out the back door of the salon, down my driveway, and across the alley to Emory's house. I knocked loudly on his door and became more miffed when he didn't answer right away.

"I know damn well you're inside, Emory. I see your black Mini in the driveway with its showy, look-at-me stripes. Answer this damn door before I call the cops and tell them I smell an odd odor coming from your house. They'll think you're dead because that's our new normal and come busting through the door." I banged some more and added, "You better have clothes on unless you want them to see you in your skivvies or buck-ass naked."

I was starting to freak out that something had happened to him, but then I saw the slight fluttering of curtains at the back door seconds before they parted to reveal Emory looking at me through the glass. He had dark purple rings beneath his eyes as if he hadn't slept in years, and the sadness in his gaze was that of a man who had seen too many terrible things. He was the epitome of bruised and broken that afternoon.

"Please let me in, Emory." I released a sigh of relief when I heard him unlock the deadbolt.

"Hey," he said softly. "I'm sorry I didn't call and cancel my appointment." I could tell by his stance that he hadn't planned on granting me entrance. *Too damn bad!* I shoved past Emory and entered his kitchen, catching him off guard because I was much stronger than people expected.

"Josh, now isn't a good time." I was happy to hear the irritation in his voice instead of sadness.

"Now's the perfect time because I happen to have an empty salon chair for the next one hundred and eighty minutes. So," I pulled out a chair and sat down at Emory's kitchen table, "why don't you tell me what's going on. Every time I turned around, you were in my face, and today I had to force myself on you. That's a big turn of events. I'm starting to get my feelings hurt that you didn't like my cooking or something."

"You know that's not the case," Emory said in a grim voice. "I just had a setback and needed time and space to deal with it."

I studied him and his surroundings. I recalled the expensive outfit that he wore the day he moved in and how he'd downplayed his wardrobe since then. His kitchen appliances and the furniture I could see were expensive, high-end stuff. His espresso machine alone cost at least five big ones. His dining room table and chairs appeared to be custom made, not something you'd find at a value furniture store. The highlights in his hair were so good that they could *almost* pass as natural, which spelled big talent and big money. I was struck again by the oddity of Emory's appearance in our lives and town. *What the hell was he doing here?*

All my suspicions and concerns vanished when I realized just how lost he looked in his kitchen. All I wanted to do right then was help him. "Talk to me, Emory. You can tell me anything, I promise you that I won't gossip."

Emory was watching his finger draw the infinity symbol on the shiny wood surface of his table. "I'm not sure talking about it will help me, Josh, but I appreciate your willingness to listen," he said after several quiet moments. I had begun to think he hadn't heard me.

I covered Emory's hand to stop the motion and hopefully get his attention. It worked because he looked up at me curiously. "I have to be honest with you, Emory. It looks like not talking is killing you. Is this about a vision?"

Emory snorted and said, "You could say that."

"It's about Jonathon Silver, isn't it?" He looked at me in surprise.

"I saw the way you reacted to him when your hands touched. Is he in trouble?"

"I don't know about that, Josh. It wasn't *that* kind of vision," he said morosely.

His tone surprised me. What could be worse than... "Oh." Emory saw something on a personal level he hadn't wanted to see; it obviously shook him.

"Yeah," he replied. "I, um... we appeared to be very happy in the vision." It was said in a voice so grave that you would've thought he just announced the end of the world was near.

"You don't want to be happy, Emory?" I asked.

"I don't deserve to be happy, Josh, and that's my problem. I just can't. Not after what happened..." Emory's words broke off, but I knew what he was going to say. He didn't think he deserved to be happy after his husband died. I couldn't possibly begin to understand the depths of his despair, as I'd never experienced something so tragic in my life. I asked the man upstairs for forgiveness for being selfish, but I hoped never to know how that felt.

"You don't think River would want you to be happy?" I asked him. I loved Gabe with every fiber of my being, and the thought of him with someone else killed me, but only if I were alive. If my time to go to the big salon in the sky came first, then I'd want him to be happy. To me, Gabe not loving seemed so much worse than him loving someone else.

Emory flinched as if I hit him when I said his husband's name. "I forgot you researched me," he said softly. "Josh, I can't... say or hear his name. If not for me, he wouldn't be dead. I don't have the right to go out and be happy after what I did."

Of course, I wanted to know what happened and why he felt that way, but I'd never ask him. That's a level of nosiness that would be unforgivable. Instead, I reached across the table and covered both his hands. "Whenever you want to talk, I promise to be here— well, unless your visions tell you differently," I added wryly. "Until then, why don't you tell me what you had planned to do with your hair today. I'll get my stuff and do it here instead."

"You don't have to do that, Josh. I can reschedule," he said.

"Honey, your roots will be grown out hideously by the time you get in again. It was a miracle you got in when you did. My skills are in high demand," I said confidently, but never arrogantly. "I've got the time and skill; you have the peace and quiet."

His lips quirked up in the first bit of humor I'd seen since I arrived. "Okay," he finally said after a long pause. "Thank you."

I rose to my feet with the intention of running to the salon and back, but then I had a better idea. I narrowed my eyes at Emory suspiciously. *How did I know he wouldn't lock me out once I left?* Instead of leaving, I called Chaz and asked him to bring the things I needed to me. He had always been a thoughtful, sensitive person and did what I asked without hesitation because he knew something was up.

"Do you need me to reschedule your next appointment?" he asked wide-eyed.

"No, I'll be back in time. Thank you, though." I could search the world over and never find better friends to share my life.

I faced Emory once more with a smile. "Color and trim?" I asked.

His eyes lost focus, and he was quiet for so long that he appeared to be in a trance. I was starting to wonder if he had another vision, but he blinked a few times then focused on me. "I want a haircut, not a trim."

"Like a few inches or…"

"Short," he replied. "I want something new." It was such a drastic change; I had to be sure. "I'm positive," he told me before I could voice my concern.

"I told you to quit reading my mind, Emory. It's just fucking rude." My prim tone was at odds with my crude language, and it caused Emory to laugh loudly. I was happy that it sounded less rusty than it had that day I ran into him during my jog. I considered it progress.

"You search for hairstyles you like on your phone while I whip up magic potions in my bowls," I said while I unpacked the bag Chaz brought to me. "It'll help me know where best to place your highlights."

"I want something chunkier this time," he said, searching on his phone. "It doesn't need to look natural. In fact, I want it to be more obvious."

"Damn, you sound like one of the dramatic before and after advertisements," I said jokingly. "If that's what you want, Emory, then that's what I'm going to do." I couldn't help but feel that his reason had something to do with his vision and reaction to Jonathon Silver rather than wanting a change.

"It's what I want," he said, that time with more conviction.

"Then that's what you shall have, Emory."

A little over an hour later, I stared down at someone I hardly recognized. Even when I was suspicious of Emory, I thought he was an attractive man, but after his haircut, I could see the beautiful bone structure of his face. His eyes looked bigger and greener, his lips seemed fuller as they smiled broadly at his reflection in his bathroom mirror.

"Holy fuck!" he exclaimed. "I look so different with short hair." It wasn't quite the Bieber look I had mentally threatened him with when I first met him, but it was pretty damn close.

"Do you like it?" I asked. I could tell from his reaction that he did, and despite the impression I gave to some, I wasn't some damn glory hog. I was proud of my talent, sure, but I wanted to make others feel good.

"I love it, Josh. It's just the change I needed too." He ran his fingers through the long bangs that cut across his forehead. He'd picked an asymmetrical cut that worked wonders for his bone structure. "There won't be any hair for him to fist," he muttered under his breath. His eyes widened when he realized what he spoke out loud. "Um…"

"You don't have to say anything else," I told him. "I'll pretend I didn't hear it." I left him alone in his bathroom and went to the kitchen to start packing up my supplies.

Emory returned to the kitchen and headed into his pantry. He returned with a broom and pink cheeks. "I saw something that I am not prepared for now, probably never if I'm honest. I just thought maybe this," he gestured to his hair, "might change the course of things."

I knew next to nothing about psychic abilities or how the universe worked. I had a feeling if Emory was destined to end up in Jonathon Silver's arms, it would happen whether his hair was long, short, or non-existent.

Emory began to sweep the hair into piles. "River didn't want to go out that night," he said softly. "He wanted to stay in, order pizza, and watch his favorite movies. I insisted we go out on the town for his thirtieth birthday. If I had just listened to him…" His words broke off, and he began to cry.

"Emory." I dropped what I had in my hands and hugged the man tight while his body shook with the force of his sobs. "I'm so sorry."

"He was my whole world, and I didn't listen to him. I put myself first and lost everything that had any meaning to me. I don't want to feel or love again. That part of me died with him in that icy water." He ran his fingers through his bangs again and said, "River loved my long hair; I just can't stand the thought of anyone touching it like he did."

"I wish I could make this better for you, Emory." I hated feeling helpless when someone was hurting. I wanted to do or say anything that might put a smile on their faces. My first reaction when those feelings bubbled up was to alleviate the emotional turmoil with my snarktastic sense of humor, but there was no place for that in

Emory's kitchen.

"Nothing and no one can help me," he said. I knew he was wrong because I had felt the same way before I met Gabe. Our situations were not in the same hemisphere of tragedy, but broken is broken, and I knew that the right man could come along and mend his heart—if only he'd let him. Emory would have to be the one to decide when and if he was ready for that. Cleary, he wasn't ready yet. After several long minutes, he pulled back and wiped his tears. He groaned as if he was embarrassed and covered his face with his hands.

"I hate to leave you here like this, Emory. I will cancel the rest of my appointments and..."

"No! Don't do that for me. I promise you that I'm okay. The whole thing with Jonathon hit me hard and has left me reeling since. Thanks to you, I feel better now."

The old Josh would have remarked that hair grew back and, unless he had a time-stamped vision, it could've been a glimpse of years in the future. The new Josh hugged his new friend once more and kept his shit together until he stood by himself in the kitchenette in the rear of his salon. Only then did I allow myself to grieve for Emory because had it been me, I don't know how I would've gone on.

I had to believe there was more for Emory than a life of loneliness, but that didn't mean I thought that Jonathon Silver was the answer to his broken heart. Emory seemed like a good man with a tender soul, who deserved to be happy. I had lived both sides of the coin, and I knew damn well which one I preferred.

"You okay?" Chaz asked, popping his head into the room. "Mrs. Tasker is here."

I wiped my tears and nodded. "I'll be right there." I could tell he wanted to know what was going on, but I couldn't share Emory's private pain with anyone, except maybe Gabe. *Gabe.*

I knew what I needed to do to feel better. I whipped out my

phone and sent a quick *I love you* text before I squared my shoulders and entered the salon. I knew it was going to be obvious as hell that I'd been crying and I didn't want to give them the wrong idea. The last thing I wanted was for their tongues to be wagging all over town and telling people that Gabe and I broke up.

"I can't believe Missy and Mark broke up," I said, rattling off the name of the latest Hollywood it-couple to call it quits.

"I know," Mrs. Tasker said. "I heard he had an affair with his nanny."

"It's always the nanny," someone said.

"Nanny? It was the young Russian co-star," another added. "I could tell there was going to be trouble when they announced that *she* was playing his wife in the movie. She's broken up about five marriages already."

Crisis diverted.

TWENTY-SIX

Gabe

Dorchester and I decided not to drive to Cincinnati unless something new developed in the case. We had already met with all the witnesses who were available to interview in person and would have to wait until the Robertson brothers returned to town to speak with them. In all honesty, Lawrence Robertson didn't like or trust his nephews, but we had found no evidence to connect either of them to his death or the others. Rick Spizer was the only one I could tie to the deaths, with Owen Smithson being the exception.

What bugged me the most was not understanding Rick's motive to commit the crimes—*if* he did. I'd been in law enforcement for too long to think that every case was going to get wrapped up in a pretty package like it did in cop shows.

Sometimes, people did things that made no sense at all. Were the homicides an example of that? I honestly couldn't say, but I was certain that the CPD would consider the cases solved soon unless new evidence surfaced that pointed to, or concluded, someone else was involved. They had the possible weapon in evidence along with a note from the man who claimed "responsibility" for their deaths before he supposedly took his life. There were too many uncertainties for me, but I didn't have the final say.

If something broke on the case, we would head to the city. Until then, Dorchester returned to his partner with the CCSD, and I was happy to sit across from Adrian's desk and get caught up with what was going on locally. There'd been a recent string of break-ins and vandalism cases that had kept Adrian busy.

"Any similarities to the break-in and vandalism at Georgia Beaumont's?" I asked. It still bothered me that we couldn't connect that to her death. I hated unsolved cases because, regardless of their size, a crime was a crime.

"No, buddy. As best we could tell, nothing was stolen from Georgia's," Adrian stated.

"According to her murderer, Wanda Honeycutt," I mumbled. Wanda confessed to everything else and had no reason to lie about ransacking the place. It was most likely someone else that Georgia had been blackmailing. What was the likelihood that her attempt to blackmail the county commissioner was the first time in her life? On the other hand, it was personal for her since his lover happened to be her ex-husband; who was also her lover at the time of her death.

Adrian's laughter reverberated through the small police department. "Oh, how I've missed razzing you about her," he remarked.

I ignored his comment and turned the conversation to my future goddaughter, as I had started to think of her. It had been less than a week since I last saw them and got updated on their health, but it felt like a year had passed. Adrian immediately started talking about the final plans for the nursery. He joked and said that Sally Ann had changed her mind at least four different times, but had finally settled on a theme. "For now," he added. "I'm sure that will change by the time I get home."

I laughed, but not too hard because I figured Josh would be the same exact way if we decided to have a family. I knew in the deepest part of my soul that I was going to marry Josh, even though we hadn't discussed it, but I had no idea where he stood on fatherhood. I did know that he would be an amazing dad to a very lucky kid if we were so blessed. If not, we'd be the best uncles on the planet.

I was just about to say something to Adrian when I noticed I had a new email from the state lab. They had finally sent back the test results of the paint transfer found on Nate's bumper. I opened the email and read it out loud to Adrian.

"The test concludes that the paint sample provided for testing is a hundred percent match to the Absolute Black color used on Ford's F-150 trucks." I looked up from my email and said, "Hot damn!"

"Does Spizer or anyone in his immediate circle own a Ford F-150 that matches the criteria?" Adrian asked.

"Damn, Adrian," I admonished. "Let me have this little victory before you go throwing cold water on me."

"Sorry, partner," he said, but I could tell he wasn't.

I pulled up the Bureau of Motor Vehicles database, and none of Spizer or his cronies had an F-150. In fact, no one involved owned… "Oh fuck!" I just realized why the photo on Spizer's desk caught my eye. I'd seen it before. "I didn't see this coming," I said.

"Saw what coming. What's going on, man?" Adrian said, rounding his desk to stand over my shoulder.

I typed a name into the database and confirmed what I knew.

"You'd think after Wanda we'd get tired of saying we didn't see something coming, but I'm with you, partner."

"I can't believe I didn't look deeper into *all* the people involved in the case or who knew the victims. Damn it!" I picked up my cellphone from my desk and called Dorchester. "It's Rylan Broadman," I said as soon as he answered. "He has the same exact photo of a baseball team hanging on his wall that Spizer had on his desk."

"You're sure?" Dorchester asked.

"Positive," I responded. "I got the paint sample results from the state lab that tell me the vehicle I'm looking for is a Ford F-150 painted in Absolute Black. Guess who has a black 2015 Ford F-150 registered with the BMV?"

"Rylan!" Dorchester said excitedly. "What the hell is his role in all of this? Money?"

"We'll find out when we ask him. I'll be there in ten minutes to pick you up," I told him then disconnected.

Adrian had gone to his computer when I called Dorchester. He looked up when I hung up the phone. "I found another connection," he said. "They served in the same army unit. Call Dorchester back and tell him and Whitworth to meet us at his office. You two aren't going in there alone if he's responsible for four deaths."

We didn't go in with blazing lights and blaring sirens because the last thing we wanted to do was tip him off and end up in a potential hostage situation. We met the two men in the dollar store parking lot a few blocks away from Broadman's office. Dorchester got in the car with me while Adrian and Whitworth headed over on foot. The deal was they'd wait for us to go inside to speak to Broadman then cover both the front and rear entrances.

The bubbly receptionist smiled broadly when we walked into the office until I pulled my gun out of my holster and slid the safety off. "Pick up the phone and ask your boss to come out here, but don't tell him why." There was no way I was going into his office not knowing what he was doing behind the closed door. Our team was

240

going home safe to our loved ones that night and that was final. The receptionist's hand shook like a leaf as she reached for her phone.

"There's no need, Lucy. I'm right here," Broadman called from down the hallway. He walked out with his hands up in the air. "I'm unarmed," he said softly and rotated slowly so we could see that he didn't have a gun shoved in the back of his pants.

"Hands above your head and don't move, Broadman," I commanded. I nodded for Dorchester to move in while I kept my gun aimed at him. I began reading him his Miranda Rights as Dorchester holstered his gun and started forward. "Rylan Broadman, you are under arrest for the murders of Nathaniel Turner, Owen Smithson, Lawrence Robertson, and Richard Spizer. You are also under arrest for arson. You have the right to remain silent. Anything you say can and will be used against you in a court of law. You have the rights to an attorney. If you cannot afford an attorney, one will be provided for you. Do you understand the rights I have just read to you?"

"I know my rights," Broadman said sarcastically, as Dorchester pulled his left arm down and bent it so that his hand rested on the small of his back. I heard the familiar sound of the handcuff locking into place.

"I'm just following the rules so you don't get off on a technicality," I told him. "With these rights in mind, do you wish..."

Broadman made a spin move and head-butted Dorchester just as he started to bring Broadman's right arm down to cuff behind his back, knocking Dorchester out cold. Broadman grabbed for Dorchester's gun from his holster, and I had no choice but to take a shot.

The receptionist screamed as the sound of the gun reverberated loudly in the tight office space. Broadman clutched his shoulder and fell to the ground. Adrian and Whitworth entered the building shouting after the gun discharged but my sole focus was making sure Broadman stayed down.

"Don't you fucking move," I shouted, "or I'll put you down."

"Call 911," he said between gritted teeth.

"We are 911 you son of a bitch," Whitworth said, as he knelt beside his partner.

"He's just been knocked out," I told the distraught detective. "Adrian, call it in." I secured Broadman's hands and used Lucy's cardigan to apply pressure to the wound that appeared to be a clean shot through the fleshy part of his right shoulder. I didn't want him to bleed out because death would be too good for him. He would need surgery to repair torn muscles and ligaments, but then he could recover and get physical therapy in the prison infirmary while he awaited trial.

I wanted to pin that fucker down and get my answers, but I knew they wouldn't hold up in court if asked while he was under duress. He whined and cried about how miserable he was and how he planned to sue. I laughed at the lawsuit portion of his comment, but not over his remarks about being in pain. I was certain that Nate, Owen, Lawrence, and Rick would've much preferred to have his injuries over their grave ones. It took everything I had not to dig my fingers in his wound and make him suffer even more. Luckily for him, the paramedics got there before I forgot that I was a decent man.

Unfortunately, the Goodville Police Department arrived and wanted to take over the crime scene and the investigation. Technically, Dorchester and Whitworth's deputy sheriff status trumped Goodville's authority, but the jackasses who showed up wanted to fight for it. My adrenaline was pumping quickly through my veins and, to tell the truth, I was spoiling for a fight. I would've preferred to fuck it out of my system, but that wasn't an option right then. I was prepared to settle for the next best thing until two loud voices rang out loudly in the office.

"I got this, Detective Wyatt," Captain Reardon said. "Stand down, Officer, our men are taking the lead in this case." I slowly released the fistful of the starched uniform of the officer I had grabbed when he implied that country people were too stupid to investigate a crime properly, acting as if Goodville was a fucking metropolis. It had one extra traffic light, two extra dollar stores, and a McDonald's.

"This man is being arrested for crimes our task force is investigating—a force that includes law enforcement agencies from Carter County Sheriff's Department, Blissville Police, and Cincinnati Police. Detective Wyatt leads the task force and will oversee this investigation also," Sheriff Tucker stated firmly. It was the first time I'd ever seen them agree on anything. "The shooting today was a result of our investigation into four homicides, and it takes precedence over your investigation. We'll inform you if we need your assistance beyond securing the outside of the premises to keep the onlookers away from our crime scene." Tucker nodded to dismiss the man, who swallowed hard then got to boot scooting it out of there.

Lucy was taken outside and questioned while we searched the office for evidence, making sure to stay out of his client files. We were coming up empty until we found a safe hidden inside a closet. Lucy provided the combination and gasped when she saw what was inside.

"That wasn't in there last night when I put the bank deposit inside," she said. I stared down at the stacks of cash that obviously came from Robertson's safe deposit box. They were the same straps that we initialed after the money was discovered and counted. "I wasn't involved in any of this," she said, tears running down her face. I wasn't falling for tears again so easily. We'd double-check everything to make sure she was telling the truth, if not, she'd be going to jail too.

I realized that I set my phone down on Broadman's desk while I was in there and went to retrieve it. I noticed that I had missed a text from Josh that simply said he loved me. It gave me the warm and fuzzy feelings, and I returned a quick message to him so he wouldn't think I was ignoring him. Tucker and Reardon followed after me for reasons I didn't know because they both got distracted by the diploma hanging on the wall.

"A Wisconsin graduate," Reardon scoffed.

"You can't ever trust them," Tucker added.

The situation was grave, but I couldn't keep the smile off my face. The only thing that could bring a Michigan fan and an Ohio State University fan together was the hatred of another rival Big Ten school. And, perhaps solving crimes too.

"Your deputy did a good job," Reardon said to his father-in-law with a tone of voice you'd expect someone to use while discussing a rectal exam, which should *never* be confused with a prostate massage.

"Your detective isn't so bad either," Tucker replied as if I was a half-step above a root canal.

I was about to leave the office for good when an idea struck me. I removed the framed picture of the baseball team from the wall and took it out of the frame to see if their names and a date had been written on the back of the photo like my mom had done for me as a kid. Sure enough, it was from when the guys were eleven years old. The names of the other members of the team were listed, and one jumped out at me big as shit: Jeffrey Smithson. I would bet Dorchester's right nut that Jeffrey was Owen's father. Somehow either Spizer and Broadman together, or Broadman alone, brought Owen into the situation then killed him to keep him quiet.

The motherload of evidence was found at Broadman's house. Not only did we find a .45 caliber gun, but we found a baggie full of mangled bullets coated in blood and other biological matter that I was sure would test positive for a DNA match to our victims. Broadman's search history on his computer turned out to be very damning as well, most especially the one about the hardest accelerants for arson dogs to detect. And like other psychotic killers, the dumbass kept something from each victim that put him at each scene, including Rick Spizer's. He kept Nate's license, a flash drive that belonged to Owen Smithson, Lawrence Robertson's dog tags, and a personalized pen with Rick's name on it. The final nail in his coffin was the damage to the front bumper of his truck that was consistent with the damage to Turner's rear bumper. We had plenty of evidence for the DA without a confession, although I planned to give it my best shot once Broadman recovered.

I went to the station after the search was concluded to write up my reports and call my task force to fill them in on what we had found. At the time, I couldn't call Mrs. Spizer and tell her that her husband's death was a homicide until after Chief Hopkins with the CPD granted me permission. My last call was to Silver to let him know what we'd found out.

He sighed in relief and said, "Thank you, Gabe." Silver's voice choked with emotion, and I knew a man like him would want some privacy to process what he'd learned. I promised to keep him posted and hung up the phone to go home to my man.

It was much later than normal by the time I arrived home. The adrenaline from earlier had never diminished; it spiked even higher when I got an eyeful of Josh in his black yoga pants doing his stretches. He didn't like to be disturbed when he was trying to decompress through yoga, and I knew when he sent the text that he'd had a rough day. It wasn't that Josh was stingy with his affection, but his texts tended to be more cutesy or sexy than mushy. Had I not been in the middle of collecting evidence, I would've called him right on the spot.

I stood quietly and watched him go through his routine. Hell, I had already waited hours to sink inside him so what was a few minutes more? I was proud of my maturity and eagerly anticipated the moment I felt his tight heat surrounding my raging hard-on. More than sex, I just wanted to kiss him and hold him in my arms and soak in the preciousness of the time we had together.

"Gabe loves Josh!" Savage squawked loudly. I had been trying to teach him that phrase for months when Josh wasn't around, but he never said it until then. Almost as if he could understand the mood of the moment.

Josh lost his balance and nearly fell over. The glare on his face made me happy it was the bird that fucked up that time. He smiled when he saw me then ran and leaped into my arms to give me a hero's welcome home—his words, not mine. I gave him a wall-banging fit for a prince—my words, not his. Afterward, when we collapsed to the floor with him wrapped tightly around me as if he was afraid to let me go, I knew what I needed to do. I also knew it would take careful planning because Josh wasn't just any guy and any old proposal would never do.

TWENTY-SEVEN

Josh

I BLINKED AND NEXT THING I KNEW IT WAS THE MOST WONDERFUL time of the year—my birthday, not Christmas. Technically, it was the Friday before, but I believe in a birthday week, not just a day. I mean, if I couldn't get a national holiday out of it then I could at least take a weeklong vacation with my guy. Honestly, it had been Gabe's idea, not mine. I joked that June 1st should be a national holiday, but I usually just took the day off from work. Gabe decided he wanted to take me on a birthday trip. What guy refused something like that? Not this one.

Besides, a week on a white sandy beach in the Bahamas was just what we needed after the chaos we lived through the past several months. Things were about to heat up when the Broadman murder trials began a little later in the summer, so I agreed that it was the perfect time to get away. I knew how much it bothered Gabe that he wasn't able to get Rylan Broadman to confess to the crimes, but I assured him that not everyone could be Deputy Brenda Leigh Johnson. He had no idea who I was talking about, of course, so I had to school him on excellent television because he still seemed to be stuck on those dang sports.

I had serious doubts that he'd confess to binge-watching all seven seasons of *The Closer*, but I didn't need that. His laughter over Provenza and Flynn's antics was all the acknowledgment I needed to know that my shows were far superior to his. He never laughed that hard while watching his ballgames. Brenda Leigh was badass and always solved her cases. Some of her outfits were less than attractive, but her hair always kicked ass. Gabe didn't seem to notice her outfits or hair, and he didn't find me amusing when I recommended that he use some of her tactics to get Broadman to spill his guts.

I had started filming the wedding series for Channel Eleven the week following Broadman's arrest. I enjoyed it far more than I ever expected to and my co-stars were amazing. I told Cindy upfront that I had no desire to be the "token gay" on the show. I was flamboyant as fuck at times, but always on my terms and only when I felt like it. I had no desire to be part of anything contrived because it was PC or showed how "cool" the station and network were. Diversity had to be real and genuine because people could see and feel fakeness; not only that, it was awkward to be included in a group that didn't want you.

Our group clicked from the very beginning. Marla Henderson was the boutique owner, Cliff Nathanson was the caterer, Brenda

Halstrom was the florist, and Juan and Joan Diaz were the photographer and wedding planner duo who were partners in business and life. Sometimes it took a few takes to film certain segments because we laughed so much. Our series was so successful that we were invited to be a big part of the wedding Expo at US Bank Arena, which generated a lot of traffic to our businesses.

My staff remarked that we had almost outgrown our location, which got me thinking about something I never thought would happen—relocating. I had purchased my childhood home from my parents with the plans of living there for the rest of my life, but Curl Up and Dye could use the upstairs space to expand the salon. If it wasn't my living space, I could move the spa services upstairs and have more room downstairs to put in more stations and hire more stylists. It was something that I needed to consider for the long-term growth of my business.

It wasn't something that I had discussed with Gabe but planned to do on vacation. I wasn't sure how he felt about house shopping and moving all over again. Once the idea of buying a new house took root, I couldn't get it out of my head. The more I thought about it, the more I thought it was the best idea I had in a long time. We could find a place that would be both of ours because it still felt like Gabe was just staying over because it had been my place without him for quite some time.

We really could use a guestroom for parental visits, a bigger yard for Buddy to run and play in, and a garage so Gabe could bring Charlotte home. As annoying as small-town life could be at times, I didn't want to move to a bigger city. I checked the internet for listings daily, but nothing screamed "forever home" at me. I knew the right one would come along if it were meant to be. *Hmm, maybe I should ask Emory.*

The Friday of Memorial Day weekend was our last shoot for our series, and it was going to end with the group sitting on comfy couches doing a kind of series wrap-up chat and answer viewer questions that were submitted online. Viewers could watch it streaming live on the website or catch clips of it over a few days during the daily news broadcasts.

By the time we got to the chat, I was amped up and ready to go. Not only did I have an amazing time filming the series with a great group of people, but I was also looking hella good, and I was leaving for the Bahamas with Gabe the next day. We already packed our bags; the only thing left to do was head to the airport at an ungodly hour the following morning. Gabe grumbled about the early hour, but to me, it just meant we'd hit the beach that much earlier. I bought special bikini trunks that I knew Gabe was going to love. I was certain he'd spend all his time trying to get me back to the hotel room and out of them. I couldn't wait!

Cliff catered a scrumptious celebration lunch for us then we took our places on the comfy set that looked like a posh living room. I sat on the ivory leather couch with Marla that was set in the center of the room because Cindy made me. I would've been happy sitting in one of the club chairs off to the right, but Cindy said the camera loved my face and my personality drew in the viewers.

"Shut up," I told her while waving my hand for her to continue.

Joan and Juan curled up on an ivory-and-gray-striped loveseat to the left of the couch while Cliff and Brenda took the dove gray club chairs that I wanted to take home with me. Don't think I didn't snap a picture of the setup for a future home I hadn't even found yet. It was always a good thing to have goals.

"Oh, we have our first question," Marla said, looking at the laptop in front of us. The two of us were to take turns reading the questions that popped up during our live event. "It's for you, Cliff. Martha S. would like to know the best entrée to offer guests at a reception."

"Thanks for the question, Martha," Cliff said. "I think it's best to offer your guests a choice of entrées, especially if you plan to offer seafood. Not everyone likes seafood and a lot of people are allergic and can't eat it. Steak and chicken are the most common, but you shouldn't shy away from them for that reason. They're popular because they're versatile so you can change yours up with a unique seasoning combination or marinade."

"Good to know," I said to Cliff. I looked at the next questions that popped up. "The next question is from Jennifer R., and she has a question for you, Marla. Jennifer would like to know if you offer a variety of sizes at your boutique or if you only dress skinny bitches." I laughed and added, "I like this girl."

Marla laughed also and said, "We want to make *every* woman look beautiful on her special day. If I don't have the dress you're looking for, then I'll find it for you, but please give me the time to do so. I can't begin to stress how important it is to start shopping for your dress at least six months in advance of your wedding. There are fittings and alterations that take time. Weddings are stressful enough without the added anxiety from poor planning." I loved how Marla could insult people without really sounding like it. Gabe said I was the only other person he knew who could pull that off.

"Okay, let's see who's next," Marla said. "Bethany J. would like to know from Brenda what her favorite flowers are."

"Oh wow, I can't pick a favorite," Brenda replied then discussed the merits of several popular wedding flowers and how she liked to pair them with less common flowers to give each wedding a unique feel to them.

The next question was for Joan, the one after was for Juan, and then another question for Marla. It seemed like no one had any questions for me about hair or makeup. I was getting a little discouraged but did my best not to show it. The questions were great, and the answers given were even better, so I just had to wait my turn and not pout that people weren't fighting over one another to hear my little pearls of wisdom.

"Here's a question for Josh," Marla said. I perked up but tried not to look pathetic. "It's from a Detective Smitten from Blissville."

A smile spread across my face as I wondered what the hell Gabe was doing. "He wants to know what you're doing for the rest of your life?"

"Huh?" There went my polish and professionalism. "He asked what?" I leaned forward and read the question for myself. A follow-up question popped up beneath the first one. "Will you marry me?" I read out loud. The guys on the set chuckled while the girls giggled happily at the shell-shocked expression on my face, which was nothing to the jaw-dropping that happened when Gabe stepped onto the set and walked toward me with a sexy grin all over his face. I noticed that he was wearing my version of a skinny jean for him that I placed in his drawer without telling him. I was briefly distracted by images of me unbuttoning his fly from my knees, but not on air.

"Hi, Sunshine," he said when he reached the beautifully patterned area rug covering the hardwood floor of our makeshift living room.

"Hi," I said shakily. "What are you doing here?"

"I think it's kind of obvious, but if not, maybe this will help." Gabe dropped to one knee and held a ring box up in front of him. "Josh, will you make me the happiest man on earth and agree to be my husband?" Gabe opened the box and showed me the platinum and diamond band inside.

Tears burned my eyes, and I had to swallow a few times before I could whisper, "It's not my birthday."

"This isn't a gift for your birthday. It's a gift to myself; you're my gift," Gabe said.

"Are you even real?" I asked him, echoing words I had used in the past.

"Me or the diamonds?" Gabe asked, taking a page from my book and using humor to lessen the tension. "Both are real." Gabe leaned forward and lowered his voice. "Um, you've left me hanging here, Sunshine." He shook the ring box a little. "We're streaming live, and our parents are watching. You think maybe you can give me an answer?"

It was the most precious moment in my life. I wanted to say the right thing, something that he would cherish forever. For the life of me, I couldn't think of a snazzy response, so I just went with genuine. "Yes, I will be honored to call you my husband, Gabriel."

Cheers and laughter broke out around us as Gabe slid the ring on my finger. He rose from his knee and pulled me into his arms for a sweet kiss that had tears running down my cheeks. I showed my ring off to the girls and shook hands with the guys before we got back to filming the rest of the wrap-up show.

"Have a wonderful vacation," Cindy said once we finished. "When you come back, you'll get to start filming your solo segments. Are you excited?"

"About many things," I answered, looking down at my ring again. I thanked her for helping Gabe pull off his surprise, then left with my fiancé.

The hour-long trip home was spent on the phone either texting, tweeting, talking, or Facebooking our big news. I could do that because Gabe had hired a car service to drive him to Cincinnati to surprise me. Gabe looked gloriously ridiculous driving Princess, but he didn't like to be driven places by anyone. *Well, he let me take his ass for a drive on occasion.*

When we got back to town, I expected Gabe to take us straight home, but he didn't. He parked in front of Georgia Beaumont's mini mansion that had remained empty since her death. He looked over at me with a proud grin on his face.

"What are we doing here?" I asked him.

"Five bedrooms, four bathrooms, a huge, fenced back yard, and a three-car detached garage for Charlotte, Charlotte II, and Princess." It still made me laugh that Gabe couldn't pick out a better name for his everyday Charger. He laughed when I looked surprised. "You think I don't notice you checking out listings for houses daily? I'm a cop; I notice things."

"Why this house?" I asked him.

"You don't like it? It has beauty and grace, but it's classic and masculine at the same time. It reminds me of you." Damn, he knew how to render me speechless. "I also thought that Georgia would approve of someone she loved living in the home she adored. You're not worried about ghosts or anything, are you?"

"No," I answered honestly. "Well, maybe if I'd smeared an ug-ly-ass pastel pink on Georgia's lips for her viewing. She would've haunted my ass no matter where I lived if that had been the case."

Gabe chuckled then asked, "What's holding you back from say-ing yes?"

"Um, the expense," I told him. "We make a good salary togeth-er, and the salon is growing faster than I can keep up with, but this house must cost a fortune. How can we afford to buy it?"

"I inherited some money from my grandparents that we could use for a large down payment to make the mortgage payments more manageable. Don't look at me like that, Sunshine." He shook his head. "They left me the money to do something amazing with, and I can think of no better way than to spend it on our future."

"That wasn't what I was thinking, Gabe, but I'm sure I would've gotten there eventually," I said saucily.

"Okay, then what's bothering you? Don't tell me nothing be-cause I know better," Gabe warned.

"I'm more worried about Internal Affairs breathing down your neck," I told him. "What small town cop can afford a mansion on his salary? They've already investigated you three times—oh, make that four with the Broadman shooting. You must like it. Your nefarious reputation could be bad..." I broke off when I realized how absurd my statement was going to sound. Bad for my business? Ha! The sketchier things were, the busier my salon became. Hmm, I began wondering what kind of rumors I could spread.

Gabe laughed hard for a few minutes. "You never fail to make me smile, Sunshine. What do you say? Do we want to get serious about buying this home when we get back?"

"Yes," I said. "This has always been my favorite house, besides mine, and I can see us being very happy here. Hell, we'd each get a wing to ourselves if we start getting on each other's nerves."

Gabe smiled and said, "I thought we could find better uses for some of the extra rooms."

"Sex room, arcade, home gym…"

"Those are all very good suggestions, but I was thinking more like bedrooms for our kids," Gabe said.

I had never permitted myself to consider fatherhood in the past because I had believed it was something that would never happen to me and didn't want to put myself through unnecessary misery. With Gabe, all things good and wonderful were possible. I didn't yet know how or when it would happen, but raising kids with him was something I saw in my future. I didn't need my psychic friend, Emory, to tell me it would happen.

"I hope they take after you," I told Gabe. "There are only so many divas a house can hold, regardless of the size."

"I'm not afraid of divas," Gabe replied with a happy, hopeful expression on his face. "I have only one worry, and this is a deal breaker, Sunshine."

"What, babe?" I asked.

"The entrances to that scary-ass hidden basement are getting boarded up forever. I will never go down those rickety motherfucking steps for any reason," Gabe said resolutely.

"Deal," I agreed. We sealed our promise with a kiss and Gabe put Princess in drive so we could head back home.

A sexy vacation, a wedding to plan, and a house to buy and furnish were on the horizon; my life couldn't possibly get any sweeter. I had to pinch myself to be certain that I hadn't died and gone to heaven.

To be continued…

I DO, OR DYE TRYING

is coming May 2, 2017

ACKNOWLEDGMENTS

First, I need to thank my husband and children for their constant support and encouragement. It's not easy living with a writer who often disappears into a fictional world for long periods of time. They do so many things to help me out so that I can realize my dream. I love you guys more than words can ever express.

Many thanks go out to my three best friends, Anne, Deena, and Kerry. They've stood by me, cheered me on, picked me up, and held my hand through some really rough patches. I love you girls so very much. I wish everyone had friends like you because the world would be a much kinder place.

To my creative dream team, thanks seem hardly enough for all that you do. Pam Ebeler of Undivided Editing thank you for your tireless work, feedback, and many laughs while editing. Jay Aheer of Simply Defined art is just an incredible artist, and I love how she brings my words to life. Stacey Blake of Champagne Formats is also an amazing artist who does incredible interior formatting and designing for e-books and paperbacks. New to my team is Judy Zweifel of Judy's' Proofreading. She does an amazing job of finding the tiniest details that make a book shine.

I would like to thank my beta readers for all the honest feedback they give me on my storyline. I appreciate you guys so much. Aimee's ARC Angels are Anne, Kerry, Jason, Jodie, Kim, and Laurel. Thank you for all that you do!

ABOUT THE AUTHOR

I am a wife and mother to three kids, four dogs, and a cat. When I'm not dreaming up stories, I like to lose myself in a good book, cook or bake. I'm a girly tomboy who paints her fingernails while watching sports and yelling at the referees. I will always choose the book over the movie. I believe in happily-ever-after. Love inspires everything that I do. Music keeps me sane.

I'd love to hear from you.

You can reach me at:

Twitter - twitter.com/AimeeNWalker

Facebook – www.facebook.com/aimeenicole.walker

Blog – AimeeNicoleWalker.blogspot.com

www.ingramcontent.com/pod-product-compliance
Lightning Source LLC
Chambersburg PA
CBHW070859250626
47159CB00003B/1116